MANGO BAY

A Mango Bob and Walker Adventure

by

Bill Myers

www.mangobob.com

Mango Bay

This book is a work of fiction. Names, characters, places and incidents are either the product of the author's imagination or are used fictionally. Any resemblance to actual persons, living or dead, or to actual events or locales is entirely coincidental.

Version 2019.10.18

ISBN-13: 978-1495298844

Second Edition: March 2017

CHAPTER ONE

"Clothing optional."

That's what Anna had said about Serenity Cove.

Clothing optional, as in a *nudist* camp.

I was pretty sure she was kidding. Anna kidded a lot. It was part of her charm. Her way of getting to know someone.

We'd met while both of us were camping at Sebastian Inlet State Park, just north of Vero Beach on Florida's Treasure Coast.

I was in my motorhome and she was camping in the space next to me in a small tent. We were both there for the same reason, to try our hand at finding gold from the Spanish shipwrecks on the nearby beaches.

An intense tropical storm had come up, bringing with it high winds, heavy rains and a flood that stranded us in the park. I was safe and sound in my motorhome, Anna was wet and miserable in her tent.

Being a gentleman, I invited her over to wait out the storm with me and my cat, Mango Bob.

She was reluctant at first, but when her tent blew away she took me up on my offer. Three days later, we had become great friends.

My name is John Everett Walker. Most people just call me Walker.

Until recently I was head of network security for a big company. You'd recognize the name if I told you, but for reasons you'll understand later, I can't reveal it.

I'm currently unemployed and living full time in a 28-foot

1

motorhome. It's not a bad life, but definitely not something I had planned.

It all started when the company decided to move their operation south of the border. They laid off 600 people, including me. I was one of the lucky ones. I got a pretty good severance package, including a big check and a motorhome.

Here's how it went down. During final inventory, the company discovered a motorhome on its books. It had been purchased five years earlier by a company executive, used a few times and forgotten.

They needed to get rid of it. At the time, my so-called marriage had just ended rather abruptly and I needed a place to stay. The company offered to sell me the motorhome at a price I couldn't resist. I bought it and moved in.

I set up camp in the Toad Suck Ferry campground near the Arkansas River until a friend convinced me to deliver a cat to her sister in Florida. In exchange I'd get a free campsite near the beach.

Being unemployed with no income, I liked the idea of living rent free. Especially close to the beach.

Just one minor detail though, I had to deliver the cat.

Sounds simple, right? Drive fifteen hundred miles in a used motorhome with a strange cat and deliver it to a woman I'd never met. Could have been a recipe for disaster, that's for sure.

After three long days on the road, Mango Bob—the name of the cat—and I arrived safely in southwest Florida. My friend's sister, Sarah, was thrilled to get her cat back and, as promised, she let me camp in the lot behind the building she rented for her kayak business.

That was six months ago. Since then I'd explored different parts of the Sunshine State, including the Treasure Coast where I met Anna.

When the big storm had passed, Anna and I hit the beaches

with our metal detectors. As luck would have it, we came away with some valuable gold and silver reales from the Spanish Fleet wreck of 1715.

Anna cashed hers in at a local coin shop, and we celebrated that evening with a fine meal and one too many bottles of wine. The next day, we parted company. I headed back to the small town of Englewood on Florida's west coast, and Anna headed back to her home north of Miami.

Or so I thought.

CHAPTER TWO

Two days after we parted company on the Treasure Coast, Anna surprised me by showing up in Englewood pulling a Casita camper trailer behind her Land Cruiser.

The first words out of her mouth were, "We're going to be roommates! I talked to Sarah and she said it was okay for me to camp next to you for a few days. Won't that be fun?"

I wasn't sure whether fun was the right word to describe it. It all depended on what Anna expected of me.

"You're moving to Englewood?"

"Sure am. Already got a job. I just need a place to stay until I can find an apartment. I figured staying in my camper next to you would work. Unless you have a problem with that."

I shook my head and smiled. "No problem. In fact, I'm happy to see you. Just a little surprised."

Anna looked at me, a gleam in her eyes. "Walker, it'll be fun. You'll see."

And she was right. It was fun. At least for a while.

Anna had been hired as a sales agent for a local real estate firm, which meant she had to get up early and go in to work each morning.

I, on the other hand, didn't have a job, so I could sleep in whenever I wanted to.

I'd see Anna when she came back to her trailer each evening and we'd usually have dinner together.

More often than not, our meal was something frozen we'd cook up in the microwave. But sometimes we'd have fresh shrimp from the nearby Gulf of Mexico or takeout from the China Garden.

Over dinner and wine we'd talk about our lives. Where we'd been, what we'd accomplished, and what we might be doing next.

Anna had big plans. And they didn't involve living in a camper trailer for much longer. She wanted to become the top selling realtor in town and eventually own her own agency. Maybe even own several agencies.

She said she didn't mind working hard and was willing to put in the hours to accomplish her goal. I wasn't surprised when two months after she moved in, she announced she was selling her trailer and moving into an apartment.

It was inevitable. And necessary if she wanted to live the life of a successful real estate agent. At the very least, she needed the extra closet space not afforded in her small camper trailer.

After Anna moved into her apartment, we stayed in touch. Partly because we were friends and partly because she was my real estate agent.

That had been one of Anna's promises to me when she moved to Englewood. She had said, "I'll find you the perfect house to buy. And you'll thank me for doing it."

You might be wondering, how does an unemployed guy living in a motorhome afford to buy a house in Florida?

Well, as it turned out, after I was laid off, the company offered me a large cash settlement to keep my mouth shut about crimes committed by one of their board members.

I hadn't asked for the money. And the company knew I'd already been interviewed by the FBI and other authorities about the matter. But the board of directors still thought it was worth paying me to keep quiet. They were worried that if I talked to reporters, it could hurt their stock price.

So even though I had no plans to go public with what I knew, my attorney said, "Take the money. You'd be a fool not to."

So I did.

CHAPTER THREE

Anna knew I had a bit of money stashed away and she knew if she found me the right place, I could afford to buy it. So she'd been checking the MLS daily and following leads hoping to find a place that would suit me.

So far we hadn't had much luck.

But Anna had been lucky with another one of her clients, a retired couple from Michigan. She'd found them a small beach-front cottage and they had just finalized the deal. This meant Anna was going to get her first big commission check and she'd invited me to join her and Sarah (the girl whose cat I delivered) to celebrate.

We met up at one of our favorite eating places, the Mango Bistro, which was within walking distance of where I lived in my motorhome. As usual the food and service at the Mango was great and, at Anna's urging, we stayed late and drank too much wine.

When it was finally time to leave, Anna and Sarah wisely caught a cab and headed back to their places. With my motorhome just two blocks away, I walked, happy that I didn't have to drive.

The next morning, way too early, I heard footsteps in the gravel parking lot outside my window. Then a voice.

"Walker, get up. Today's the day."

It was Anna. The early riser, the one who was always ready to go.

"Walker, get your clothes on, we need to talk."

I rolled over, pulling a pillow over my head. I didn't want to talk to anyone. Not that early. Not that morning. I just wanted to stay in bed until the pounding in my head went away.

I had a hangover and, as far as I was concerned, it was Anna's fault. She was the one who kept the wine flowing the night before. She was the one who kept saying, "Drink up, Walker. We're celebrating!"

Maybe she was there to apologize. Maybe that's why she was banging on my door.

"Walker, I know you're in there. I'm not leaving until we talk. Trust me; you'll want to hear this."

I was pretty sure I didn't want to hear anything. But it was obvious that Anna wasn't going to let me sleep. Not even on that special day, the day I had to move, was she going to let me get the few extra minutes of sleep I desperately needed.

Anna was like that. Persistent. In business and in her personal life, she didn't take no for an answer. Normally, it was one of the things I liked best about her. But not so much that morning. I would have been perfectly happy had she just gone away and let me sleep.

But I knew she wouldn't. She wouldn't leave until I got up and talked to her. And if I didn't get up, she'd unlock the door and come in on her own. Because she had a key.

I'd given it to her when we first met, over on the Treasure Coast, brought together by a tropical storm. After her tent blew away and she started sleeping on my couch, I'd given her a key so she'd feel at home, free to come and go whenever she wanted.

That was more than three months ago and she still had the key. She could still come and go as she liked.

CHAPTER FOUR

One of the advantages of living in a motorhome is if you get tired of your neighbors or bored with the view or just want better weather, you can pull up stakes and move. There's no need to pack. You just get in the driver's seat, turn the key and go.

Drive until you find a better place. One with a better view, nicer weather, and different neighbors. Then set up camp and stay as long as you like—provided you pay the camping fees and abide by park rules.

For the past several months, I hadn't had to worry about any of that. I was camping for free, in a place with no rules and no neighbors.

My motorhome was parked in an old storage yard. The place had been closed for more than seven years, and not much remained, except for a tall privacy fence that kept my little home hidden from the rest of the world.

Sarah, the woman who I had delivered the cat to, rented the boat yard and the small building in front of it, and used it as her office for her kayak tour business.

The out-of-state owner Sarah rented from had agreed to let me stay, as long as I watched over the property and did minor repairs as needed.

In return for keeping the vagrants out, I got a camping spot with full hookups close enough to the beach that I could hear the surf at night. The place was well hidden behind the privacy fence, and walking distance to nearby shops and restaurants. And, as I mentioned before, it was free. I couldn't ask for much more.

But I was being forced to leave.

The local government had decided the old boatyard would make a great city park. They had offered the owner a deal she couldn't refuse. They'd given her more than the place was worth, and promised to name the new park after her much beloved deceased husband.

It was going to be Bob Snyder Park. And everyone was happy about it except me.

I'd been given thirty days to move. It went by quickly. The thirty days was up and I needed to be gone no later than midnight.

For the past month I'd been calling all the local RV parks trying to find a new place to live. I hadn't had any luck. All the parks said the same thing. "We're full and have a waiting list."

That happens during snowbird season in Florida. Retirees from up north wanting to escape the cold weather quickly fill up all the RV parks. The demand is so great that many people make reservations years ahead just to be sure they have a campsite when they arrive.

This is good news for park owners but bad news for people like me who don't have a reserved site and need a place to stay.

From outside, I could hear Anna. She was getting impatient. "Walker, either open the door or I'm coming in. You've got one minute."

Like I said, she is persistent.

I pulled on a pair of shorts and a T-shirt and made it up front just as Anna opened the door and stepped in.

She saw me and smiled, then frowned. "What's wrong with you? You look like death warmed over."

"I didn't get enough sleep and my head is pounding. And it's your fault."

She laughed. "Poor baby. Got a hangover on moving day."

"Yeah, I've got a hangover. Hope you and Sarah had fun getting me drunk last night."

Anna shook her head. "We didn't force you to drink. You could have stopped anytime."

She was right. They didn't force me. But they knew I wasn't much of a drinker. And they kept ordering refills. For me as well as them.

The worst part of this was Anna had drunk more than I had. She went to bed later than I did. She got up earlier than me, and instead of a hangover, she had a smile on her face, and looked like she had just stepped out of a fashion magazine.

I ran my hand through my hair. "So other than coming by to harass me, what's up?"

She smiled. "I found a place for your motorhome. It's not far from here, it's on the water, and they even have a pool. It's $550 a month with a three-month minimum. No kids, no pets over forty pounds. And normally no one under fifty-five years of age."

She was smiling, knowing I'd be pleased. She had found me a place.

"Anna, if they don't allow anyone under fifty-five to live there, why would they let me in? I'm way too young."

She smiled again, knowing that her smile alone could win almost any argument. "Here's the thing. I know the owner of the park and she's thinking about selling it. But she wants to wait until the end of the season to list it.

"In the meantime, she wants someone there working 'under cover' to figure out why the park isn't earning the kind of money it should be. She thinks the manager might be stealing.

"I told her I knew someone who might be perfect for the job —you.

"We could tell the other residents you were hired to upgrade the park's wireless internet system, and you'd be living there while you were doing it. Everyone in the park would be so happy the Wi-Fi was being updated they wouldn't care if you were twenty years under the minimum age.

"The owner thought it was a great idea. She even said you could live there rent free—as long as you agree to be her undercover man.

"So, what do you think? Are you interested in working undercover at Serenity Cove?"

Anna was waiting for my answer.

"Serenity Cove? That's the name of the place? It sounds like the name of a cemetery."

Anna shook her head. "It's not a cemetery. It's a nice park. And you really can't be too picky at this point. If you don't take this, you'll be sleeping in the Walmart parking lot tonight."

She was right. I needed a place to stay starting that day.

"So let me get this straight. All I have to do is move in, check things out and report back what I find. Nothing else, right?"

Anna nodded. "That's all you have to do. Just look around, talk to some of the residents and write up a report on what you find.

"The only catch is the owner wants you there for three months. And she really does want you to figure how much it's going to cost to upgrade the park's Wi-Fi.

"You can do that, can't you?"

Anna had hit all the right buttons. She knew I needed a place to stay. She knew I liked the idea of free rent, and she knew I wouldn't have any trouble with the park's Wi-Fi system.

She had set it up perfectly. And I'd be a fool not to take the deal.

"Okay, I'm in."

CHAPTER FIVE

Anna was on the phone with the owner of Serenity Cove, the place I would soon be calling home. I could only hear her side of the conversation.

"Yes, he said he'll do it.

"Yes, he can move in today.

"Okay, I'll be sure to tell him that.

"Noon today, no later. Got it.

"Okay, I'll call you later this week."

Anna ended the called and turned to me.

"It's all set. You have a site reserved at Serenity Cove. You have to check in before noon today. If you show up after that, the office will be closed and you'll be sleeping on the street tonight.

"When you check in, tell the manager you're the Wi-Fi guy. He'll be expecting you. He'll know your rent has been taken care of. Got it?"

I nodded. "Yeah, get there before noon. Tell them I'm the Wi-Fi guy."

Anna smiled. "Walker, you're going to like this place. It's a lot nicer than the old boatyard. It even has a swimming pool.

"You'll get three months free rent and all you have to do is sniff around and see if you can figure out why the place isn't making money. And to keep your cover from being blown, you'll want to check out the problems with the park's Wi-Fi.

"With your computer background, the Wi-Fi part should be easy."

She pointed to the clock over the kitchen sink. "You've got less than two hours to check in over there. So shower, shave, and go.

"Call me tonight. Tell me how it went."

She turned and headed for the door.

"Anna, wait. I really appreciate you finding me a place. So thanks. But I've got a feeling there's more to this than what you've told me."

She smiled. "You're right. There is one thing I may have left out. Serenity Cove is a clothing optional resort."

With that bombshell, she left before I could ask any more questions.

As I mentioned before, Anna is a kidder. I was hoping she was kidding about this. There was no way Serenity Cove was a clothing optional resort. Especially not in Englewood, Florida, a small town of less than twelve thousand people, most of whom are over sixty years of age. Almost all are retirees who moved to Englewood to escape the cold winters up north.

Unlike other areas of Florida, this place is not a tourist destination. There are no theme parks, no roadside attractions, not a Mickey or Minnie Mouse to be found anywhere.

It's just a small beach town halfway between Sarasota and Fort Myers.

It's not on the interstate and it's unlikely you'll end up in Englewood by accident. Your GPS is not going to route you through it unless it's your final destination. You're either coming on purpose or you'll never know it exists.

But if you do visit, you won't see any traffic jams, no rush hours, and so little crime that Englewood doesn't even have its own police department. Life is slow; the big attractions are the weekly farmer's market on Dearborn Street and the sixteen miles of sandy beaches on nearby Manasota Key.

For some, it's too tame. But I discovered I liked the place. In fact, it didn't take me long to figure out Englewood was where I wanted to park my motorhome and stay awhile. But not if it meant I had to live in a 'clothing optional' resort.

After Anna left, I fired up my computer and searched Google for "Serenity Cove, Englewood Florida". According to the search results, it was true that Serenity Cove had been established as a nudist resort. A place where people could camp in their RVs and run around naked if they wanted to.

But it hadn't worked out well.

The owners of the place had failed to factor in the average age of people visiting Englewood. Mostly retirees over sixty. And there weren't many of them interested in seeing the private parts of other senior citizens.

After two years of high vacancy rates, the Serenity Cove Nudist Resort went out of business. New owners came in and immediately dropped the 'clothing optional' rule and removed "Nudist Resort" from the name of the park.

The new Serenity Cove was relaunched as an upscale RV resort catering to snowbirds who wanted to spend their winters camped under palm trees near the Gulf of Mexico.

It had forty-eight spacious RV sites, each with full hookups and paved parking area. Amenities included a swimming pool, a tennis court, a covered picnic area, and a small boat dock on Lemon Bay.

All this sounded good to me.

Satisfied I wasn't really heading into a clothing optional campground, I heeded Anna's advice and took a quick shower and changed into clean clothes.

After the shower, I packed up the motorhome, freshened up Mango Bob's litter box and unhooked from shore power. The only other thing I needed to do was bring in the motorhome's slide room, but before I could, I had to find Mango Bob.

He's the cat that started all this. He's the reason I was in Florida and the reason I'd been able to park my motorhome in the old boatyard for free.

Officially, he's Sarah's cat. She'd found him as an abandoned kitten and taken him in. They had lived happily for two years until Sarah's new boyfriend gave her an ultimatum.

"Either the cat goes or I do. Choose one."

Sarah chose the boyfriend and Mango Bob was shuffled off to live with Sarah's sister in Arkansas.

Not long after, Sarah discovered she'd made the wrong choice. She should have kept the cat and dumped the boyfriend. She eventually kicked the guy out and decided she wanted Mango Bob back from her sister.

That's where I came in.

The deal offered to me by Sarah's sister was simple. "Deliver the cat to Sarah in Florida and you can live in your motorhome in her back yard close to the beach for free."

I'd never owned a cat before and wasn't sure about traveling across the country with one. But getting the chance to live in my motorhome near the beach sounded pretty good. So I accepted the offer.

Traveling to Florida with the cat turned into a real adventure. He'd never been in a motorhome before, and every time we stopped, he tried to get out. I didn't blame him for trying. I probably would have done the same thing had some one locked me up with a stranger and sent me on a trip across the country.

Only once was he able to get out. We were parked in Mississippi and when I opened the door to go out, he made a break for it. He got out before I could catch him, and ran under a car parked nearby. There was a lot of traffic and I was afraid I was going to lose him.

Fortunately, some very kind folks saw what was happening and they helped me get the cat back inside the motorhome. Had they not come to my aid, I'm not sure it would have ended well.

After that, I was very careful entering and leaving the motorhome. I didn't want to lose the cat. Especially in traffic.

In the end, everything turned out okay. I was able to deliver the cat to Sarah, and, as promised, she let me park my motorhome in her back yard. Which as it turned out, was an old boat yard she was renting for her Dolphin Kayak tours business.

Three months later, she closed her business and took a job in Venice, moving into an apartment where cats weren't allowed. She asked me to take care of Mango Bob until she could work out better living arrangements. I couldn't turn her down, and he's been with me in the motorhome ever since.

The funny thing is, the cat seems to like living in a house on wheels. It's got plenty of cubby holes he can use to hide, a soft bed he can sleep on, and lots of windows from which he can view the world outside. And even though it took some work on his part, he's got me pretty much trained to do his bidding.

He's been living with me for three months now, and I've kind of grown attached to him. That's why I needed to find him before I brought in the motorhome's slide room.

When the slide room comes in, it moves the driver's side wall about three feet into the motorhome. If Bob is near the wall when it is moving, he could get squished. So I never move it without first finding and locking him in the bedroom where he'll be safe.

To find him that day, I picked up his food bowl and gave it a shake. "Bob, I've got something to show you."

From behind the couch I heard, "Murrph."

He had heard me but wasn't ready to come out just yet.

I rattled the bowl again. "Come on, Bob, we're going on a road trip. You know what that means."

Again, I heard Bob say, "Muurrph?"

He was getting interested but wasn't coming out just yet. I put the bowl down and went up to the front of the motorhome

19

and pretended not to care what Bob might be doing in the back.

A few moments later, he came out and I heard him crunching on his food. When I turned to check on him, he yawned and trotted back to the bedroom. He knew what was going to happen next.

I closed the bedroom door behind him and pressed the switch to bring the slide in. Once it was all the way in, I opened the bedroom door and let Bob out.

With the outside utilities disconnected and the slide room in, I did a final walk through to make sure all the cabinet doors were closed and the TV antenna was cranked down. Satisfied that we were ready to roll, I sat in the driver's seat and called out, "Bob, we're going to be moving soon. You'll want to get up here."

I started the motor and this got his attention. He knew that when the motor started, things were going to happen. I patted the passenger seat. "Up here, Bob."

He understood. He came running from the back and jumped up on the seat and settled in. I put the motorhome in gear, and we headed out.

CHAPTER SIX

It took us ten minutes to get from the old boatyard on Mango Street to the front gate of Serenity Cove. My first impression of the place was not good. It didn't look anything like the photos on the web.

Instead of a nicely paved drive that led past a well-kept office building, I found a potholed and muddy lane leading past a rundown cinder block shack desperately needing a coat of paint.

Maybe this bad first impression was one of the reasons the park was losing guests. I'd mentioned it in my notes to the owner.

I parked in front of the shack and headed into what I presumed was the office. A bell attached to the door announced my presence. There was no one at the front desk, but I could hear a TV in the back room.

I waited a few minutes, but no one came out to greet me or check me in. Seeing a bell on the desk, I hit it twice with the palm of my hand.

From the back room I heard a grunt, followed by the sound of a chair scraping against the floor. Soon after, the door to the back opened just enough for a man to show his face. He looked at me and said, "What?"

I nodded. "My name is Walker. I'm the Wi-Fi guy. You have a spot reserved for me."

Saying nothing, the man shook his head and shuffled up to the counter. He appeared to be in his late thirties, hung over and unshaven, with greasy unkempt hair. He was wearing oil stained cargo shorts and a gray T-shirt that might have once been white.

Reaching under the counter, he pulled out a paper form and slid it over to me. "Fill this out."

I didn't have one on me, nor did I see one on the counter, so I pointed to the form. "You got a pen I can use?"

The man looked at me as if I had just insulted his sister. "What did you say?" he asked.

Speaking slowly, I repeated my request. "Do. You. Have. A. Pen. I. Can. Use?"

He stared at me for a moment. A prison yard stare. The kind you see just before someone gets knifed. He coughed into his hand, then reached under the counter and came up with a pencil. He dropped it on the registration form. "Ring the bell when you're done."

He turned and walked into the back room leaving me alone in the office.

At most RV parks, the people working the front desk usually go out of their way to make you feel welcome. But not this guy. I got the feeling I might get stabbed by the desk clerk if I asked the wrong question.

Clearly this wasn't the Hilton.

If this was the way all new guests at Serenity Cove were treated, it might be another reason so many were leaving to go somewhere else. I'd make a note about it for the owner.

After I completed the check-in form, I rang the bell.

There was no response from the man in the back room.

I waited two minutes then hit the bell again.

This time, he came out, looking pissed. Like I was interrupting his day. He reached across the counter, picked up the bell and tossed it toward a trash can on the other side of the room. The toss went wide; the bell hit the wall behind the can and bounced onto the floor.

I was tempted to say something but thought better of it.

The man turned to me, picked up the form I had filled out,

looked it over and held out his hand. "Six hundred dollars."

I shook my head. "No, I'm the Wi-Fi guy. I'm here to work. My spot has been reserved by the owner of this place. She said I could stay rent free."

He shook his head and moved his open hand toward me. "No one stays here for free. Six hundred dollars. Cash. Or leave."

I smiled. "You don't understand. The owner of Serenity Cove has arranged for me to stay here while I work on the Wi-Fi. Rent free."

I reached for my phone. "Maybe I should call her and straighten this out."

The man's demeanor suddenly changed. No longer surly, he smiled. "No need to bother her. We're good. Your rent is paid up. You'll be in eighteen."

He slid a sheet of paper over to me.

"Park rules. Read them."

I picked up the paper and scanned it. The rules were pretty straightforward.

1. 1. Residents and guests must adhere to all state and local ordinances.

2. 2. Sites must be kept clean at all times.

3. 3. Cars are to be parked in designated areas only.

4. 4. No open containers of alcoholic beverages outdoors except within the pool area.

5. 5. Quiet hours are from 8:00PM to 8:00AM and are strictly enforced.

6. 6. Pets must be on a leash and owners must clean up after pets.

7. 7. Speed limit is five miles per hour.

8. 8. Motorhomes must stay in assigned site during

stay. No day travel in motorhomes.

9. 9. No firearms, BB guns or bows and arrows permitted.

10.   10. Fighting, profanity, public intoxication and drugs strictly prohibited.

Scrawled across the bottom were the words, "*Report problems to the park manager, not the police!*"

When I looked up, the man behind the counter was staring. "You understand? If you have a problem, don't call the police. Come up here and report it at the office."

I nodded. "Yeah, I understand. No police. Anything else I need to know?"

"You'll need this."

He handed me a slip of paper.

Gate Pass Code: 2013

Wi-Fi Password: serenity

Without waiting to see if I had any more questions, he turned and went into the back room closing the door behind him. A moment later, I heard the TV volume go up, followed by the sound of a beer can being opened.

He was through with me.

Back out in the motorhome, Bob was sitting in the front seat waiting. I got in and explained the situation.

"Bob, we'll be staying here tonight."

He said, "Murrrph."

He didn't care where we were as long as there was food in his dish.

I put the motorhome in gear and we headed into the park looking for our site. It was easy to find. The site numbers were clearly marked, and space eighteen was the only empty space I saw.

I pulled past it, and then backed onto the paved parking pad, using my rear view camera to make sure I didn't hit anything. The site was wide and getting in was easy.

I killed the motor and grabbed Bob. I held him as I ran the slide room out. When I was done, I put him on the top of the couch, where he could look out the window and see his new surroundings.

A tall palm tree sat between our site and the next, providing both shade and a bit of privacy. Beyond the palm in the site next to us sat a late model Airstream trailer.

Little did I know that the person living in that Airstream would change the course of my life forever.

CHAPTER SEVEN

When it comes to motorhomes, there are several different kinds.

There are the big buses that the rich and famous have, the rolling palaces that can cost upwards of two million dollars. And then there are the Class A motorhomes, which are typically thirty five to forty five feet long and look like buses but are more affordable and within the reach of the not so rich.

On the other end of the size scaled, there are the small Class B camping vans. Ideal for day trips and maybe for two people who don't mind spending time in a cramped space. These little vans are quite popular these days but are a little too small to live in full time.

In between these two sizes, there are the Class C motorhomes. These are built on a standard heavy duty truck chassis and range in size from twenty to thirty-four feet. They have all the amenities you'd find in a Class A motorhome, but in a somewhat smaller package.

That's the kind of motorhome I have—a Class C.

It's a 28-foot Winnebago and even though it is six years old, it's pretty nice. Kind of like a small condo, it has granite counter-tops, solid oak cabinets, a double door fridge, full bath with shower and a private bedroom in the back.

There's a dinette table across from the kitchen and couch just behind the driver's seat. The couch can be folded out to make a guest bed.

All in all, it's a nice little package and has just about everything a person would want or need while on the road. While it'd probably be too small for a family of four, it suits me just fine.

The only problem with living in a motorhome is if it's your only vehicle, it means you have to unhook from shore power, bring in the slide and drive the motorhome everywhere you go. If you need to pick up groceries, you drive the motorhome. If you want to visit the local hardware store, you drive the motorhome. If you want to eat out at a restaurant, you drive the motorhome.

This can be a problem because you have to plan ahead and make sure the streets you take and the parking lots you pull into have enough room to get a motorhome in and out of without getting stuck.

I'd gotten used to this, driving my motorhome to grocery stores and other places to pick up supplies. It was inconvenient but doable.

Now that I was living in Serenity Cove, I wouldn't be driving my motorhome that often if I were to abide by the rules on the sheet of paper I'd gotten in the office.

Like a lot of longer term RV parks, Serenity Cove didn't want you driving your motorhome in and out of the park every day. They wanted you to keep it parked until you get ready to check out.

This "keep it parked" rule actually makes sense, especially in parks where people are staying for months at a time. Without this kind of rule, you might end up with motorhomes and trailers coming and going at all times of the day and night, creating lots of traffic and noise. That wouldn't be good for anyone.

So parks have the rule and many enforce it.

This 'keep it parked' rule is one reason many motorhome owners have a 'toad'—a small car they tow behind their motorhome. The toad gives you a way to leave the park and drive to the store or mall without having to rely on the motorhome.

So far, I'd been able to make do without having a toad, but

now that I was living in Serenity Cove, I'd need to get one—
and soon. Otherwise I'd have to call a cab to take me into town
to get groceries and supplies.

Fortunately, the solution to my toad problem was just a few
steps away.

CHAPTER EIGHT

She said her name was Polly. Polly Sparks.

Five foot tall and rail thin with light blonde hair pulled back into a ponytail. White cotton shirt, faded jeans. Looked to be in her mid-fifties.

In her hand, a plate of brownies.

She smiled and pointed to the silver Airstream trailer next door. "Welcome to Serenity Cove. I'm your neighbor and these are for you."

She handed me the brownies, and without hesitation, I invited her in. I had to. She had brownies. And I've always had a policy of never turning anyone away who's holding a plate of brownies.

I guided her to the kitchen table. She sat on one side, and I sat on the other. The plate of brownies sat in the center of the table between us.

I smiled. "These look really good. Mind if I try one?"

She shook her head. "No, you can't have one yet. Not until you tell me your name."

I smiled. "I'm John Walker. But everybody calls me Walker."

"Glad to meet you, Walker. Have a brownie. I think you'll like them. They're from my special recipe."

I picked one up and took a bite. The brownie was still warm from the oven and without a doubt the best I'd had in years.

She watched me eat it and smiled. Then asked, "You live here alone?"

"Yeah, just me. And my cat, Mango Bob."

"Mango Bob? What kind of name is that for a cat?"

"It's a long story."

"Let me guess. It involves a woman."

I nodded and she laughed.

"That's what I thought. There's always a woman. You married?"

I shook my head. "No, not anymore."

Polly nodded. "A lot of that going around.

"So not to get too personal, but I've got to ask. I'm guessing you're a lot younger than fifty five. Am I right?"

I nodded. "Yeah, you're right. I'm in my thirties."

She smiled. "That's what I thought. So what brings a single thirty-something guy into a 55+ retirement park?"

I reached for another brownie. "Work. I'm here to work on the Wi-Fi."

She smiled again. "Wi-Fi, huh? That's a good cover story. Some people might even believe it. But not me. I think you're really an undercover cop."

CHAPTER NINE

"You think I'm a cop? What makes you think that?"

She looked at me not answering. Then said, "Don't worry. I won't blow your cover. Your secret is safe with me."

I smiled, "Polly, I assure you I'm not a cop. And even if I were, why would I be here, in Serenity Cove?"

She leaned forward, a mischievous look in her powder-blue eyes. Then she looked around, as if checking to see if anyone else might be listening in on our conversation. "Walker, we've had a crime wave here lately. There have been a few break-ins and some drug dealing. There's a rumor an undercover cop was going to move in and check things out.

"Since you've just moved in and are a lot younger than everyone else here, I figure you're the cop. You sure fit the profile. Clean cut, physically fit, no visible tattoos."

I smiled. "Polly, like I said, I'm not a cop. I'm here to work on Serenity Cove's internet and the owner's letting me stay for the summer."

She nodded. "Well, the internet does need work. It's slow most of the time except when it's not working at all.

"Course, if you were an undercover cop, that'd be a good cover story—telling people you were working on the internet while doing your undercover investigation.

"But, just so you know, it wouldn't bother me a bit if you *were* a cop. In fact, it'd be nice to have police protection living next door to me. You'll be a whole lot better than the last people who lived over here.

"They had a couple of grown kids hanging around all the

time, always getting into trouble."

While Polly was telling me this, I grabbed my third brownie and quickly finished it off. I wanted another but didn't want to look like I was starving.

I wiped my mouth. "These are good. Hard to stop at just one."

Polly smiled. "Yeah I know. It's my special recipe. Everybody loves them."

She paused for a moment. "Walker, whether you're a cop or not, I need to ask you a favor.

"One of my prescriptions has run out and I need to go to Publix to pick up the refill. But my eyes are a little crazy this morning and I'm afraid to drive. I wonder if you would drive me over to Publix?"

Now, normally I don't mind doing favors. Even for people I've just met. And Polly had already won me over with her brownies so I was ready to do her a favor.

But I couldn't.

"I'd be happy to drive you to Publix. But I don't have a car. Been meaning to get one, just haven't gotten around to it yet."

She smiled. "That's okay. You can drive mine. You do have a driver's license, don't you?"

I nodded. "I do. And if you want me to drive you to Publix, I'd be happy to. When do you want to go?"

She rubbed her eyes. "Right now would be good. My eyes are starting to sting and that medicine would help. But if you can't do it now, we can go later."

"No, now is fine. Give me a minute or two to lock things up here, and I'll meet you out by your car."

After Polly left, I grabbed my wallet, cell phone, keys and sunglasses—everything I figured I needed. Then I stepped outside and locked up the motorhome.

Polly was outside by her car. At her feet was a dog. Short,

stubby legs, low slung body, shiny, brown coat. Eager to go for a ride.

"Who's this?"

"Oscar. My faithful companion."

Upon hearing his name, the dog trotted over to the side door of the white Toyota minivan that was parked next to Polly's Airstream trailer.

Polly pressed a button on her remote and the minivan's rear passenger door slid open. Oscar climbed in and settled in on the back seat.

Polly pushed another button on the remote, and the door glided to a close. She handed me the keys and said, "You're driving."

Before getting in, I walked to the passenger side and opened the door for her. She smiled. "It's been years since someone has done that for me. But don't do it again. Especially when we're out in public. I don't want people thinking I'm old."

Having learned a quick lesson, I climbed into the driver's seat, adjusted the mirrors and buckled my seat belt.

The minivan started easily. Before I backed out, I checked the rear view mirror. Oscar was stretched out in the backseat, apparently asleep.

"He sure looks comfortable back there."

Polly smiled. "Yeah, he loves to ride in the car. Usually he hops in and goes right to sleep."

"So how'd he get the name Oscar?"

"It's from the song."

"What song?"

"The wiener song."

"The wiener song?"

"You know the one. It goes like this."

Polly started singing. *"Oh, I wish I was an Oscar Mayer*

wiener, that is what I'd truly like to be, 'cause if I were an Oscar Mayer wiener, everyone would be in love with me."

By the time she had finished singing, we were both laughing. She had sung the song to perfection, and on the very last line, Oscar had joined in from the back seat.

He sang, "Wooo wooo eeeeee wooo wooo wooo eeeee."

When Polly quit laughing, she said, "I should have warned you. That's Oscar's favorite song. He always sings along."

That put us both in a good mood. Polly and Oscar's duet had made my day.

"Are we going to the Publix on Dearborn or the one at Merchants Crossing?"

Polly smiled. "I was wondering if you were going to ask. I figured a newcomer wouldn't know there were two Publix on this side of town. But an undercover cop would."

I shook my head. "Polly, I'm not a cop. I've been living here long enough to know where the grocery stores are. So which one?"

"The one on Dearborn."

It was an easy drive from Serenity Cove. Almost no traffic and only one stop light.

I pulled into the parking lot and found a place to park under the shade of a palm tree. In Florida that's one of the first things you learn. Park in the shade when you can. Even if it means a longer walk to the store.

As soon as I turned off the motor, Polly reached over and touched my arm. "If you don't mind, stay here in the car with Oscar. I'll go in and pick up my prescription and be right back."

I smiled. "No problem."

Polly got out and headed into the store. Oscar didn't seem to mind. He was in the backseat snoring loudly.

Ten minutes later, Polly had yet to return. Oscar grunted

then sat up. In the distance we could hear the sound of a siren heading in our direction.

CHAPTER TEN

As the siren grew louder, Oscar began moving his head from side to side. His mouth opened, and a groaning sound came out. Like he was either in pain or deeply worried about something.

He was still in the back seat, standing, watching the front door of Publix where Polly had gone in.

When the Englewood Fire and Rescue truck pulled into the parking lot, Oscar climbed up on the console between the passenger and driver seats, and put his front paws on the dash so he could get a better look at the action.

His groaning sound became louder and he looked in my direction, as if he were expecting me to do something. I tried to calm him down.

"It's okay, Oscar. Polly is fine. She'll be back in a few minutes."

As we watched, two paramedics in blue uniforms climbed out of the rescue truck and rushed into the store. A crowd of curious onlookers gathered outside.

A few moments later, one of the paramedics came back out and got a stretcher from the back of the truck, and then went back inside.

Polly was still in the store and Oscar was quite concerned. He stood looking at the rescue truck, whimpering.

I stroked his back. "Oscar, she'll be back. She's okay."

But I wasn't sure. She'd been in there a long time. Maybe Oscar knew something was wrong.

Three minutes later, the paramedics exited the store pushing a gurney with an older woman strapped onto it.

It wasn't Polly.

The woman on the gurney was much larger and had long, dark hair. The paramedics put the woman in the back of the emergency vehicle and drove off.

A minute later, Polly exited the store carrying a small, white bag in her right hand. As she walked toward us, Oscar's little tail went wild, wagging faster than I thought possible.

Polly got in on the passenger seat and said, "Did you see that? That lady was checking out and had a seizure. She fell to the floor and no one knew what to do."

While she was telling me this, Oscar was doing his best to get into her lap. He was happy she was back safe and sound. And he wanted to be close to her.

Polly stroked his head. "Oscar, were you worried I wasn't coming back? You know I'd never leave you."

Oscar licked her face and wagged his tail, while Polly continued to stroke his back and rub his ears trying to calm him down.

Finally she said, "Oscar, time to get in the back seat."

He groaned, not wanting to leave her lap.

"Oscar, back seat."

This time he stood and climbed into the back seat.

"That's a good boy."

With Oscar out of her way, Polly opened her shopping bag and pulled out a small vial of pills and a bottle of Zepherhills water. She opened the water first then tapped out a single pill and popped it into her mouth. She washed it down with water.

She put the pill bottle in her purse and turned to me. "That'll help. Won't take long now. So, was Oscar a problem?"

"No, he was good. He was worried when he saw the EMTs go into the store. But as soon as he saw you come back out, he was happy."

She smiled. "Oscar is smart. He knows I'm not going to ever leave him, but he does worry when I'm not around."

I started the minivan, planning to head back to Serenity Cove. But before I could back out of our parking spot, Polly asked, "Where do you want to go next?"

I shrugged. "I don't know. Where do you want to go?"

She smiled. "You mentioned you didn't have a car and wanted to buy one. What kind you looking for?"

I'd been thinking about getting a car for a while, so I had a ready answer. "I want something to pull behind my motorhome. Like a small pickup with a manual transmission."

"New or used?"

"Used."

"Good. Used is good. I know just the place to go. My daughter, Lucy, works at the Truck Depot in Venice. They always have a good selection of used trucks. I bet she could find you just what you are looking for. Mind if I call her?"

I smiled. "Not at all, give her a call."

Polly pulled her phone from her purse and made the call. I could only hear her side of the conversation.

"Lucy, I'm sitting here with my new neighbor, and he says he's looking to buy a used truck. I think you might be able to help him.

"Yes, I know, but he seems nice. At least talk to him."

Polly handed me the phone.

"Say, 'HI,' to Lucy."

CHAPTER ELEVEN

I took the phone. "Hello?"

"Hi, this is Lucy. Who am I speaking with?"

"Hi Lucy, I'm Walker. Your mom's new neighbor."

"Walker, I hope my mother isn't being a bother. She's always trying to push people to buy cars from me. So let's save us both some time. If you're not really interested in buying a car, say so now."

"Lucy, I really *am* interested in buying a car. Actually a truck."

"Good. Tell me what you want."

"Something I can tow behind my motorhome. Maybe an older Toyota Tacoma. It has to have a manual transmission because I can't tow an automatic."

"Got it. What's your budget?"

"I'd like to stay under fifteen thousand."

"That sounds doable. Let me check our inventory and I'll get back to you. What's a good number to reach you?"

I gave Lucy my number then handed the phone back to her mother. She spoke to Lucy for a moment then disconnected.

After she ended the call, she turned to me and smiled. "That went well. Lucy said she might be able to find you something."

I nodded. "It would be good if she could."

We were still sitting in the Publix parking lot. I was waiting for Polly to say she was ready to go home. But apparently she wasn't because what she said was, "Start driving. There's something I want to show you."

CHAPTER TWELVE

We turned left out of the Publix parking lot and headed south on Indiana Avenue until we reached Beach Road. At the light, we turned right and crossed over the Intracoastal Waterway via the Tom Adams Bridge.

When we reached the roundabout at Manasota Beach, Polly said, "Go left. Then slow down because we're almost there."

I started through the roundabout, but had to stop when a snowbird with Jersey plates ignored the rules and blew through the intersection, just barely missing a VW convertible.

Polly shook her head. "These people get down here and forget how to drive."

Then she said, "Just ahead, turn left into Chadwick Park. Then drive back to the boat ramp."

I'd been over the Tom Adams Bridge leading to Manasota Key many times. The first time was with Sarah. We'd walked on the beach, held hands and watched the sun set. Since then, I'd visited Manasota Beach often. Usually carrying my metal detector. But I'd never noticed Chadwick Park. Probably because there were no signs leading to it, just a small driveway across from the public beach parking lot.

Following Polly's directions, I turned left and drove to where the road ended in front of a small open air pavilion overlooking the Intracoastal Waterway.

Polly pointed toward the water. "It's over there."

I looked at where she was pointing. All I could see was water and a few boats tied up in the mooring field.

"What am I supposed to be looking at?"

"See that white houseboat, the one with the blue curtains?"

I scanned the boats. "Yeah, I see it. The *Escape Artist*?"

"Yeah, that's it. It's my boat."

I was surprised. "You have a houseboat out here on the water?"

She nodded. "Sure do. Bought it a year ago with plans to travel up and down the Intracoastal Waterway—just me and Oscar.

"But on our first outing, I discovered Oscar isn't much of a sea dog. He doesn't like being on a boat. Especially a moving boat. He got seasick.

"And let me tell you, being on a boat with a seasick dog with no one around to help isn't much fun. So my plans for the boat have changed. No sailing away on the Intracoastal for me and Oscar."

She paused for a moment, then said, "I'm thinking of selling it."

I didn't know what to say, so we sat there in silence, looking out over the water, listening to Oscar snore in the back seat.

I started thinking about the boat. It looked to be in pretty good shape. And it would be a good way to get away from it all. And a way to travel up and down the Intracoastal Waterway and see the sights.

I was kind of interested, so I asked the obvious question. "How much are you going to ask for it?"

"I'm thinking thirteen thousand. That's what I've got in it."

"Anything wrong with it?"

She laughed, "It's a boat. There's always something wrong. But not anything serious that I know of. I start it at least once a month, and it seems to run just fine."

"What's it cost to keep it over there?"

"Nothing. It's a public mooring field. All you have to do is tie up to a mooring ball and make sure the boat doesn't float away. Think you might be interested in buying it?"

Before I could answer, Polly's phone began playing the first few bars from an old Beatles's song, "Lucy in the Sky with Diamonds".

Polly answered. As before, I could only hear one side of the conversation.

"Lucy, what's up?

"Yes, he's right here."

Polly held the phone out for me. "My lovely daughter wishes to speak with you."

I took the phone. "This is Walker."

"Hey Walker, this is Lucy. I think I found something you might like.

"I know you were looking for a Tacoma, but this might work better. We've just got this on trade—a Jeep Wrangler. Four wheel drive. Black on black with a factory hard top. It's got the six-cylinder motor and the six-speed manual transmission.

"And get this; the original owner set it up so he could pull it behind his motorhome. It's got a base plate, a tow bar, and even a Roadmaster brake system.

"Like I said, we just got this in. It's at our Sarasota lot, and it's priced right so it's going to go quickly. Think you might be interested?"

I'd owned a lot of four wheel drive trucks over the years but never owned a Jeep. But my friends who had Jeeps seemed to like them. Having one in Florida might be fun, especially since this one was already set up for towing behind a motorhome.

"Lucy, I'm interested. But I don't have a car, which means I have no way to get over to your Sarasota lot to take a look at it."

There was a pause. Then Lucy said, "That's not a problem. I'm having dinner at Mom's tonight. I can drive the Jeep and you can take it for a test drive. Will that work for you?"

"Yeah, that'd be great."

"Then it's a date. I'll be there around six. Let me talk to Mom."

I handed the phone to Polly. And again I could only hear one side of her conversation.

"Yes dear, he's nice. You'll like him. And he's single.

"I don't know about that, but you can ask him when you see him this evening.

"Okay, bye."

Polly looked at me with a twinkle in her eye. "You're going to meet my daughter tonight. That should be interesting."

She turned her attention back to the houseboat. "Any time you want to see the boat, just let me know. I haven't put the 'for sale' signs on it yet, and if you think you might be interested, I'd rather show it to you than deal with strangers."

In the back seat, Oscar snorted. Then farted.

Polly laughed. "Sounds like I need to get Oscar back home. He's on a strict poop schedule, and I don't want him to miss his window of opportunity."

I started the minivan and we headed back.

CHAPTER THIRTEEN

Back at Serenity Cove, I thanked Polly for her brownies and she thanked me for driving her to Publix. Oscar came over and sniffed my shoes then snorted. I didn't know if it was a snort of acceptance or derision. Perhaps he smelled Mango Bob.

Speaking of which, as soon as I opened the door to my motorhome, Bob was there. He had things to show me.

First, he led me back to his food bowl, which needed topping off. Then he led me back up front where he jumped on the back of the couch and leaned against the window sill.

From his perch, he had spied birds. Watching birds was one of Bob's most favorite things. He'd watch them until his little mouth would start a strange chattering sound and his stub of a tail would begin twitching back and forth.

As far as I knew, Bob had been an inside cat since being rescued at a very early age. But his instincts for hunting were deeply ingrained and I had no doubt that if he could get out, he'd soon be chasing birds instead of just chattering at them.

Since the weather was mild, I opened the window so he could better hear the birds and perhaps get their scent. The screen on the window would keep him inside, while the open window would let him feel closer to nature.

As soon as I opened the window, Bob looked up at me and said, "Murrph." His 'thank you' sound.

Then he returned his gaze to the birds in the tree just out of his reach.

While Bob watched the birds, I checked the fridge for something to eat. I'd missed lunch, and other than the three brownies, I hadn't had much else that day.

Seeing that the fridge was almost bare reminded me that as soon as I got a car, I'd need to go out and restock with fresh food.

Until recently, I'd been buying food at Walmart. Their large parking lot was a lot easier to get into and out of than most other stores, so that's where I shopped. But I wouldn't be taking the motorhome to Walmart or anywhere else for a while. The rules at Serenity Cove prohibited those kinds of in and out trips.

I really did need a car, and soon.

Maybe the Jeep Lucy was bringing over that evening would be the one.

Since my cover story at Serenity Cove was that of a specialist brought in to upgrade the park's Wi-Fi and since I had a few hours to kill before Lucy showed up with the Jeep, I figured I might as well fire up my computer and do a quick check on their system.

Back when I worked in the corporate world, my specialty was setting up secure Wi-Fi networks and finding ways to hack into them. Finding weak spots in the network before hackers did, gave us a chance to plug the holes keeping the bad guys out.

To test our network, I had put together a set of software tools which I still had on my computer. These tools made it easy for me to quickly analyze a Wi-Fi network and see what was wrong with it.

I logged into the Serenity Cove network and ran the analysis. The entire process took less than five minutes. The results showed the park was using an older and slower Wi-Fi transmission protocol and had limited bandwidth and spotty coverage.

It was typical with older systems, especially those with hotspots and repeaters installed outdoors. Fortunately, bringing the Serenity Cove system up to date wouldn't take much. A new router and repeaters, an updated firewall, and new cabling.

At current prices, probably less than $3,000 in hardware. And three days of labor to get it installed.

I'd write up a report with my recommendations and a cost estimate. My realtor buddy Anna could give it to the park owner and get approval before I started spending any money on new equipment.

While waiting for approval, I could make a few changes to the router and get a major improvement in the system without spending much money. But I'd wait a few days before I did that. No need to get the work completed the first day on the job.

While on the computer, I browsed over to eBay and checked the prices of Jeeps like the one Lucy would be bringing over that evening. There were plenty for sale, in every shape and condition. Many had been customized with lift kits, big tires, and off road accessories.

These didn't interest me. I wanted something close to factory stock.

The bid prices for low mileage, good condition, unmodified Jeep Wranglers were pretty much in line with what I wanted to pay. Lucy hadn't mentioned a price, but knowing what they were going for on eBay, I knew what they were worth.

I printed out a few of the listings, turned off my computer and spent the rest of the afternoon, getting settled into my new campsite.

Around six o'clock, a shiny, black Jeep Wrangler pulled into the parking in front of Polly's Airstream. The driver's door opened and a woman, late twenties to early thirties, wearing cargo shorts, white T-shirt, dark sunglasses, and a ball cap, stepped out. She looked in my direction and smiled.

Lucy Sparks. The car salesman who made house calls.

I started to go outside to introduce myself, but she turned and walked to the front door of the Airstream where her mother greeted her.

They had a short conversation then both started walking

toward my motorhome.

I went outside to meet them.

Polly introduced us. "Walker, this is my daughter, Lucy."

I reached out and shook her hand. "Glad to meet you, Lucy. I see you brought the Jeep."

She nodded. "Sure did. Just like I promised."

She turned toward the Jeep. "It's a beauty, isn't it?"

Before I could answer, she said, "Let me show you why you're going to like it.

"It's got new tires all the way around. New battery. No dents and no rust."

She patted the roof. "Factory hardtop. A two-thousand-dollar option. Well worth it in stormy weather. Plus it keeps the interior nice."

She opened the passenger door. "The seats and dash are in perfect condition. The air conditioning is ice cold."

Lucy was in car salesman mode, excited she had a prospect and a decent car to sell.

I smiled and asked a question. "So Lucy, where's the tow bar you mentioned?"

She pointed over her shoulder. "We took it off back at the sales lot. It comes off easily and there was no need to drive around with it mounted to the front grill."

I nodded but didn't say anything. I was interested in the Jeep but didn't want to seem too anxious.

Lucy looked at her mom then back at me. "So, Walker, you want to take it for a test drive?"

"I do. You coming with me?"

"Yeah, I'm coming with you. Someone's got to make sure you'll bring it back. That'll be me."

She tossed me the keys. "You drive, I'll ride shotgun."

Turning to Polly, she said, "If we're not back in thirty

minutes, call the sheriff."

After Lucy got in, I climbed in on the driver's side, adjusted my seat and mirrors and scanned the dash. The controls were pretty much what I expected. Nothing fancy, but easy to understand.

Pushing in the clutch, I started the motor, eased the transmission into reverse, and backed out onto the road. I put it in first gear and we headed out.

The Jeep handled well. A little stiff over the bumps, but pretty much what you'd expect in a Jeep. It had plenty of power and a rugged feeling that just begged to be taken off road.

When we reached Dearborn Street, Lucy said, "Turn left here. Head toward River Road. When we get to Pine Street, turn right, and we'll loop back around. That'll give you a chance to see how well it handles at speed and in traffic."

I nodded and kept driving.

The Jeep surprised me with how much pep the six-cylinder motor had. If I wasn't careful when letting out the clutch, I could chirp the tires in first and second gear.

The first time I did it, Lucy shook her head. "It's not yours yet, so don't tear it up."

"Okay, I'll be gentle with it."

But I wasn't. I hit the speed bumps on Dearborn a little faster than I should have. Then I tested the brakes at the second stop sign with a hard stop.

The brakes worked well, I was happy we both had our seat belts on. After the brake test, I drove normally. Listening for problems, making sure the steering felt tight and there weren't any unexpected rattles.

Inside, the seats were comfortable, not cushy but firm.

"So what do you think?" asked Lucy.

I didn't want to let her know how much I liked it, so I said, "It's not bad. For a Jeep."

She smiled but didn't say anything as I continued on River Road.

As we neared the Pine Street intersection, I moved over into the right lane so I could make the turn at the light. It was red when we got there, and the car in front of us wasn't turning, so we had to stop and wait for the green.

Just as the light turned, a boy on a bicycle shot across the intersection, trying to outrun the row of stopped cars.

He almost made it.

The car to the left of me had accelerated as soon as the light had turned and had hit the bike broadside, throwing the kid over the hood and onto the road in front of oncoming traffic.

The driver of the car that hit the kid, an elderly woman, came to a full stop in the center of the intersection.

The driver in the car behind me honked his horn, wanting me to make my right turn and get out of his way. I wasn't sure whether he had seen the accident or not, but he was in a hurry to go somewhere.

I turned right to get out of his way, pulled to the side of the road, and, as soon as the waiting car passed, did a U-turn. This put us in the lane opposite and to the left of the kid lying in the center of the road, exposed to oncoming traffic.

Turning to Lucy, I said, "Hold on."

I accelerated into the intersection, jerked the steering wheel hard to the left, slid the Jeep sideways then stomped on the brakes as we closed in on the fallen rider.

Lucy looked at me wide-eyed. "What the hell are you doing?"

I pointed to the oncoming traffic. "I'm creating a road block so that kid doesn't get run over."

After asking Lucy to call 911, I released my seat belt and jumped out to see how badly he had been hurt. He was lying on his back in the middle of the road, not moving.

It looked bad.

Preparing for the worst, I ran toward him, hoping he was still breathing. As I got closer, I was surprised to see that he wasn't a kid. He was a middle-aged man, probably in his late forties, maybe early fifties.

It looked like he had led a hard life. Deep creases on his unshaven face, tattered shirt and pants. Scars on his hands and legs.

Still not moving.

I'd gotten close enough to see that there was no blood. No seeping wounds. But he wasn't breathing.

Looking around, I could see that people had stopped and were getting out of their cars. But they were staying back, not wanting to get too close. Not wanting to get involved.

I couldn't really blame them. Accidents like this are messy. You never know who you are dealing with or what diseases the victims might be carrying.

But if it were *you* on the ground, you'd want somebody to get involved. To take a risk to save your life.

In the military we had been trained how to react in situations like this. Check the airway for obstructions, check for open wounds, stop the bleeding and, when necessary, perform CPR to get the heart restarted.

I checked the man's pulse. There was nothing there. He wasn't breathing and his heart had stopped. If he were to be saved, it had to happen now. Someone needed to start CPR.

No one else was coming to his aid. So it was left to me. Either I could stand by and watch him die or I could try to save his life.

It was an easy decision.

I knelt down beside him and put both hands near the center of his chest. Pushing hard, I began the compressions. Fast and to the beat of the Bee Gees' *Staying Alive*. One compression for each word in the chorus.

"*Ah, ha, ha, ha, stayin' alive, stayin' alive.*

Ah, ha, ha, ha, stayin' alive."

Twelve compressions in a row. I hoped it would be enough. Else I'd have to do it over and over until help arrived.

He hadn't revived, so I started again, humming the Bee Gees' song.

"Ah, ha, ha, ha, stayin' alive, stayin' alive. Ah, ha, ha, ha, stayin' alive."

On the final 'stayin alive', the man surprised me. His eyes popped open and he took a deep, noisy breath.

Then, with a toothy grin, he said, "Wow, that could'a been bad!"

The paramedics arrived moments later. I stood and got out of their way.

Looking around, I saw that Lucy was standing with the woman who had been driving the car that had hit the cyclist. They were talking with a sheriff's deputy who was taking notes.

Lucy motioned me over.

When I got close, she asked. "How is he?"

I shrugged. "Don't know for sure, but I think he's going to be okay. Doesn't appear to have any broken bones. Just had the wind knocked out of him. He's sitting up and talking to the EMTs."

She smiled. "Good. We were worried."

She introduced me to the woman standing beside her. The driver of the car that had hit the man.

"I never saw him. The light turned green and he was just there."

Lucy touched the woman's shoulder. "It's all right. It wasn't your fault."

Lucy had already told the deputy what had happened. How the cyclist had come off the curb against the light, right in front of the woman's car.

The deputy took me aside and asked me to tell him what I'd

seen. I told him the same thing Lucy had. The cyclist had come off the curb against the light, directly into traffic.

"So it wasn't the woman's fault?" he asked.

"No. She didn't do anything wrong. The cyclist ran the light; no way she could have avoided him."

The deputy got our names and contact info and said, if needed, they would get in touch. But, at the moment, it looked like that wouldn't be necessary.

As I was walking back to join Lucy, her phone chimed with an incoming call. She looked at it and said, "It's Mom, checking up on us."

After Lucy assured her mom that I hadn't kidnapped her, she told her about the accident and said we were heading back and should be home in a few minutes.

Our Jeep was still parked in the middle of the road. The deputy was directing traffic around it. It was time for us to go.

The cyclist was now standing, arguing with the paramedics. They wanted to take him to the emergency room and he didn't want to go.

He glanced over at me, smiled, and gave me a big thumbs up. I nodded and drove off.

CHAPTER FOURTEEN

"You're staring at me."

Lucy shook her head. "No I'm not."

"Yes, you are. Do I have blood on me or something?"

She smiled. "No, it's nothing like that. It's just I've never seen anyone do what you did.

"Most people wouldn't have gotten involved. But not you. You took charge. You almost wrecked the Jeep trying to keep the guy from getting run over. Then you got out and saved his life.

"Mom thinks you're an undercover cop. Maybe you are. I can't think of anyone else who would do something like that."

I shook my head. "I'm not an undercover cop. Not a cop of any kind. But that guy needed help. And you just don't walk away when someone needs your help."

I changed the subject. "This Jeep. I like it. What's the asking price?"

Lucy smiled. "We weren't talking about the Jeep. We were talking about you. Where did you learn first aid? At the Police Academy?"

I shook my head. "I've never been to the Police Academy. I was in the Army. Did two tours. Saw a lot of action."

We rode in silence for a few minutes.

"Seventeen thousand. That's what the sales manager told me to tell you. Seventeen thousand for the Jeep."

Before I could reply, she continued.

"Blue book retail price would be about thirteen five. Add in the hardtop and the tow bar, and you're up to fifteen. But I think I can get you into it for fourteen. With sales tax, title and fees, you'll be fifteen five out the door.

"And we can finance with 20% down."

I liked the Jeep. And I liked Lucy's honesty about the price. I probably would have paid the higher price, but the lower one was better.

"Fifteen five out the door works for me. I'll take it."

Lucy smiled. "Good. When we get back to my mom's, I'll write up a sales contract. Tomorrow I'll take you to our Venice sales lot and we'll finalize the deal."

When we got back to Polly's trailer, Lucy pulled a sales contract out of her purse and said, "I'm going to go inside and let Mom know we're here. Don't go anywhere, I'll be right back."

Before she got out of the Jeep, she reached over and took the keys out of the ignition.

I laughed. "You don't trust me?"

She shook her head. "No offense, but I don't trust anyone until I have a signed sales contract and payment in hand."

With that, she went into her mother's trailer while I waited in the Jeep for her return.

A few minutes later, she came back out with the sales contract, and after I looked it over, I signed it.

"Mom wants you to join us for dinner. She said I couldn't take 'no' for an answer."

I smiled. "Well, in that case, I guess I'll be eating dinner with you. But I need to clean up first. I'll meet you over there in a few minutes."

I went back to my motorhome, washed up and changed into some clean clothes, then headed over to Polly's.

Lucy was waiting for me at the door. She escorted me to the dining table.

Over dinner, she retold the story of how, in her mind, I had single-handedly saved the cyclist's life. I tried to explain that I hadn't done anything special, certainly nothing heroic.

But Lucy wasn't having any of it. She told her mom that had I not been there, the man would have surely died.

Upon hearing the story, Polly was more convinced than ever that I was an undercover cop.

CHAPTER FIFTEEN

The next morning, I was up early. Mango Bob hadn't slept well and had patrolled the motorhome all night. Every once in a while he'd let out a worrisome howl, telling me things looked different outside.

This was to be expected.

Bob and I had spent most of the last six months camped out in the old boatyard where we were completely surrounded by an eight-foot privacy fence. At the boatyard, Bob's view was limited; there were no other people, no pets and no cars to be seen.

But here at Serenity Cove, Bob could see a new landscape out every window. There were trees above us with birds and squirrels. Motorhomes beside us with people and pets. Cars, golf carts, and bicyclists on the driveway in front.

All this new activity required Bob to be on full alert.

So while neither of us had slept well, Bob's appetite hadn't suffered. By early morning, his food bowl was nearly empty and he felt it important to make sure I knew about this. He did so by hopping up on the bed and tapping my ear with his paw until he got my attention.

After getting up and filling his bowl, I ate a quick breakfast of cold cereal and white grape juice. My normal breakfast. Easy to make and easy to clean up.

Lucy had said to expect her around eight and I wanted to be ready. I took a quick shower, shaved and put on clean shirt and shorts.

Right on schedule, Lucy showed up with the Jeep. She

looked sharp in her cargo shorts, powder-blue Columbia fishing shirt, sunglasses, with a dark blue ball cap pulled over her ponytail.

When I stepped out to greet her, she had a big smile on her face and dangled the keys in my direction.

"You want to drive?"

I shook my head. "No. You drive while I enjoy the view."

She smiled. "Suits me. But before we leave, make sure you have your driver's license, insurance card, and check book."

I patted my back pocket where I carried my wallet. "Got it all. I'm ready whenever you are."

She nodded. "Good. Give me a minute to talk to Mom, and I'll be right back."

While Lucy visited her mom, I locked up the motorhome and inspected the Jeep.

It had looked pretty good the previous evening; it looked even better in the early morning light. No scratches, dents or blemishes. Even though it was several years old, it looked new.

It was clear the previous owner had taken good care of it. I was happy it would soon be mine.

From behind me, I heard my name. It was Polly, Lucy's mother. "Walker, after you get done with Lucy, come by and see me. There's something I want to talk to you about."

"Sure, no problem."

Lucy drove us to the Truck Depot lot in Venice. She introduced me to Ed, the sales manager and gave him the sales agreement I had signed the night before.

At first Ed smiled then he shook his head. "She let you have it for fourteen? That's crazy. I would've never done that. Should have been a couple thousand more. You got a steal."

I was pretty sure he told every customer the same thing, regardless of what kind of deal they got.

We went into Ed's office and he started on the paperwork

needed to close the deal. "So, how much do you want to put down?"

I smiled. "Not going to put anything down. I'll just write you a check for the full amount. If that's okay."

I pulled out my checkbook and waited.

Ed smiled. "Paying in full does make it easier. Is it a local check?"

"Yeah, drawn on Sun Trust bank. There's a branch across the street if you want to see if it's good."

He nodded. "I'm sure it's good. Make it out to Truck Depot. Here's the amount."

He slid the sales agreement to me from across his desk. At the bottom of the form, he had added in sales tax, title and license fee. The total was just over fifteen thousand five hundred dollars, right in line with what Lucy had said. I wrote out a check for the full amount and slid it over to him.

He picked the check up and smiled. "I'll be right back. Don't go anywhere."

He left his office door open and walked over to Lucy. I could see him pointing at me and asking her a question, to which she replied, "Yes."

He shook his head and walked away.

A few minutes later, he returned to the office and closed the door behind him. Smiling, he reached out to shake my hand. "Congratulations. The Jeep is now officially yours. Lucy has the keys."

I thanked him and went outside where Lucy was waiting for me with a big smile. She handed me two sets of keys and a folder with sales documents. "It's all yours now. Try not to wreck it. But if you do, call me and I'll find you another one."

She handed me her business card. Turning it over, I saw she had written her phone number on the back.

I started to get into the Jeep but remembered it didn't have the tow bar that was supposed to be included.

"Lucy, where's the tow bar?"

"Oh yeah, that's supposed to go with it. It's at the Sarasota sales lot. I'm going over there this afternoon and I'll get it for you. I'm picking up Mom for yoga on the beach in the morning and I can drop it off with you then if you'd like."

I nodded. "That works for me. As long as you stop by and say, 'Hi.'"

"Will do. Now be safe in your Jeep. Don't get hurt playing super hero."

She was smiling as I drove off.

CHAPTER SIXTEEN

My drive back to Serenity Cove took me by the offices of Beach Realty where Anna worked as a sales agent. Anna had been the one who'd gotten me into Serenity Cove and I'd promised her I'd call as soon as I got checked in.

I'd forgotten to do it and that wouldn't sit well with Anna. Since I was out and about in the Jeep anyway and since her office was just ahead, I decided to stop in and thank her in person.

Pulling into the Beach Realty parking lot, I saw Anna's white Land Cruiser which meant she'd probably be inside working at her desk.

Parking in the open space beside her Cruiser, I climbed out of the Jeep and went inside looking for her.

This wasn't the first time I'd been inside Beach Realty. Anna was my real estate agent and I'd stopped in at her office several times to confirm appointments, review listings, and just shoot the breeze.

When I walked in, Janet, the cute receptionist behind the front desk, greeted me. "Walker, you're looking good. Life must be treating you well."

I smiled. "Can't complain. Is Anna in her office?"

"Yes, she's back there. I'll let her know you're here."

She tapped some keys on her phone, then spoke into her headset. "Anna, you have a visitor. Your friend Walker."

Janet nodded then spoke into the headset, "I'll let him know."

"She'll be right up."

From the back offices, I could see Anna coming my way. Wearing Florida business casual. Light tan capri pants, a sleeveless white blouse, a smile on her face.

"Walker, I've been wondering what happened to you. You were supposed to call and let me know about Serenity Cove. I was worried maybe you didn't get in, maybe you were living in the Walmart parking lot."

"Anna, you know better than that. Before I'd camp at Walmart, I'd move in with you."

"In your dreams. So why didn't you call?"

"Totally my fault. After I checked in, the woman in the site next to mine asked me to take her to the drug store, and that took a lot longer than I expected.

"Then we went out and looked at her boat. Then she introduced me to her daughter."

Anna stopped me. "Let me get this straight. Minutes after you move into Serenity Cove, you met a woman and went out with her? That's moving pretty fast, even for you, Walker."

I smiled. "Anna, it's not like that. The woman is old enough to be my mother. She needed someone to drive her to the store. So I volunteered. And, yes, I forgot to call you. To make up for it, I'm here to take you to lunch. In my new Jeep."

She looked surprised. "You broke down and bought a car? Finally spending some of that money you keep stashed away?"

Anna knew about the settlement I'd gotten from the company I previously worked for. To her, me having money was no big deal. She'd also come into a comfortable sum—and she too was keeping a low profile about it.

"So where's this Jeep you bought? Is it new?"

I pointed to the door. "It's right outside. And it's not new. You know me better than that. I'm not spending the money on a new one. It's definitely used."

We went outside and I pointed out the Jeep.

"Wow, that's nice."

She walked over to the driver's side door, opened it and climbed in. She grabbed the steering wheel and said, "I like it. I can see you driving the back roads of Florida in this."

She reached over and fondled the gear shift. "Glad to see you didn't wimp out and get an automatic."

After inspecting the interior, she got out and smiled. "Walker, you did good. This Jeep suits you."

I nodded. "I think I'm going to like it. The previous owner set it up so it can be towed behind a motorhome. Do you want to go for a ride? I'll buy you lunch."

Anna shook her head. "Not today. I'm supposed to show a house in about fifteen minutes. The client is meeting me here. Maybe some other time."

I nodded and started to get into the Jeep.

"Wait. Tell me about Serenity Cove. What's your first impression of the place?"

I thought for a moment then said, "My first impression wasn't good. The office building is run down and the office manager is a real jerk. But once you get past the front office, it's pretty nice. The sites are large and level with plenty of space between them. There are palm trees everywhere and plenty of shade. The place has a nice, old Florida vibe.

"The park's Wi-Fi system definitely needs work. Most likely one or more of the repeaters need replacing. Probably the router as well. But it won't be real expensive. I can probably fix everything for less than three thousand dollars."

Anna nodded. "I'll let the owner know. But I won't say anything to her about the park manager just yet. Maybe he was just having a bad day.

"Speaking of which, I'd like you to keep a list of the things you'd do if you were the owner of the place. Improvements you'd make, personnel changes, park rules and regulations—that kind of thing.

"It doesn't need to be a formal write up, just a list of notes and ideas about making it a better place. Will you do that for me?"

I nodded. "Sure, no problem. Anything else?"

She smiled, "No, that's pretty much it. Just keep an eye on the place for the owner. If anything serious comes up, let me know. But don't get the police involved.

"And, Walker, guess what? I've got a date tonight. One of the agents I met on a home tour asked me out. He seemed nice, so I said, 'Yes.'"

I smiled. "I hope the guy knows what he's getting into."

Anna playfully punched me on the shoulder. "Walker, if you're lucky, one of these days I'll show you exactly what he's getting into."

She turned and walked back into the Beach Realty office, leaving me in the parking lot wondering what I might be missing.

CHAPTER SEVENTEEN

After leaving Anna's office, I headed south on state road 776 toward the Publix grocery store at Dearborn Street. I needed to stock up on food for me and Mango Bob.

The Publix in Englewood is different than most grocery stores. It's not that the building is different, it's the people who work and shop there. With Englewood being a retirement town, just about everyone who works there is over fifty, and a lot of the people shopping there are over seventy.

This creates a kind of slow motion shopping experience. No one moving too fast, no one in a hurry, no one talking too loud. Just a peaceful place to shop.

Of course, if you *are* in a hurry, this kind of place can drive you crazy. Shoppers will strike up conversations with total strangers and talk for twenty minutes, not realizing they have created a roadblock for others in the store.

It could be worse though. If you visit the Sam's Club down in Port Charlotte on the day they are handing out food samples, it's kind of like standing in line at a senior citizen buffet. No one's in a hurry and everyone is making sure they don't miss out on any of the free food samplings.

Compared to that, shopping at the Publix on Dearborn isn't bad at all.

Knowing what to expect and what to avoid, it only took me about twenty minutes to roll my shopping cart up and down all the aisles, stocking up on supplies while dodging senior citizens who somehow were stuck in place.

Since I wasn't in any hurry, none of this bothered me. I was living the good life in Florida. I had money in the bank, a motorhome parked near the beach, a Jeep to get around in, and some interesting friends.

From Publix, I headed back to Serenity Cove. I was taking the last of the six bags of groceries I'd bought inside when I heard a door close nearby.

It was Polly, my neighbor in the Airstream next door. Oscar the Wiener Dog was with her, pulling at the leash she was holding.

"Walker, glad to see you're back. Oscar and I are going for a walk around the park. Would you like to go with us?"

I did. "A walk sounds good. Let me get these groceries put up and I'll join you."

I went inside, put the frozen food in the freezer, and headed back outside to join Polly and Oscar.

As we began our walk, it was clear that Oscar was calling the shots. He'd drag Polly from one side of the road to the other, sniffing out spots marked by other four-legged guests at Serenity Cove.

As we walked, Polly pointed out the features of the park and gave me background info about some of its more colorful residents.

"That big bus over there belongs to a famous Hollywood actor. They say after his fifth divorce, the only thing he had left was his tour bus. He was too old for Hollywood so he moved to Serenity Cove, threw away his toupee, and has been living here ever since.

"Next door to him is the former mayor of Chillicothe, Ohio. He only lives here during the winter. The rest of the time he's back in Ohio. Some people say he's gay, but I don't know about that."

She pointed out another motorhome.

"The people who live in that one are from Minnesota. They have two cats and seven grandchildren. The cats they keep with them, the grandkids they leave back up north."

Polly pointed out almost every trailer or motorhome and told me about the people who lived in it. She'd say things like, "The man who lives there is a writer," or, "That couple is from Canada where they own a string of beauty parlors," or, "That man's wife died last year," or, "The woman who lives there is a famous artist."

Polly told me that for the most part, people kept their trailers or motorhomes in Serenity Cove year round. Even the people who went back up north during the summer months would leave their trailers there.

It was easier and less hassle for them to leave the trailer and know they had a reserved spot in Serenity Cove than to call around to all the different RV parks trying to find an available space when they came back.

So they paid their site rent even when they were up north, just so they had a place in Florida they could return to whenever they wanted to. This meant Serenity Cove stayed booked up year round. There weren't many vacancies, except when someone died.

Polly also told me that before she moved to Serenity Cove she had been a registered nurse.

"My last job was in the cardiac care center of Tampa General. It was a good job with good pay, but I didn't like the stress of living in a big city like Tampa.

"Jack, promised me that when we retired, we'd move back to Englewood. But that never happened. On his sixtieth birthday, driving home from work during rush hour, he had a heart attack on the Gandy Bridge. It took the EMTs eighteen minutes to get to him. Twelve minutes too long. There was nothing they could do to save him.

"I was alone after that. Living in Tampa. In a big house, without Jack. Just me and Oscar.

"After I got over the shock of his death, I put our house on the market, and when it sold, I bought an Airstream trailer and set it up here in Serenity Cove. Been living here ever since."

"Jack was your husband?"

"Yes, we were married forty years. He was a good man. A good father to Lucy. I really miss him. But Oscar here keeps me company these days. It's because of him that I get out and walk around the park. He needs his daily exercise. So I get out and walk with him.

"When I'm out with Oscar, everybody wants to stop and talk. They want to know what kind of dog he is, and then, after we get to talking, they tell me their life stories.

"So Oscar is kind of like the ice breaker. Everyone here knows him and most admire his regularity."

I laughed.

Polly laughed as well. "You'll find out that Serenity Cove is a nice place to live. There are nice people here. And there wasn't much crime until recently."

"Something happen?"

"Yes, a few things have gone missing. A couple of trailers were broken into."

CHAPTER EIGHTEEN

"It started right after PT and Spider showed up. I thought they were part of the Monday mowing crew. But these guys didn't seem to do any work.

"They drove a beat up pickup truck. Black with dark-tinted windows. Busted front windshield. A camper shell on the back.

"Never saw them working with the mowing crew. They'd drive up to the office, go in with a twelve pack of beer and hang out for a few hours.

"You'd occasionally see them walking around the park, acting like they were looking for something. I figured they were casing the joint, so I reported them to the park manager.

"He said not to worry about them. They were old friends of his. Just hanging out.

"I never saw them do anything illegal, but it wasn't long after they showed up, that things started to go missing around here.

"I saw them in the park after midnight once. Oscar needed to go out to take care of business, and while we were standing in the grass over there, we saw them driving slowly with their lights out.

"They pulled up to the dock and parked. Not sure what they were up to, but when Oscar was done with his business, we went back inside and those guys were still there."

I could see why Polly would be suspicious of these two guys. Especially if they were in the park around midnight.

"Polly, you called these guys PT and Spider. Is that their real names?"

She shook her head. "No, we don't know their real names, first or last. So we made up names for them.

"The taller guy has a ponytail. It's kind of funny because his hair is gray, like an old man. But he has this long ponytail, so we dubbed him PT, for Ponytail.

"The other guy is covered with tattoos. He's got them everywhere, except his face. A big spider web tattoo covers his arms, legs, and neck. So we call him Spider.

"We never call them that to their faces. They don't seem real friendly and have never said anything to me or anyone else in the park that I know of—except for the manager.

"Of the two, PT seems to be the leader. He always drives the truck. Spider seems more like PT's sidekick. Always a few steps behind him. Maybe it's because he is younger, in his forties."

I nodded, thinking about PT and Spider. They certainly didn't fit in with the older crowd living in the park. But just because someone looked a little different didn't automatically make them a criminal. These guys could have been good old boys who liked to drink beer and hang out in the manager's office.

Nothing criminal about that.

"Polly, when was the last time you saw PT and Spider?"

She thought for a minute. "I guess it's been about two weeks. Come to think of it, I haven't seen them since that night I saw them hanging out by the dock."

I nodded. "Maybe they're gone. Headed back to where ever they came from."

Polly smiled. "I hope so. It just felt like they were up to no good. If you *are* an undercover cop, feel free to check those guys out."

I smiled. "Polly, I assure you I'm not any kind of cop."

We had walked the full circle around the park and were back at Polly's Airstream. Oscar was tired from the walk, and he promptly plopped down on the small patch of grass in front of her trailer.

"Walker, do me a favor. Give me your cell number so I can call you if something comes up."

We exchanged numbers. Almost immediately Polly's phone started playing "Lucy in the sky with diamonds".

Polly answered her phone. "Hi Lucy, what's up?"

Stepping away so Polly could talk with her daughter in private, I walked around my motorhome looking for any anything that needed to be tended to.

A motorhome is a house on wheels, and like any house, it will need occasional maintenance to keep it in tip top shape. But unlike a normal home, a motorhome is subjected to the equivalent of a continual earthquake as it is being driven down the road.

Stop and go traffic, potholes, and taking hills and corners at sixty miles an hour puts a lot of strain on the motorhome's bits and pieces.

Even if you never drive the motorhome, things wear out. Especially the rubber seals around the roof vents and windows.

Because I live in mine full time, I keep an eye on everything. I want it to be in good shape because I never know when I might need to hit the road in it unexpectedly.

That's what I was doing while Polly was on the phone. Walking around my motorhome, looking for things that might need fixing. When I completed my walk-around, Polly motioned me over to her.

When I got close, she said, "Walker, I want to ask you a big favor. Feel free to say no.

"That was Lucy on the phone, and she's having a bad day at the car lot. A customer came in screaming about something wrong on his title, and Lucy's boss blamed her.

"The thing is, Lucy wasn't involved in the sale. She didn't have anything to do with the title mess. But her boss still blames her and she's feeling kind of bad.

"So here's the favor. Call Lucy and ask her out to dinner tonight. Take her somewhere she can relax, somewhere she can have a drink or two, a place to help her forget about work. Think you could do that?"

I nodded, "Yeah, I can."

Polly smiled, "Good. Just one thing though. You can't tell her it was my idea to ask her out."

CHAPTER NINETEEN

So I called Lucy, and asked her out to dinner. She said, 'No', which didn't surprise me. She was having a bad day.

I didn't give up, though. I tried a little harder.

"Lucy, we can go to Zekes. We can sit outside under the tiki hut and watch the sun go down over the gulf.

"We'll eat some shrimp, drink some wine and watch the dolphins play in the bay.

"You won't have to do anything. I'll come pick you up, and whenever you get tired, I'll take you home. No strings attached.

"So how about it?"

Lucy paused then asked, "Walker, did my mother put you up to this?"

I laughed. "Of course she did. But even if she hadn't, I would have eventually asked you out. This way, we make your mother happy, and if it turns out badly, we can blame her.

"But if you don't want to go out with me, just say so. I'll be able to deal with it. It'll mean I'll be all alone eating by myself tonight. But don't you worry about that."

It was my pity play.

Lucy wasn't buying it.

"Walker, don't try the pity routine with me. It won't work. But if it'll make my mom happy, I'll go to Zekes with you. Just know that I'm not getting dressed up or anything. I'm coming the way I am."

She gave me her address on Harbor Drive. I agreed to pick her up at six thirty. That would get us to Zekes early enough to grab an outside table, with a water view over Lemon Bay.

That time of year, the weather in southwest Florida is just about perfect. Sunny, with deep blue skies, temperatures just barely hitting seventy, and almost no humidity.

Since Lucy and I would be dining waterside with a good chance of a cool breeze coming off the gulf, I decided to wear jeans and a button up Columbia fishing shirt.

This is considered 'dressed up' in that part of Florida.

I arrived at Lucy's as scheduled, right at six thirty. She lived in a small cottage. Local realtors would call it "Florida chic"— the kind of place tourists from up north would take photos of but probably wouldn't live in themselves.

I parked my Jeep behind a late model Toyota 4Runner in her driveway. I presumed it was Lucy's.

Walking up onto her porch, I rang the bell and soon after, Lucy opened the door. She was wearing faded jeans, a loose, white shirt, and a smile on her face. In one hand she had her house keys, in the other, her cell phone.

"Walker, right on time. I like that in a man."

Without inviting me in, she walked out onto the porch and locked her front door behind her. Pointing at my Jeep, she said, "We're taking yours, right?"

"Yep, that's the plan."

I walked over and opened the passenger door and Lucy climbed in without saying anything. Unlike her mother, she didn't tell me to never open the door for her again.

When I got in on the driver's side, she said, "Nice Jeep you got here."

I nodded. "I hope so. The salesperson said it was in good shape. But you can't ever trust them. They'll tell you anything to make a sale. The wheels fall off tomorrow."

Lucy laughed. "Maybe you should have bought the extended warranty."

Then she pointed at her car. "Your tow bar is in the back of my 4Runner. I'll drop it off in the morning before I go to the beach with Mom."

I nodded. "Sounds good. But there's no hurry. I probably won't need it until late this summer, when I move out of Serenity Cove."

Lucy smiled, "I don't want it rolling around in the back of my 4Runner, so you're getting it in the morning, whether you need it or not.

"I'm picking Mom up for yoga at eight and I'll drop it off then."

"Yoga? On the beach?"

She nodded. "Yeah, they have it every morning. I try to go at least three times a week, depending on my schedule and the weather. Mom likes to come with me whenever she can.

"I'd invite you to join us, but you don't seem the yoga type. And the class is mostly women."

I smiled. "So you're telling me there will be a bunch of women on the beach in the morning, without many men around, and you don't think I'd be interested in being there? It sounds like something I wouldn't want to miss."

She laughed. "Great, I'll expect you to be ready at eight. Be sure to wear your yoga pants."

Yoga pants? What had I gotten myself into?

Zekes on the Bay is a small, open air cafe perched on a seawall behind Royal Palm Marina in Englewood. To get to Zekes, you drive down Wentworth Avenue until it dead ends at the large boat warehouse.

You park in the dirt parking lot, walk around the marina, and when you see the building with a tiki hut, you've reached Zekes.

When you walk in, you'll be asked whether you want to eat inside or out under the tiki hut. We chose to eat outside and found an empty picnic table overlooking the Intracoastal

Waterway and Lemon Bay.

A young woman wearing cutoffs brought us menus. "Welcome to Zekes. What can I get you to drink?"

I nodded at Lucy. "You first."

She shook her head. "I haven't decided. You go ahead."

"I'll have an unsweetened iced tea."

With a quizzical look, Lucy asked, "You're drinking tea? Not wine or beer?"

"Yeah, I'm drinking tea, if that's okay with you. I'm not much of a drinker, and since I'm driving tonight, I figured I'd play it safe."

Lucy smiled. "Well, that's one point in your favor. I'll have unsweetened tea as well."

The server nodded and said she'd be right back.

Turning to Lucy, I asked, "You said that's one point for me. So I'm on a point system? And I get a point for asking for tea? How many points do I have so far?"

She shook her head. "Not anywhere near enough."

When the server returned with our drinks, she asked for our order. Lucy suggested we share a pound of steamed shrimp, and I agreed.

While we waited for our shrimp, we sipped tea and looked out over Lemon Bay as small fishing boats returned to the marina. Dolphins followed some of the boats, surfing the wakes they left behind.

The sun was still above the horizon, but it wouldn't be long before we'd see a spectacular sunset over the gulf.

Our steamed shrimp arrived in a tin bucket and we were provided with paper plates, a roll of paper towels and fresh shrimp sauce. We were both hungry and we dug right in.

It didn't take long before we had a tower of discarded shrimp shells and a mountain of wadded paper towels in the center of the table.

Between bites, we talked about the weather, the snow birds, which boats in the marina we'd like to have, and whatever else came to mind.

The friendly server returned several times, refilling our glasses and removing the discarded shells. After we'd finished most of the shrimp, we took a break from eating to watch the sun slowly disappear over the horizon.

Lucy patted the bench on her side of the table and said, "Come over here so you don't have to strain your neck."

I moved over, and we sat side by side as the sun went down and the sky above changed color.

When the sun finally disappeared over the horizon, there was a smattering of applause from the growing crowd of diners and wait staff.

Our server returned. "Would you like some dessert?"

I looked at Lucy then asked the server, "Do you have Key lime pie?"

"We sure do. Made fresh here every day. It's really good."

Looking at Lucy, I asked, "What do you think? A slice of Key lime pie?"

She smiled. "Yes. Please."

After our server walked away, Lucy said, "That's another point for you."

I was still sitting beside Lucy and had no intention of moving back to the other side of the table unless she asked me to. On this side of the table, not only was I closer to Lucy, I had a better view of the marina below and the waters of Lemon Bay spread out before us.

There was a row of small live-aboard boats docked in the marina. Most were unoccupied, stored there by wealthy snowbirds who rarely used them but were able to tell their friends up north they had a yacht in Florida.

To the left of the live-aboards were slips for much smaller fishing boats. Further back, the pumps for the marina fueling stations.

At this time of the day, with the sun having set, there wasn't much going on in the marina. Most of the smaller boats had already come in from the gulf. But there was still some activity.

Two men were loading what looked like medium-sized black suitcases into a small cabin cruiser. One of them had a long, gray ponytail. The other had tattoos on his arms and legs.

"What are you looking at?" asked Lucy.

I nodded toward the dock and whispered, "Down there, those two men. They fit the description of PT and Spider. The men your mother told me about."

Lucy looked in their direction. "I can only see one of them. The one with the ponytail. It could be PT, but I can't tell for sure."

As we watched, the man who looked like Spider climbed into the boat and quickly went into the cabin. After a few seconds, the inboard motor came to life, and the tall man with the ponytail cast off the line that held them in the slip.

The boat moved away from the dock and slowly headed out into the Intracoastal Waterway, heading north toward Venice.

Lucy shook her head. "Probably just going out fishing."

I nodded. "Probably."

But I wondered why fishermen would be loading black suitcases into a boat.

Our server returned and we turned our attention to the two slices of pie she placed in front of us. After her first bite, Lucy smiled. "This pie is amazing. Best I ever had. Wait till I tell Mom."

I smiled. Lucy was happy. And that made me happy.

After we finished our meal, our server returned, picked up our plates and asked, "Are you staying for the live music? It'll be starting in about twenty minutes."

I looked at Lucy and she shook her head.

"No, I think we'll be going."

Our server returned with our check and placed it on the table. I paid with cash, leaving a twenty dollar tip.

When we stood to leave, Lucy grabbed my hand. "Let's not go right away. I want to walk around the marina for a bit, look at the boats."

I nodded. "I was hoping you'd say that. I'd like to get a closer look at those live-aboards."

The docks at Royal Palm Marina are well lit and we had no problem finding our way around. We strolled up and down the metal walkways looking at the large boats and checking the prices on the ones with 'for sale' signs.

Lucy pointed to a forty-foot Mainship. "I like that one. If I win the lottery, maybe I'll get something like that."

"Yeah, that one looks big enough. Plenty of room for two people. Probably nicer inside than my motorhome."

Lucy stopped and looked at me. "Walker, speaking of which, there's something I've been meaning to ask.

"Why exactly are you living in a motorhome? Why not a house? And what do you do for a living? As far as I can tell, you're unemployed. But you had no problem paying cash for the Jeep.

"So what gives?"

I thought carefully before I answered. I liked Lucy but didn't want to tell her too much about my background.

CHAPTER TWENTY

"Lucy, for most of my life I've worked. Either at a job or in the military. I didn't take vacations, didn't take sick days, just showed up and worked.

"About a year ago, the company I worked for decided to move operations to Mexico and laid off six hundred people, including me.

"My wife had just filed for divorce. Said she was doing me a favor. Giving me a chance to do something else with my life.

"We didn't have any kids, so we split things right down the middle. She got the house. I needed a place to stay so I bought and moved into the motorhome. I drove it to Florida and have been living in it ever since.

"I haven't quite figured out what I'm going to do next, but I'm working on it. If it matters, I'm happy."

Lucy looked up at me. "So you're really not an undercover cop?"

"No Lucy. I'm not an undercover cop."

We walked around the marina for about twenty minutes until Lucy said, "Okay, that's it for me. It's been a long day, it's time to go home."

After driving back to her house on Harbor Drive, I turned off the motor and reached for my door. My plan was to get out and open the door for her. But before I could get out, Lucy put her hand on my shoulder. "Don't get out. Dinner was nice. We probably ought to do this again. But I'm beat. I'm going inside and going to bed."

She leaned over and kissed me on the cheek then stepped out

and walked to my side of the Jeep. "Yoga tomorrow morning. Eight o'clock. I'll be knocking on your door."

Without waiting for my reply, she turned and walked to the front door of her home, unlocked it and went inside.

Seeing that she was safely in, I started the Jeep and drove back to Serenity Cove.

It had been a nice evening.

Bob was waiting for me at the door. He said, "Muuuuurrph," in his outside voice and headed straight for his food bowl.

I knew what he wanted.

He had been home alone most of the day, probably sleeping and when he woke up, I wasn't there. Worse, when he checked his food bowl, he could see it was almost empty.

To Bob, this meant starvation was imminent. It didn't matter to him that there was still food in the bowl. It didn't matter that in all the time Bob had been with me he'd never gone hungry.

What mattered was that if he could see the bottom of his bowl, it meant he'd soon be out of food. And that meant he needed to let me know about it in his sternest voice.

"Muurrrphhh!"

Bob has a vocabulary of about thirty different sounds he uses to express his feelings. This latest one meant he wanted me to fill his food bowl. Immediately.

To show him I understood, I spoke to him. He likes it when you respond.

"It's okay, Bob. You're not going to starve. There's still food in your bowl, but I'll put in some more. Would you like that?"

Bob responded with, "Muurrph." His almost happy voice.

While he watched, I topped off his food bowl with fresh kibble.

When I stepped away, he sniffed the bowl, and then, without

taking a single bite, he strolled off, proud he was able to get me to do for him. As he understood it, I was there as his manservant, to handle his every wish.

Of course, he was right. All cats understand this is how it works.

After washing my hands, I found Bob on the couch in the living room. He saw me walk up and said, "Murrph?" as if he was asking, "Where have you been today?"

Since he'd asked, I felt obliged to tell him the story.

"I went to dinner at Zekes with Lucy. You'll probably meet her tomorrow, I think you'll like her.

"We had shrimp then watched the boats in the bay. Then I came home to see you."

Bob said, "Murrph."

Then he curled up beside me and purred as I rubbed his big ears. We stayed that way for almost an hour, him sleeping and me trying not to.

Around eleven, I locked up, turned off all the lights and went to bed.

CHAPTER TWENTY-ONE

It was still dark when my phone chimed me awake. I rolled over and picked it up off the night stand. The time showed 12:43. Just after midnight.

Too early for Lucy to be calling about yoga.

The caller ID said, "Anna."

I answered. "Anna, what's up?"

In a tired voice she said, "I've got a problem and need a favor."

"Okay, tell me what you need."

"Remember earlier today when I told you I had a date?"

"Yeah, I remember."

"Well, the date isn't working out. We're at Rusty's Raft on Dearborn, and the guy I'm with is hammered. He started drinking before he picked me up and he's been drinking all night.

"It got ugly and he got kicked out for picking a fight with the bouncer. I think he's still outside. Waiting for me.

"I don't want to be around him. He's too drunk to drive. So I need a ride home."

I sat up with the phone to my ear.

"Anna, stay inside the club. I'll be there in ten minutes. I'll call you when I pull up to the door. Stay inside until then."

"Thanks, Walker. I'll owe you."

Pulling on the clothes I had worn earlier, I grabbed my keys, wallet, and cellphone, and headed out. Rusty's Raft is on

Dearborn Street, just a few minutes from Serenity Cove.

That late in the evening, there wasn't much traffic. Almost no one out, and I made good time.

When I arrived at the Raft (as locals call it) the parking lot was half full. I didn't bother pulling in. Instead, I did a quick U-turn and pulled into the loading zone at the front door, then pressed redial on my phone to reach Anna.

When she answered, I said, "I'm right outside."

A moment later, Anna stepped through the front entrance of the Raft. She looked around, saw me and headed for the Jeep. Almost immediately, a man stepped from behind a palmetto bush and moved toward her. His disheveled hair, wrinkled shirt, and the large wet spot on the front of his pants suggested he might be the date Anna was trying to avoid.

I quickly exited the Jeep and stepped between Anna and the obviously drunk man.

"Hey," he slurred. "She's with *me*."

Then he took a swing.

People who are drunk should never fight. They almost always have a distorted depth perception and are usually off balance.

Avoiding the man's swing was easy. I stepped back as his arm went by and watched as the momentum of the missed swing carried him in an arc that ended with his knees on the ground.

Putting my arm around Anna's shoulder, I walked her to the Jeep, got her inside and closed the door behind her.

I walked back to the drunk. "Give me your car keys."

He was still on the ground with a confused look on his face. I repeated myself, "Give me your car keys."

The man started crying but made no effort to give me his keys.

From behind I heard a deep voice. "Is there a problem here?"

Turning, I saw a muscular man wearing a tight fitting

Rusty's Raft T-shirt. Arms on his hips in a classic defensive position. The bouncer.

I pointed to the man on the ground. "He's too drunk to drive. He got that way inside your place. He's your problem now."

I walked back to the Jeep, got in and drove off.

Before I had driven a mile, Anna reached over and touched my shoulder. "Walker, I feel sick. Pull over."

CHAPTER TWENTY-TWO

Anna threw up before I could get the Jeep stopped. Fortunately, she had the presence of mind to roll down the window and lean out before letting go.

It wasn't pretty, but it was understandable. Too much to drink, too little to eat, combined with the stressful situation of dealing with an obnoxious drunk.

After she stopped throwing up, I put the Jeep in gear and headed toward her condo on Manasota Key, about five miles away. We were driving south on Indiana Avenue and in the distance I could see the lights were still on at the Shell station. One of the few places still open late at night in Englewood.

I pulled in and parked.

"Anna, I'll be right back. Don't go anywhere."

She mumbled something that sounded like, "Mar riiight."

Inside, I grabbed two bottles of cold water and a package of chocolate chip cookies. I put a five dollar bill on the counter. Not waiting for change, I headed back out to the Jeep. Just in time to see Anna stick her head out the window and throw up again.

I got in on the driver's side and handed her a bottle of water. "Drink this. All of it. And eat some cookies. It'll make you feel better."

Turning toward me, she groaned, "I feel bad. Real bad. I don't want to go home. Take me to your place."

"Anna, are you sure? You'll sleep better at your condo. In your own bed."

"No. I don't want to spend the night alone. I want to sleep

at your place. Please."

She looked miserable. Her skin was pale, her eyes watering, her hands shaking. "Please, take me to your place."

She was shivering. "I can't feel my legs. They're numb."

I reached over and touched her arm. She was cold. I could see panic in her eyes.

"Anna, it'll be okay. I'll take you to my place. You can sleep on the couch."

She smiled then slumped back in her seat. Eyes closed, mouth wide open.

The drive back to Serenity Cove went quickly. No traffic to slow us down.

I had a bad feeling about Anna's condition. When it came to drinking, she could hold her own. I'd never seen her like this. Passed out. Shivering.

Turning into Serenity Cove, I switched off the Jeep's headlights and coasted to my site. No need to announce my arrival to those who might still be up this late at night or disturb those who were sleeping.

Parking in front of my motorhome, I saw there would be a problem getting Anna out of the Jeep, up the stairs and through the front door.

She wasn't heavy, but, being passed out, she was about one hundred ten pounds of dead weight.

Opening the passenger door, I unbuckled her seat belt and leaned in close. In a whisper, I said, "Anna, we don't want to wake the neighbors, so keep quiet."

No response.

I started to reach around to lift her, but realized that if I carried her to the motorhome, I wouldn't be able to unlock the front door without putting her down first.

I released my hold on her, went to the motorhome, unlocked it and went inside. Mango Bob was at the door. Waiting for me.

Seeing me hesitate at the open door, he said, "Murrrph?"

He was wondering if I was going to leave the door open for him, giving him an opportunity to go outside and do some nighttime hunting.

"Sorry, Bob, I'm going to have to put you in the bedroom for a few minutes. You'll be okay back there, it'll be fun."

Bob followed me as I made my way to the back. I sat on the bed and patted the mattress. "Up here, Bob. There's something I want to show you."

Bob looked up, not sure whether this was some kind of trick or not. But his curiosity got the better of him and he jumped on the bed.

I stroked his back twice and he started to purr. I then eased off the bed. "Bob, I'll be right back."

With Bob safely out of the way, I went back up front and propped open the front door using the baseball bat I kept tucked behind the couch.

Looking out and seeing that Anna hadn't moved, I took a few seconds to fold the couch out into a bed. This was where Anna would be sleeping. From the overhead cabinet, I grabbed a sheet and pillow and tossed them on the couch.

When I went back outside, she was still out cold. Breathing heavily with drool on her chin. In a soft voice, I said, "Anna, I'm going to carry you up the steps, please don't struggle."

Reaching under her arms, I pulled her toward me. Her head facing mine. Holding her tightly, I lifted her through the Jeep door.

I was taller than Anna by almost six inches, and I was able to slip my arms under hers and lift her so that her feet were off the ground. We stood together, as if we were doing a slow, sensual dance. My arms around her, her head over my shoulder.

If anyone had been watching, they would have thought we were lovers in a deep embrace.

They would have been wrong.

As we reached the steps leading into the motorhome, I tightened my grip. This got Anna's attention. She hugged me back and said, "Umm, that feels good."

It would have been funny had the situation been different.

Seeing a porch light come on two trailers down, I quickly carried Anna inside and set her down on the couch. She immediately fell over, head on the pillow, feet on the floor.

I went back outside and closed and locked the Jeep. Looking around, I didn't see anyone watching. That was good. No telling what they would think about me carrying a passed out woman into my motorhome after midnight.

As soon as I got back inside, I closed and locked the door. Behind me I heard a thump. Anna had rolled off the couch and was on the floor, snoring.

Remembering I had locked Bob in the bedroom, I went back and let him out. He quickly ran to the front to see what was going on. While he cautiously sniffed Anna, I went to the bathroom and got a clean wash cloth and ran cold water on it.

After wringing out the cloth, I grabbed the plastic trash can that sat in the corner of the bathroom. If she had to throw up again, this would be better than the floor.

Back up front, Bob was circling her. He had met Anna months before when she'd spent four days sleeping on this same couch while we were camping on the Treasure Coast.

He liked her company and during those four days he had slept beside her every night. I didn't know if he'd be doing it that night, but if he did, I was sure she would appreciate it.

Using the damp wash cloth, I cleaned the drool and vomit from Anna's face. In case she needed it, I put the plastic trash can on the floor nearby.

When I reached under her arms to lift her back onto the couch, she groaned. "Don't bother. I'm awake. I can get in bed by myself. But I need to go to the bathroom first."

She struggled to her feet, and then wobbled back to the

bathroom, closing the door behind her.

A few minutes later, she came back up front. Wearing one of my T-shirts. Nothing else except panties.

She wobbled to the couch and sat down. "Walker, I'm not drunk. I only had two glasses of wine and that was hours ago. With dinner.

"Nothing else. Except ginger ale.

"When I called you to come pick me up, I felt fine. After that, I went back to my table and had a few more sips of ginger ale. It tasted funny so I didn't drink much of it. There were other people sitting at the table. People I didn't know, so I left.

"A few minutes later, just when you showed up, I started feeling strange. My legs and arms were feeling heavy. Almost numb. I couldn't feel my fingers.

"I couldn't focus my eyes, my head started spinning. But I wasn't drunk. I didn't throw up alcohol. Just ginger ale."

She tried to swallow but couldn't.

"My throat hurts."

I handed her a bottle of water. "Drink this."

She took a drink then spit it out into the plastic trash can I had set near the couch. "That's nasty. Tastes like copper."

She put the bottle down and began rubbing her legs. "My legs are tingly. Like they've fallen asleep."

She lay down on the couch, pillow under her head. "I'm so tired."

Her eyes closed. A few moments later, she was breathing heavily, in a deep sleep.

I pulled the sheet up over her shoulders. Then sat down in the chair across from the couch and watched over her as she slept.

CHAPTER TWENTY-THREE

A knock at the door woke me. I had fallen asleep in the chair and slept there through the night. Anna was still asleep on the couch. Mango Bob at her side.

Outside, another knock at the door. Then, "Walker, you in there?"

It was Lucy.

The night before, I'd agreed to go to yoga on the beach with her. She had said, "Yoga tomorrow morning. Eight o'clock, I'll be knocking on your door."

Looking at the clock, I could see it was just a few minutes before eight. She was right on time. Ready for the beach.

Knock, knock, knock.

"Walker. I know you're in there. Come on out. It's time to get some exercise."

This could be bad. A half-naked woman was sleeping on my couch. There was no way Lucy wouldn't see her if I opened the door.

The good news, if there was any, was I was still fully clothed —and that should count for something.

Knock, knock, knock.

"Walker, get up."

I got up and walked to the door, opening it just slightly. "Lucy, I'm not going to be able to make it this morning. Something's come up."

From behind me, Anna mumbled, "Go away. We're trying to sleep in here."

Upon hearing Anna's voice, Lucy's eyes opened wide. A look of surprise. Followed by a look of hurt. She turned and walked away.

"Lucy, wait. It's not what it looks like. Let me explain."

She turned and looked at me. Tears in her eyes. "No, Walker, I'm sure it's not what it looks like. But there's no need to explain."

She got into her 4Runner, started the engine and backed out of her parking spot. Before pulling away, she rolled down her window. "Tell my mom I'm not going to yoga this morning. I just remembered I have something else I need to take care of."

Without waiting for a response, she drove off.

A moment later, Polly came out of her Airstream carrying her yoga mat. Looking around and not seeing Lucy, she asked, "Where's Lucy? And why aren't you dressed for yoga?"

I shook my head. "Lucy left. And it's my fault."

I pointed behind me. "There's a half-naked woman in there. I need your help to sort things out."

"You've got a woman in there? Are you saying after your date with my daughter last night, you went out and picked up another woman and brought her here?"

Before I could answer, Polly slapped me hard on my cheek. It stung.

Rubbing my face, I said, "It's not like that. A friend had a medical emergency last night and called me to help.

"She was too sick to leave alone. So I brought her here. But nothing happened. Come over and ask her yourself."

Polly looked at me. "I think I'll do just that. If it isn't like you said, I'm going to kick your butt."

She went into to my motorhome, while I stood outside trying to rub the sting out of my face.

CHAPTER TWENTY-FOUR

I half expected Polly to come back out with the baseball bat I had left by the door.

But she didn't.

Instead, after about ten minutes, she stuck her head out the door and said, "Walker, don't you have any normal food in this place? Coffee, eggs, bacon? All I can find is grape juice and cereal."

I smiled. "So you're not mad at me?"

"No, I'm not mad at you. Just wondering why you don't have any food in here. Come on in, you're off the hook."

Inside, Polly filled me in. "Anna told me what happened last night. Sounds like she was drugged. Somebody probably put roofies in her drink.

"It's a good thing she only took a few sips, else she would have really been out of it. No way she could have made it home by herself. As it is, it'll take a few hours, some food and lots of fluids to get it all out of her system. We saw a lot of this in Tampa."

I interrupted. "Roofies?"

"Yeah, the date rape drug. Someone probably dosed her drink. If you hadn't rescued her, she would have been easy pickings."

I looked at Anna. Her hair was a mess; she had bags under her eyes, her make-up smeared. But she had a slight smile on her face.

"Walker, you saved me. It could have been bad if you hadn't come and got me."

Then, shaking her head, "I'm so sorry about getting you in trouble with Lucy."

Polly patted Anna's hand. "Don't worry about Lucy. I'll call and explain it. Walker will come out looking good."

Then she looked at me, "But Walker, if this happens again, if Lucy finds another naked woman in your motorhome, you're going to be on your own.

"Anna and I are going over to my place. I'm going to fix her breakfast and get her into some clean clothes. While we're gone, you might want to clean this place up. And add coffee, bacon and eggs to your grocery list."

As they were heading for the door, I said, "Wait a minute. What about the guy who drugged her? He shouldn't get away with this. I want to go see him. Have a talk with him. Man to man."

Anna shook her head. "My date last night was kicked out of the club long before my drink was doctored. I don't think he had anything to do with this. He's a world class jerk, but I think he's in the clear."

I nodded. "If he didn't do it, who did?"

She shook her head. "Probably someone who saw my date getting kicked out. They figured I'd be alone and would need a ride, so they targeted me. But I don't know who it was."

It made sense. "Maybe they have surveillance cameras in the club. Maybe they'll have it on video."

Polly was standing at the door, waiting to take Anna to her trailer. "Walker, if you want to go down to the club and see if they have video, fine. Do that. But don't get the police involved. You don't want Anna's name on a police report. No good can come out of that."

Anna nodded. "I agree. I don't want the police involved. I don't want my name in the paper. I don't want anyone to know about this."

"Okay, no police. But I am going to talk to the manager of

the Raft. See what he has to say."

"You do that. But right now, I'm going next door with Polly so I can clean up. After that, you can drive me to my condo so I can get my car."

She gave me a hug and went out the door arm in arm with Polly.

CHAPTER TWENTY-FIVE

An hour later, Anna appeared at my door. She was freshly showered, wearing clean clothes. Her hair had a scent of strawberries. With a smile on her face, she looked and smelled a whole lot better than she had just a few hours before.

She noticed me looking at her. "Yeah, I know. I look pretty. Now quit staring. Take me to my condo so I can get my car and go to work."

"Yes ma'am. Your wish is my command."

I grabbed my keys and wallet and we went outside. After locking the motorhome, I walked over to the Jeep. The outside of the passenger door was streaked with vomit.

Pointing at the mess, Anna said, "You need to get this cleaned off or I'm not going to ride with you."

I thought she was kidding. Normally, I would have said, "You made the mess, you clean it up."

But she'd already had a rough night and there was no need for me to make it worse.

I had a water hose in one of the motorhome's outside storage compartments. I'd been using it to wash off road grime after each trip, and the high powered spray head would make short work of the mess on the Jeep.

As I went about the process of hooking up the hose and washing down the Jeep, Anna watched without saying anything.

When the job was done, I put the hose back in the storage compartment, locked it up, and came back to the Jeep.

Anna was standing near the passenger door, smiling. "Come here," she said.

Walking over to her, I expected to hear her tell me I had missed a spot. But, instead, she leaned in and kissed me on the cheek. "Walker, I'm so sorry about the trouble I caused last night. Can you forgive me?"

I gave her a hug. "Anna, there's nothing to forgive. You did the right thing by calling me."

She smiled, got into the Jeep, fastened her seat belt, and said, "I'm waiting."

Shaking my head and laughing, I walked to the driver side, got in and we headed over to her condo on Manasota Key. About half way there, I asked her, "What about work? Aren't you worried about coming in late?"

She shook her head. "I called and said I was out showing you property. Told them to expect me around noon. They like it when I show property. My boss said as long as I continue to bring in new listings and sell a few houses every month, I can come and go as I like.

"In fact—"

She was interrupted by an incoming call on her phone. She looked at the caller ID, and quickly rejected the call.

"Can you believe that? The asshole from last night. He's called six times so far this morning. Left messages saying he's sorry."

She continued. "Before I'm done with him, he's going to know the real meaning of 'sorry'. I'm going to let all the women in the office know how he got drunk and thrown out of the bar.

"It won't be long before he won't be able to get a date with any woman in this town."

I smiled, knowing that being on the wrong side of Anna was going to put this guy in a world of hurt.

Two months ago, Anna was living in her small camper trailer parked next to my motorhome in the old boatyard. It had been fun for a while, but she soon realized that living in a small, fourteen-foot trailer while trying to build a career in real estate wasn't practical.

She needed more space. A place with a large closet, a real kitchen, and a real bathroom. As it turned out, it didn't take her long to find a great place to move into.

One of her real estate clients had purchased several beach front condos on Manasota Key as a long-term investment. When he learned that Anna was looking for a place to rent, he offered her one of his condos at below market rates.

That meant Anna was able to afford a two-bedroom luxury unit overlooking the gulf in an almost new building with all the amenities one would expect, including a pool, exercise room and tennis court.

Having been to Manasota Key several times, I knew exactly where Anna's condo building was. A four-story, white block building, half a mile past the public beach.

Even though I knew where the building was, I'd never been inside Anna's condo. She had invited me in several times, but I'd never taken her up on it.

As I pulled into the parking lot, she pointed. "Over there. The parking spot with thirty-three on it. That's mine."

I pulled up behind her white Land Cruiser, which was already parked in the spot, and killed the Jeep's motor. I started to get out, but she stopped me.

"Walker, someday soon you need to come see the view from my balcony. We'll watch the sun go down, have a few drinks and tell each other stories.

"But not today. Today I need to rest."

She opened her door and walked around to my side of the Jeep. "Call me later. Let me know how things work out with Lucy."

Before I could reply, she turned and walked to the front entrance of her condo. I watched to make sure she was going to get in safely and, in doing so, I noticed that I'd come to appreciate the way she moved when she walked.

When she reached the door, she turned and waved at me and then went inside.

CHAPTER TWENTY-SIX

It was still early in the day. Too early for the Raft to be open. But the manager might be in. I wanted to talk to him to see if they had any video from the night before.

These days, a lot of bars have video cameras recording everything that goes on inside. They use the recordings to make sure employees aren't stealing and guests aren't faking injuries. The videos can come in real handy if needed as evidence in lawsuits.

Unfortunately, these surveillance videos are often low resolution and poorly focused. But not always. Some places have newer cameras, which produce high quality video making it easy to see who may have dosed a patron's drink.

I was hoping to find that at the Raft—high quality video from surveillance cameras showing what had happened to Anna the previous night.

Englewood doesn't have many night clubs. The few they do have are located on Dearborn Street, in a section of town known as Old Englewood Village.

That section of town was established more than a hundred years ago when Englewood was a small fishing village. Back then, there were no major cities nearby, no tourist attractions in Florida, no reason to visit Englewood and no easy way to get there except on horseback or by boat.

These days, things have changed. The federal government dug the Intracoastal Waterway through Englewood, which brought more boat traffic, more businesses and more residents.

Paved roads from Venice and Fort Myers made it easier to get to Englewood, which brought more people and along with them new hospitals, schools, and shopping centers.

Even with all the modern improvements, Old Englewood Village and Dearborn Street remained virtually unchanged. Many of the old, wood frame buildings built to service the fishing fleet still stood, but most have been converted into restaurants and art galleries, catering to the wealthy clientele from Manasota Key, Venice, and Boca Grand.

A few of the older buildings had been converted into drinking establishments like Rusty's Raft. They aren't what you would call 'gentlemen's bars', where well-dressed men sit around sipping martinis while talking about polo ponies.

They are, instead, places blue collar workers go to have a drink, dance, and maybe get lucky.

Like most of Englewood, these places weren't dangerous and weren't exclusively blue collar. Everyone is welcome, and most come just to have a good time.

When I arrived at the Raft, there were only four cars in the parking lot. Probably belonging to the cleaning staff.

I backed into an open slot far away from the other cars, a habit I picked up years ago. Backing in makes for a quick exit when required.

After locking the Jeep, I headed across the lot to the main entrance. A sign on the two massive, wooden doors said, "Closed."

Pushing on one of the doors, I wasn't surprised to find it unlocked. Even though the place was closed, the doors would be unlocked for the cleaning staff and for the delivery guys restocking the bar.

When I walked in, I saw an older lady with a spray bottle in one hand and a cleaning cloth in the other, wiping down a table near the door. She saw me but said nothing.

On my left, a man with an apron around his waist stood behind the main bar counting bottles. Seeing me, he just nodded and returned to work.

Looking around the room, I saw that beyond the rows of tables, there was an elevated stage for the band with a small dance floor in front.

To the right of the stage, a hallway led to the restrooms, the supply areas, and the manager's office.

That's where I headed.

I made my way through the tables, across the dance floor and down the hallway. No one bothered to ask who I was or why I was there. Everyone was working, minding their own business.

After passing the rest rooms, I continued down the hallway until I reached a closed door with a small sign on it that said, "Manager."

Inside the manager's office I could hear two people arguing. One was saying, "I told you he was trouble. Now we've got to deal with it."

The other voice said, "We don't know for sure. We haven't heard his side of the story."

Then, "I don't want to talk about it. Get out, go do your job."

The door opened, and a short, red-faced man hurried out. He looked at me quizzically, shook his head and walked away.

From inside the office, a man's voice asked, "Who are you and what do you want?"

Stepping into the room, I introduced myself. "John Walker. Here to talk about security video from last night."

The man behind the desk looked to be in his mid-fifties, maybe six feet tall, with thin, graying hair. "You a cop?"

"No, I'm not. I'm checking on something that happened here last night. A girl was drugged. I'm trying to find out who did it."

"Roofies?"

"Yeah. How'd you know?"

113

"Sheriff's detectives came in this morning. Said a woman filed a complaint. Said someone drugged her drink. That the girl you asking about?"

"No. The girl I'm working with didn't go to the police. She wants me to find out who did it. Thought maybe you'd have videos."

The man shook his head. "You're too late. The detective that came in this morning had a warrant. He took all the videos from last night.

"Even if I still had the videos, there's no way I could let you see them. My lawyers would be all over me. Invasion of privacy or something like that."

He picked up his coffee cup and took a sip. "You say she was drugged in here last night?"

"Yes, around midnight. She was drinking ginger ale. She left her table to make a call. When she came back, she took a few sips and became ill.

"Someone put roofies in her drink. I'm here to find out who."

The man shook his head. Then said, "We need to talk. Close the door. Have a seat."

I closed the door and sat in the chair in front of his desk.

"Mr. Walker, what I tell you next is off the record. If you tell anyone I told you this, I'll deny it. Is that understood?"

"Yes."

"Good. Because I don't want you to do something stupid. I don't want you to get caught up in something that's already being taken care of.

"Last night, someone in our club made a mistake. A big one. One of our bouncers saw it happen.

"A guy came in late, alone. Acting strange. Not drunk, but like he might be up to something.

"Our bouncers are trained to look for weirdos, and this guy

fit the profile. We were watching him as he stood off to the side.

"Four ladies left their table to go to the bathroom and the guy walks over and waves his hand over their drinks. Then walks away.

"The ladies didn't come back. We had one of our runners clear the glasses from the table.

"Our bouncer continued to watch the guy. It wasn't long before the guy did it again. He squirted something into a woman's drink right after she left a table.

"Our guy saw it happen, grabbed the man and escorted him back here where I detained him.

"Our guy then went back up front and had a runner clear the drinks from the table. But in all the commotion, he may have missed your friend's drink.

"We sincerely regret this. I've got daughters and if something like this happened to one of them, I'd be down here with a gun and somebody would get shot. So I can understand if you're upset.

"But the man who did this isn't going to get away with it. After we detained him, we called the sheriff and they sent someone down here.

"When the detective interviewed him, he denied putting anything in anyone's drinks. But when they searched him they found three vials of roofies. Enough to hold him overnight.

"This morning the sheriff's department came and watched the videos from last night. They saw the guy squirt something into the drinks. That along with the roofies will be enough to keep him in jail for a long time.

"So if you're looking for the guy who dosed your friend, he's already in jail. He won't be out for a while."

I nodded. "What's his name?"

"I can't tell you. In fact, I've already told you more than I should. But know this; if he gets out and ever steps foot in here again, he's in for a long boat ride out into the gulf without a return ticket."

I smiled. "My friend will feel better knowing the guy is off the streets."

We shook hands; I left his office and headed out to my Jeep.

It was nearly noon. I was hungry, tired, and ready to go back to the peace and quiet of my motorhome.

CHAPTER TWENTY-SEVEN

My quick wash job hadn't completely cleaned the mess off the Jeep's passenger door and I knew if I didn't get it cleaned the stomach acid from the vomit would damage the paint. So I headed to the only car wash in Englewood, the Soap & Suds.

Pulling into the lot, the attendant greeted me and asked what kind of wash I wanted.

"Wash and wax, exterior only."

He punched a code into the terminal and handed me a ticket. "Leave the keys in the ignition, pay inside, and we'll have it done in ten minutes."

After going into the office and paying, I stood by the large picture window and watched as my Jeep was slowly pulled through the car wash. Automatic brushes swooped down and cleaned the top, sides, hood and back. Then a rinsing shower washed away the suds followed by a fine mist of hot wax.

After the wax, a loud blower blew gale force winds over the Jeep removing the remaining water droplets.

As the Jeep exited the wash tunnel, one of the attendants got in and drove it to the drying area, where two men with towels and chamois cloths wiped it down.

I tipped them five dollars, happy to see my Jeep shiny and clean again. I'd only had it a day and wanted the 'new to me' feeling to last as long as possible.

Back at Serenity Cove, Bob met me when I opened the door with a loud "Mee-oooww!"

He was obviously upset about something. I could understand why. He'd been awakened in the middle of the night, locked in the bedroom away from his food, and found a stranger (Anna) sleeping on his couch.

This morning, another stranger (Polly) invaded his space. To make matters worse, I'd left him alone most of the day and hadn't topped off his food before I left.

As I walked back to his bowl, I reassured him. "It's okay, buddy, it's alright. You're not going to starve."

He trotted in front of me, his stubby tail up in the air, pleased I was home and about to feed him.

After I topped off his food bowl, he sniffed it and walked away. It wasn't that Bob wasn't hungry. He probably was. But he didn't want me to see him eat right away. He was funny that way.

Bob's a real character with a distinct personality. He'll let you know when it's time to feed him or pet him. He'll also let you know when you better leave him alone.

I like that in a cat. You don't have to guess what he wants because he'll tell you. If you ignore him, he'll make you pay.

After I'd fed Bob, I made myself a quick sandwich, poured a glass of tea, and sat down to eat. I'd skipped breakfast and was plenty hungry.

After eating, I realized how tired I was, having not slept much the night before while watching over Anna. I figured a quick nap might be in order, so I headed back to the bedroom and lay down.

It didn't take long before I was asleep.

Sometime later, I was woken by a loud beeping sound outside my door.

Beep. Beep. Beep. Beep.

Figuring it was a garbage truck backing up, I ignored it. But the sound continued.

Beep. Beep. Beep. Beep.

The volume was constant, like someone was parked right

outside my door honking a toy horn. It was annoying but I figured, whatever it was, it would soon go away.

And it did. After a few minutes the beeping stopped.

It was replaced by a loud tapping sound.

Tap. Tap. Tap.

Tap. Tap. Tap.

Someone was at my front door. Tapping instead of knocking. I had no idea who it could be and really didn't want to get up and see. I'd only been in Serenity Cove for two days, and no one except Anna, Polly and Lucy knew. If any of them were at my door, they wouldn't be tapping. They'd knock.

I thought if I ignored whoever it was, they'd go away.

But they didn't. The tapping continued.

Tap. Tap. Tap. Tap.

Followed by more beeping.

Beep. Beep. Beep. Beep.

Figuring that someone outside wanted to see me really bad, I gave in. I got up and looked out the window and saw an older man wearing a white cowboy hat, white cowboy shirt, white linen pants and dark sunglasses. He was sitting in a shiny, black golf cart.

The man had driven his cart up the shell path leading to the front steps of my motorhome. Close enough so he could use the black walking stick he held in his right hand to tap on my door.

As I looked out the window, the man tapped the horn on the golf cart.

Beep. Beep. Beep.

I was pretty sure the neighbors would get tired of hearing the beeping, so I went to the front door and opened it to see what the guy wanted.

Before I could say anything, he looked at me and asked, "What took you so long, son? You doing drugs in there?"

119

I shook my head. "No, I was sleeping. What can I do for you?"

"You the guy who is supposed to fix the internet around here? That's what they told me down at the office."

I nodded. "Yeah, that's me."

"Good. You're the one I'm looking for. My internet is broken, and I need it up and running now."

The man looked to be in his late sixties and something about him was familiar. I'd seen him before, but I couldn't place his face.

Impatiently, he said, "Well, don't just stand there. Come fix my internet."

I shook my head. "Look, the internet is slow everywhere in the park. Fixing it is going to take some time. At least a month before the new equipment can be installed."

He shook his head. "That won't do. Can't wait a month. I need to get on the internet within the hour. And you're going to get off your butt and come down to my place and get it fixed."

I had to admire the guy. He wasn't going to take 'no' for an answer. I had nothing else to do, so I gave in. "Okay, I'll come down and take a look, but I can't promise anything."

He pointed at the passenger seat in his golf cart. "Hop in."

I shook my head. "Give me a minute. I need to get a few things."

I grabbed my cell phone off the kitchen counter along with my keys. Stepping back outside, I locked the motorhome and reluctantly climbed into the passenger seat of the golf cart.

The man smiled. "My name's Buck. Better hold on."

He floored the cart and it took off like a rocket. The momentum threw me back in my seat, and if I hadn't grabbed the hand hold in front of me, I probably would have been thrown out. I looked over and Buck was grinning as we zoomed down the road.

In less than a minute we reached his home—an old forty-five foot Prevost Marathon bus, the kind owned by movie stars. His was silver and black, with a wall of tinted windows stretching from the front to the back. The bottom half of the bus was rolled stainless steel, which shined brightly in the Florida sun.

I was impressed.

Prevost builds the most expensive motorhomes sold in the world. Absolute luxury on wheels with no expense spared in their construction. Buck's would have easily cost more than a million dollars new. Even as old as it was, it would still be worth at least a quarter million.

During our walk around the park, Polly had told me about a bus that belonged to an aging movie star who had settled in Serenity Cove after losing most of his assets through a series of divorces.

She hadn't told me the star's name, but seeing him in person, I realized who he was. Buck Waverly. A leading man from the seventies and eighties who had starred in many successful action adventure movies.

Back then he was a superstar. As famous as anyone could be. Even had his own TV show for a while. The Buck Waverly Hour.

But that had been thirty years ago. After his TV show ended, his star faded. To the best of my knowledge, he hadn't appeared in a movie or TV series in a decade.

He had gotten older and Hollywood had cast him aside. Now he lived in Serenity Cove.

Buck hopped out of the golf cart and opened the door to the Prevost. Inside, it was like a palace with the kind of luxury you expect in a movie star's trailer. Marble floors, mirrored ceiling, leather everything. Expensive and over the top.

He settled in on the large, leather couch and nodded toward the dinette table across from him. On it sat an expensive Dell laptop computer with a small video camera on a tripod behind it.

He pointed at the laptop. "There it is. See if you can get on the internet because I sure can't."

CHAPTER TWENTY-EIGHT

It took just three minutes for me to find the problem with Buck's computer. When I clicked on the network icon, it showed four available wireless networks. One belonged to Serenity Cove; the other three were fringe networks belonging to neighboring properties.

The signal strength for the Serenity Cove network showed three bars—not bad considering we were sitting inside a Prevost bus, which is essentially a metal box.

This was a problem with these high end motorhomes. Their all metal frame and skin, along with thousands of feet of internal wiring, often blocked incoming Wi-Fi signals.

But that wasn't the problem in this case.

The problem was Buck's computer was trying to connect to one of the fringe networks, not the Serenity Cove network.

This was an easy fix. Using the drop down list of available networks, I selected Serenity Cove. In less than twenty seconds, we were connected to the web.

From behind me, Buck asked, "Any luck?"

I nodded. "Yes, I've got you back on the internet. Things should run smoothly now."

"What? You got it fixed? I worked on it for an hour this morning, and couldn't get anything."

"Well, it's up and running now."

I stood and headed for the door.

"Wait, don't go yet. I'm supposed to do a Skype video interview in an hour. Will this be fast enough for that?"

I shrugged. "Don't know. Maybe, maybe not."

He looked worried. "This is important. One of my friends passed away and the network wants to do a live video interview with me this afternoon.

"Is there some way you can test to make sure it works?"

Back when I worked in the corporate world, I'd set up lots of video conference calls and knew what needed to be done.

"Yeah, I can do some testing. It might take a few minutes."

"Good. You do that. We've got an hour until the call."

When I worked as a systems analyst, it seemed like everything had to be done on short notice, with a 'do or die' deadline. This was no different.

With just an hour to get things going, I got to work. First thing was to download the latest version of Skype. It handled video better than earlier versions.

Next I ran the Skype video compatibility test. The results showed that the internet upload speed was just barely adequate for HD video.

Looking at the network signal strength bars, I could see the problem. Unless I could get at least four bars, Skype video might not be reliable.

I turned to Buck. "I need to go back to my place and get something. I'll be back in ten minutes."

He tossed me a set of keys. "Take the cart, it'll be faster."

Months earlier, right after purchasing my motorhome, I'd ordered a high gain wireless antenna adapter for my computer. The small device bypasses the laptop's low power internal antenna and lets you connect to an amplified external antenna.

With it, I'd been able to get internet in places most others couldn't. I was pretty sure that if I hooked this adapter to Buck's computer and mounted the remote antenna on the outside of his bus, he'd get a much stronger signal.

I drove his golf cart to my motorhome, grabbed the adapter and headed back. Inside his bus, I plugged the high gain adapter into his laptop and routed the cable out the nearby window. Outside the bus, I used the suction cup mount on the antenna to position it in direct line of sight to the nearest Wi-Fi repeater.

Back inside, I checked the wireless signal strength on Buck's laptop. It showed four and a half bars. I reran the Skype video test and it showed the signal was strong enough for HD. Everything was good to go.

I turned to Buck and let him know. "Looks like you're ready. Signal strength is good, video is connected and Skype confirmed the test."

He smiled and reached out to shake my hand. "Son, you did good. And right on time. My call starts in ten minutes."

I headed for the door, but he stopped me. "You can't leave. You need to be here during the call. In case something goes wrong."

He pointed to the couch. "Sit over there. Stay out of the camera view. Don't say anything once the interview starts."

He sat down in front of the laptop and began preparing for his interview. He put on his cowboy hat, dusted his face with a make-up brush, checked his teeth, and arranged the laptop so it looked like he was looking directly into the camera.

A few moments later, his computer announced an incoming Skype call.

He clicked on "Answer with video", and he was immediately connected with a producer for *Entertainment Tonight*. The producer explained the interview would start in about three minutes, would last no more than five. The questions would be about Sally Land, a woman who had co-starred with Buck in several feature films.

The producer asked him to do a sound check, which Buck did by speaking a few words. "Howdy, I'm Buck Waverly. I'm coming to you from sunny Florida today. How's that?"

The producer said, "Video is good. Audio is a little weak. Bring up the volume of your microphone just a bit."

Buck complied then repeated the sound check. "Howdy, I'm Buck Waverly. I'm coming to you from sunny Florida today. Is this better?"

"Yes, that's perfect. Stand by for a countdown to go live."

Four minutes later, the interview started.

Buck was warmly greeted and was asked about the actress who had recently passed away. He answered questions easily and offered heartfelt remembrances and some humorous anecdotes about working with the woman.

After four and a half minutes, the interviewer signaled that time was almost up. He asked Buck about his health and whether he was working on anything new.

Buck laughed and said his health was fine and he was always looking for new projects but was currently just enjoying life at his home in Florida.

The interviewer thanked him, and moments later the producer came back on and said, "Buck, we're off the air. You did a great job. Our audience loved you. We may want to do another one of these soon. We'll stay in touch."

Before Buck could answer, the producer ended the call.

Buck took off his microphone and turned to me. "Tell me the truth. How'd I do?"

CHAPTER TWENTY-NINE

"You did great. Very professional and quite entertaining."

Buck smiled. "Did I look old? Because I don't want viewers to think I'm old and washed up."

He was old. But he didn't look washed up. So I said, "You looked tanned and healthy. You smiled a lot. People will remember that."

Rubbing his hands together, Buck said, "Well good. That's all I can ask for."

He stood, went to the fridge and got a bottle of apple juice. "You want something to drink?"

I shook my head, "No thanks. I need to head back home. It's been a long day."

I walked over to his computer and started to disconnect the antenna cable.

Buck stopped me. "What are you doing?"

"Disconnecting the antenna. You don't need it."

"Yes I do. You heard the producer. They may want me for another call. Tell me how much it costs. I'll pay for it."

I shook my head. "Buck, it's not the cost. It's the way it's connected. It's only attached with a suction cup. First good wind and it'll be gone. It's not designed to be outside in the weather full time."

He frowned. "But I need it. What if I get another Skype interview request? I gotta have that antenna."

I thought for a moment then came up with a solution. "How about this. I'll order you something that'll work a whole lot better. It costs a little bit more, but if you need high speed internet, it'll get the job done."

He smiled. "Order whatever you think I need and I'll be happy to pay for it. In the meantime, let's leave that little antenna out there until the new one gets here. Is that okay?"

I nodded. "Yeah, that'll work."

I headed for the door.

"Wait son. What's your hurry? I owe you something for today. Will a hundred take care of it?"

I laughed. "Buck, you don't owe me anything. I really didn't do much. Plus, I got to see you in action—live—and didn't even have to buy a ticket."

Buck shrugged. "Well, if you won't take money, how about dinner tonight? I'm buying."

I shook my head. "I appreciate the offer, but tonight there's a woman and her mother I need to make amends with."

Buck grinned. "Woman trouble, huh? I'm pretty much an expert on that. I've had woman trouble of all kinds, and most of the time it was my fault.

"But I've learned you can't give up. No matter how much trouble they are, it's usually worth it.

"So are both these women single?"

I nodded. "Yes, they are."

"Well, son, that'll make it easier. You call and invite the woman and her mother to join us for dinner tonight. We can go to the Mango Bistro and have a nice meal. I'll entertain the mother while you try to make amends with the daughter. Who knows, maybe we'll both get lucky."

I shook my head. "I'm not so sure. It might be that neither of these ladies will want to go out to dinner tonight."

Buck handed me his phone. "Call the mother. Tell her you're sitting here with me and that I've asked you to call and see if she and her daughter would like to have dinner with us tonight. Be sure to mention my name."

Reluctantly, I took his phone and punched in Polly's number.

She answered on the fourth ring.

"Polly, this is Walker. I'm sitting here with one of your neighbors and he's wondering if you'd like to join us for dinner tonight at the Mango Bistro.

"Before you answer, check the caller ID."

There was a pause as Polly looked at her phone.

"Walker, is this a joke?"

"No, it's not. Buck Waverly is sitting across the table from me, and he asked me to call and see if you'd like to go to dinner with him tonight.

"And just so you'd feel safe, he wants Lucy and me to tag along. Kind of like a double date."

Polly hesitated. "This is pretty short notice. What if I already have a date tonight?"

"Well, Polly, if that's the case, Buck will be pretty disappointed. Should I let him know you have a previous engagement and won't be joining him for dinner?"

She laughed. "Don't you dare tell him that. I'm in. What time are you going to pick me up and what should I wear?"

It was agreed we would eat early, around six, and we'd all dress casual.

With Polly still on the phone, I asked, "What about Lucy? Should I call and ask her to join us or would it be better if you made the call?"

Polly laughed. "Lucy was pretty mad at you this morning. She found a half-naked woman in your motorhome. If it were me, I'd be mad at you too. But now that I know the full story, I'm actually proud of you. You did the right thing.

"I've already talked to her and filled her in on what really happened. She's not nearly as angry as she was this morning.

129

But I don't think she's ready to talk to you on the phone. So let me call her. I'll make sure she joins us for dinner."

I was relieved. I wasn't looking forward to calling Lucy. We said our goodbyes and ended the call.

Buck leaned back, smiling. "So I take it we have dinner dates?"

After I filled Buck in with the details, I headed back to my motorhome. Bob met me at the door, gave my shoes a quick sniff then headed back to the bedroom to resume his nap. Like all cats, Bob is nocturnal—meaning he sleeps most of the day and prowls most of the night.

He was catching up on sleep so he'd be sharp later on that night. I should have been doing the same thing, considering what little sleep I had gotten the night before.

But sleep would have to wait. I had to shower and shave and get ready for my dinner date.

CHAPTER THIRTY

At exactly five thirty, I left my motorhome, locking the door behind me, and walked across the driveway to Polly's Airstream. Oscar the Wiener Dog must have heard me coming because before I got to the door, he started barking.

Almost immediately, I heard Polly's voice. "You're right, Oscar. Someone's out there. Let's go see who it is."

The door opened and Polly said, "Look Oscar, it's Walker. From next door."

Oscar danced around the floor then walked over to his leash, which Polly kept on a nearby table.

"Sorry, Oscar, you won't be going with us tonight. Walker and I have a date. You'll have to stay here and protect the place while we're gone. Can you do that?"

Oscar didn't look happy. He wanted to go with us.

Polly pointed to the couch. "Oscar, get in the bed."

He snorted his disappointment then walked over to the couch and jumped up on it.

"Good boy. You stay here until I get back, and then we'll go for a long w. a. l. k."

Upon hearing the word 'walk' spelled out, Oscar sat up, wagged his little tail and smiled as only a dog can. He was happy. He had been promised a walk.

Polly stepped out and locked the door behind her. "It's so rare that I go anywhere without Oscar. I don't know who feels worse about it, him or me.

"But he'll be fine. I've already walked him this afternoon,

and when we get back I'll walk him again before bedtime."

While Polly was telling me this, I was doing my best not to stare at her. She had untied her ponytail and combed out her hair so that it flowed over her bare shoulders. That combined with the white, gauzy dress she was wearing gave her the appearance of someone twenty years younger.

"You look great!"

"You don't think I overdid it, do you?"

"No, not at all."

Looking around, Polly asked, "Where's Buck? When do I get to meet him?"

"He's on his way. I called him just before I came over. He said he was going out the door heading this way in his black chariot."

Looking down the drive toward Buck's bus, we could see him coming our way in his golf cart, cowboy hat on his head, a broad smile on his face.

As he approached, Polly waved timidly. He waved back and parked his golf cart behind my Jeep.

I did the introductions. "Polly, meet Buck Waverly, your neighbor."

Buck tipped his hat in Polly's direction, "Polly, the pleasure is all mine."

She blushed and said, "You're a real charmer, aren't you?"

He nodded. "I try to be, especially when there's a pretty woman involved."

Both Polly and Buck were smiling, like teenagers going out on their first date. I stood back and watched as they got acquainted.

After five minutes, I tapped my wrist where there'd be a watch if I wore one. "It's about time to go. Where's Lucy?"

Polly turned to me. "She said for us to go without her. She'll meet us at the restaurant."

Then she asked, "Who's car we going in?"

I pointed at my Jeep. "Mine."

She looked at Buck, then back at me. "No, we're not going to ride in that thing. Too hard to get in and out of. Probably rides like a garbage truck."

She tossed me the keys to her minivan. "Let's take mine. Buck and I'll ride in the back, you can drive."

"A take charge woman," said Buck. "I like that."

It was a little early for the dinner crowd when we got to the Mango Bistro. The parking lot was nearly empty, so I parked close to the door.

Buck got out first and held Polly's hand as they headed into the restaurant. When he walked inside, the manager came over and greeted him. They spoke a few friendly words, and then the three of us were ushered to a private table in the back.

As soon as we were seated, a server appeared and welcomed us. She told us about the evening specials, took our drink orders and left.

Before she returned, another server brought over a tray of appetizers. Compliments of the owner. Moments later, our drinks arrived.

It was clear we were getting special treatment. Apparently eating with Buck Waverly, at least in this restaurant, had its perks.

Normally, when I go out to eat, I like to sit so I have a view of the front door. Call me paranoid, but I don't want people sneaking up behind me. Buck is the same way, and it was he who was sitting with his back to the wall that evening, giving him a clear view of the front of the restaurant. Polly sat beside him, and I sat across with an empty chair to my right for Lucy.

As we started our appetizers, I saw Polly look over my left shoulder and smile. "There she is. I knew she'd come."

Turning around, I saw that Lucy had just walked into the restaurant. Wearing blue shorts and a white button up shirt, she looked like she had just left work and had driven without stopping at her home.

As she approached the table, I stood and helped her with her chair. "Lucy, glad you made it."

She returned my smile then leaned over and whispered in my ear. "I'm doing this for mom."

During dinner, Buck was a superb host. He shared stories from his past, listened intently when Polly or Lucy spoke, and was the perfect gentleman throughout.

After we finished our desserts, Buck suggested that he and Polly take the minivan back to Serenity Cove while the young folks (Lucy and I) went out and did whatever young folks did these days.

Polly smiled. "Lucy, you don't mind driving Walker, do you?"

Lucy started to object, but Polly gave her a look and shook her head. Apparently, Lucy got the message. "I'll be happy to drive Walker home. In fact, I have something in my car I want to give him."

"Good, it's settled. Buck and I'll take the minivan, and Walker, you'll ride with Lucy."

After I handed the minivan's keys to Polly, Buck stood and held her chair as she got up. They said their goodbyes and left.

Lucy and I were alone at the table. She gave me a fake smile and said, "You ready to go?"

I nodded and looked around for our server. She saw me and quickly came over.

"I think we'll be leaving. Can we have our check please?"

She shook her head. "It's already been taken care of. Earlier today. Is there anything else I can get you?"

"No, we're fine. The meal and service were excellent."

After she left, I pulled two twenties and placed them on the table.

When I looked up, Lucy was smiling. "Can you believe it? My mom is out with Buck Waverly. They're probably going back to his place. This is not at all like her.

She continued. "So I'm betting you're involved in this somehow. It was you who got them together. Right?"

I smiled. "If you'll take me home the long way, by the beach, I'll tell you the whole story."

Lucy got up from the table, jangled her car keys and said, "Oh, I'll take you home alright. But I get to choose the route."

She then walked through the restaurant, out the front door and into the parking lot. I followed closely—fearing she just might leave me behind if I didn't keep up with her.

After she unlocked her 4Runner and slid behind the wheel, I tried the passenger door. It was locked. I couldn't get in.

From the driver's side, Lucy looked up at me and smiled. She put the key in the ignition and started the motor.

I stepped away, assuming she was going to leave me standing in the parking lot as she drove off. But after a moment I heard the click of the passenger door unlocking.

"Come on, get in," she said. "I'm not going to wait all night."

CHAPTER THIRTY-ONE

Lucy was driving and I was in the passenger seat. We were headed down McCall Road, which was good. It meant she *wasn't* taking me straight back to Serenity Cove. She was taking me the long way. We'd get to spend more time together.

"So, Walker, how do you know Buck Waverly? And how did you get him to ask my mom out?"

I smiled. "You probably won't believe this, but here goes. Earlier today I was helping Buck do a live interview with Mary Hart on *Entertainment Tonight*, and—"

"Wait. Mary Hart? *Entertainment Tonight*? You and Buck were on TV today?"

"No, not me. Just Buck. I was just there to help set things up.

"So, anyway, after the *Entertainment Tonight* thing, Buck and I started talking, and he asked if I could get your mom to go to dinner with him.

"So I called her and she said, 'Yes,' but only if you and I went along."

Lucy looked at me and shook her head. "Walker, I've only known you for three days. In that time, I've seen you save someone's life, I've caught you with a naked woman, and you set my mom up on a date with a movie star.

"All this in just three days. Is this normal for you?"

I thought about it and she was right. A lot had happened in three short days.

I was about to answer her question, but before I could, she said, "So mom called and told me about the woman on your

137

couch this morning. She said you were a hero last night. Said you rescued that woman after someone drugged her drink.

"So in addition to saving lives of strangers, you rescue damsels in distress? Do they always end up on your couch half naked?"

I made sure Lucy was finished talking before I answered. I wanted to give her time to change the subject, maybe give me an escape route. But it didn't happen.

So I answered. "It's not every day that I rescue a damsel in distress. And no, they don't usually end up on my couch."

She shook her head. "So, Walker, who is this woman, and why did she call *you,* of all people?"

I hesitated, then said, "She's my realtor. And she's a friend. I owed her—she rescued me once, probably saved *my* life.

"She called me because she knew I'd come. She knew I'd protect her.

"If *you* called me, I'd do the same for you. I'd even let you sleep in my motorhome. Even let you get half naked on the couch if you wanted to."

Lucy laughed. "Hold on there, cowboy. You're getting way ahead of yourself. I won't be getting half naked on your couch any time soon."

She took a right and started heading back toward Serenity Cove.

"Walker, I'm not mad at you. I just don't know if I can trust you. Too many things happen when you're around."

I understood. "Lucy, it's not usually like this. Most of the time I live a pretty boring life."

Little did I know how much that was about to change.

We arrived back at Serenity Cove a few minutes later and Lucy drove to my motorhome. Looking next door at her mother's place, she said, "That's interesting. Mom's minivan is not there. They're not back yet."

I smiled. "Maybe they're down at Buck's. Maybe they parked down there."

Lucy looked at me. "You don't think my mom would go down there with him, do you? God help her if she did."

I shrugged. "They're both adults. They can do whatever they want to."

She shook her head. "No they can't. Not on the first date. Not my mom. I'm going down there to see."

Lucy put her 4Runner in gear and drove slowly toward Buck's bus. As we got closer we could see there were no lights on inside, and the minivan wasn't parked in the driveway.

"Walker, this is starting to bother me. They should be back by now. It's only a five-minute drive from the restaurant and it's been almost half an hour. So where are they?"

I didn't say anything. Lucy didn't either. We just sat in silence for a few moments listening to the quiet of Serenity Cove.

Lucy kept glancing up at her rear view mirror, hoping to see Polly's minivan heading in our direction. After what seemed like five minutes, I spoke up. "Maybe they drove to the beach. It's nice out there after dark."

Lucy looked at me hard, shook her head then put the car in gear. We were moving again, following the loop through Serenity Cove, which would take us back to the entrance.

When we reached the street, Lucy stopped and put the vehicle in park. "Okay. So they're not back. What should we do next?"

"How about this," I suggested. "Call your mom, ask her where she is."

"No, I can't do that. I don't want her to think I'm checking up on her."

"But you *are* checking up on her. "

"I know, but I don't want *her* to know. So what else do you suggest?"

Before I answered, I thought it through. Lucy was worried something had happened to her mom. If I suggested that they had probably just stopped somewhere, it wouldn't settle anything.

So I said, "Let's drive back to the restaurant and make sure they're not broken down somewhere between here and there. If we don't find them, we'll come back here and wait until they show up."

Lucy nodded. "Right, maybe they broke down. We'll go check."

She put the 4Runner in gear and we took off toward the restaurant. While she drove, I checked every driveway and parking lot looking for her mom's minivan.

A lot of older people in Englewood drive minivans, and there were plenty of them parked in the driveways of the homes we passed, but none were Polly's.

When we got to the restaurant, Lucy pulled into the parking lot. There were more cars now, but Polly's minivan wasn't one of them.

"They're not here. Now what?"

I shook my head. "Look, if she was in trouble, she would have called you by now. Or Buck would have called me. Both of them have phones. They would call us if there was a problem.

"So let's do this. We'll go back to Serenity Cove and wait for them to show up. They may already be back there for all we know."

Lucy said nothing. She backed out of the lot and drove slowly back to Serenity Cove. We both kept our eyes peeled for Polly's minivan but didn't see it along the way.

Back at Serenity Cove, she pulled up to her mom's trailer. The minivan wasn't there. It wasn't at Buck's bus either. She drove the road that circled through Serenity Cove, making sure that the couple hadn't returned while we were out looking for them.

On our second loop through the park, Lucy pulled into my driveway. She turned to me and said, "Okay, sport. We're going to wait for them here."

I shook my head. "Not out here. It'll look suspicious. Let's go inside. I'll introduce you to Bob."

Without waiting for an answer, I hopped out of her car and headed to my motorhome.

As I unlocked the front door, I heard Lucy open the driver's door and step out. "Who's Bob?"

I turned. "He's my cat. I told you about him yesterday. You'll like him."

She reluctantly walked over and followed me inside. I turned on the lights and pointed at the couch, "Make yourself comfortable. You want anything to drink?"

"No, I'm fine. I'm not staying long. Just until Mom shows up."

I shrugged. "Fine with me. But I'm going to have a glass of wine. Are you sure you don't want any?"

She stifled a yawn. "No. No wine for me. It'd put me to sleep."

In the kitchen, I located the bottle of Merlot I had purchased at Publix and poured myself a glass. While I was putting the cork back in the bottle, Mango Bob showed up. He looked up at me, eyes blinking. Apparently, he had just woken up.

He rubbed up against my ankles, a sign that he wanted to be petted. I bent over and stroked his back and he purred loudly. He turned his head so I could rub his ears, and as he did he noticed Lucy sitting on the couch.

She had been watching us silently. Bob took a few tentative steps in her direction then stopped and looked back at me.

"It's alright, Bob. She won't hurt you."

Bob said, "Murrph?"

Then he walked over to Lucy and stopped at her feet. He sniffed her shoes then hopped up onto the couch beside her. She smiled and began stroking Bob's back. "What's the deal with his tail? It seems to be missing."

I nodded. "He's an American Bobtail. They all have short, stubby tails like that. Makes them look like bobcats."

Bob could tell we were talking about him. He rewarded us by twitching his little stump of a tail each time we said his name.

Lucy noticed. "That's cute. Each time you say his name, he moves his tail."

I nodded. "You try it. See if he does it for you."

She smiled. "Bob. Do you know your name?"

He did. He twitched his tail as soon as she said Bob.

She tried again. "Bob, you're a good kitty."

Again, he twitched his tail.

I smiled. "Lucy, pat your hand on your lap three times."

She looked at me curiously.

"Just do it. See what Bob does."

She shrugged then patted her lap.

Bob knew what it meant. It was an invitation for him to take a seat on her lap. And he did.

Lucy smiled at me and silently pointed at Bob.

I nodded.

She closed her eyes and slowly stroked Bob's soft fur.

It had taken less than two minutes for Lucy to fall under Mango Bob's spell. His purring was having an amazing effect on her. It was like she had taken a very strong sedative.

The anxiety she had displayed earlier about not knowing where her mother was had been replaced with a deep calm.

Picking up my glass of wine, I headed to the couch intending to sit down beside her, but my plans were thwarted when my phone chimed with an incoming call.

I put the glass of wine on the side table nearest the couch and went to get the phone, which I'd left on the kitchen counter.

"Is it them?" asked Lucy.

The caller ID showed it was Anna, the half-naked woman Lucy had found in my motorhome earlier that morning.

"No, it's not them. But I need to take this call. I'll be in the back bedroom for a few minutes. Make yourself comfortable."

CHAPTER THIRTY-TWO

In the privacy of the back bedroom, I answered the phone. The first words I heard were, "Walker, you want some company tonight?"

I knew right away this could be trouble.

"Anna, you sound like you're feeling better."

"I am. After you dropped me off at the condo, I slept for an hour then showered and went into work. I wasn't expecting much to happen. Just wanted to show up for an hour or two.

"But a client I showed a home to yesterday called and made an offer. We filled out the forms, and the seller accepted.

"So out of the blue, I made another big sale. In thirty days, I'm going to get one heck of a commission check.

"So, yes, I'm feeling pretty good. But you didn't answer my question. Do you want some company tonight?"

I hesitated, thinking how best to answer. After going through the possible choices, I came to the conclusion that, in this case, an honest answer would be the safest.

"I have a previous engagement."

"A previous engagement? With a woman? Could this be the same woman who knocked on your door this morning?"

"Yes. And she's over here right now."

"Well, congratulations, Walker. Glad to see you got things straightened out with her. It'd probably be best if I call you back some other time."

"Anna, wait. I visited the Raft today. Found out what really happened last night."

"Really? Tell me, and don't leave anything out."

I told her what I had learned. It took me almost fifteen minutes to get through the entire story because she continued to interrupt me with questions.

After I finished telling her everything, she said, "Well, I'm glad you went down there. I feel a lot better knowing they caught the guy."

Realizing I had left Lucy alone in the living room for more than twenty minutes, I said, "Anna, I've got to go. I need to get back to my guest before she bails on me."

"I understand. We'll talk later."

We ended the call and I went back up front to check on Lucy.

The first thing I noticed was she had kicked off her shoes and stretched out on the couch. The next thing I noticed was the full glass of wine I had set on the table was now empty. Apparently Lucy had gotten thirsty.

And it looked like the wine, along with Bob's purring, had put her to sleep.

Bob is magical this way. One minute you're wide awake with him at your side. The next minute he's in your lap and you're petting him. Before you know it, his purring and kneading has lulled you to sleep.

Lucy had fallen under his spell and was out like a light. Bob was curled up in the crook of her arm, still purring.

Not wanting to disturb either of them, I turned off the overhead lights, leaving just the night light on. Peeking outside, I could see that Polly had returned. The minivan was parked next door and Buck's golf cart was gone. It meant they had made it back safely.

The only question was whether I should wake Lucy and send her home or let her stay and sleep. I decided to let her sleep. Pulling a sheet from the overhead bin, I covered her and Bob, locked the front door, and headed back to my bedroom.

It had been a long, stressful day, and I hadn't gotten much sleep the night before. I planned to catch up on it now.

If Lucy woke during the night, she could choose to go home or stay. It was up to her.

CHAPTER THIRTY-THREE

It's rare that Bob lets me sleep through the entire night without waking me up. Usually around three in the morning, he'll loudly announce his plans to use the litter box. He'll then do his business and spend a few minutes rearranging the litter to bury the evidence.

After he's satisfied that his deposit is sufficiently hidden, he'll run around like a nut for a few minutes and then settle down on a window sill where he can stealthily monitor the nocturnal wildlife just beyond his reach.

But not that night.

Instead of making his presence known, he kept quiet all night long and didn't bother to wake me.

I'm not sure whether this was because he knew I needed the sleep or whether he simply enjoyed being cuddled up with Lucy. Whatever the reason, he let us both sleep through the night undisturbed.

When I finally woke, the dim light of the morning sun was peeking in under the privacy shade of the small window in my bedroom. I hadn't heard Lucy leave during the night, and I wondered if she might still be asleep on the couch.

I crawled out of bed, pulled on the jeans and T-shirt I'd worn the day before, and went out to check.

As I walked up front, the sunlight filtering in through the windows silhouetted Lucy's shape, still sleeping on the couch. The digital clock over the fridge showed 6:45am. I had gotten almost eight hours of much needed sleep.

Bob had moved from under the sheet covering Lucy and was

now sitting close to her face, watching her breathe.

He was purring loudly and had one paw raised above her cheek. I knew what he was about to do, so I whispered, "Bob, don't do it. Let her sleep."

He looked at me then slowly placed his paw on Lucy's face, just to the right of her nose. After a moment, he withdrew it. Then he repeated the process, lightly tapping her with his paw.

With Bob, this was a game. See how many times he could touch her face before she woke. He had played this game with me before and I knew how it was going to end.

After the fourth touch, Lucy brushed her face with her hand. Realizing that somebody or something had been touching her, she opened her eyes and saw Bob.

Still lying on the couch, she looked around and saw me. "What the hell is wrong with your cat? He's putting his feet on my face."

I tried not to laugh. "It's because he likes you. He wants you to get up and play."

Lucy looked confused. "What time is it?"

"A quarter to seven. Time for breakfast."

She sat up. "No, this is wrong. I shouldn't be here. What's my mom going to think? Did they ever get back?"

"Yes, they made it home just fine. Drove up a few minutes after you and Bob crashed on the couch."

She picked up her shoes. "I can't be here. I've got to go. I've got to get ready for work. Mom can't know I spent the night."

Before I could reply, there was a knock at the door.

"Lucy, you in there? Everything all right?"

It was Polly, Lucy's mom.

I smiled at Lucy and then opened the door, "Come on in, Polly. Lucy's just getting up. We were talking about breakfast. Would you like to join us?"

Looking up at her mom, Lucy said, "It's not what you

think."

CHAPTER THIRTY-FOUR

Lucy was trying to explain. "We were worried. You and Buck weren't here last night when we came back from the restaurant. We thought you might have had car trouble or been in an accident.

"So Walker suggested I wait here until you made it home. I had a glass of wine, and I guess I fell asleep. Next thing I know, it's morning and that crazy cat of his is tapping me on the face."

Polly looked at Lucy with a knowing smile. Then she looked at me and said, "You know, before she met you, she wasn't like this. She rarely spent the night with a guy on the first or second date."

Lucy protested. "I didn't spend the night. Nothing happened. I just fell asleep on the couch."

She changed the subject. "What about you and Buck? Why'd it take you so long to get back here?"

Polly smiled. "Buck and I had a lovely evening. We talked, we laughed, and we drove around some. Then we came back here; we each went to our own homes and slept in our own beds. That's more than I can say about some people."

Lucy picked up a pillow and threw it at her mother. Polly caught it and looked up at me with a grin on her face.

"Walker, thank you so much for arranging my evening with Buck. It's been a long time since I enjoyed myself so much.

"We're going out again this evening, and if you'd like to join us, we'd be happy to have you."

I shook my head. "Thanks for the offer. But after last night with your daughter, I need my rest."

Lucy pleaded, "Mom, I'm completely innocent. I fell asleep on the couch. That's it."

Polly walked up to Lucy, peered closely at her face and asked, "Is that cat litter on your cheek?"

Lucy sputtered as she brushed the small grains of clay off her face. "It's that crazy cat's fault. He lulled me to sleep, and then this morning he had his paws on my face."

She headed for the door. "I'm going home. I've got to take a shower and go to work."

Polly and I stood grinning as Lucy stomped out the door, shoes in hand.

Moments later, she returned. "I meant to give you this last night."

She handed me a small picture frame then went back outside, got into her 4Runner and drove off.

Looking at what she had given me, I saw it was a framed article from the *Englewood Herald*, the local newspaper. The article headline read, "Good Samaritan Aids Fallen Cyclist."

Below the headline, the article mentioned a 'mystery man' who had come to the aid of the fallen cyclist and saved his life. The photo accompanying the article showed me giving CPR to a man lying on the ground. In the background, you could clearly see my Jeep.

I handed the article to Polly who quickly scanned it. "Nice. My neighbor, local hero and good Samaritan."

She set the frame down on the kitchen counter and turned to me. "So tell me what really happened here last night."

I smiled. "It was pretty much what Lucy said. We came back here to wait to make sure you made it back safely. While we were waiting, I got a phone call and went to the back bedroom for about fifteen minutes.

"When I came back up front, Lucy was asleep on the couch with Bob curled up beside her. I didn't want to disturb them, so I just let them sleep."

Polly laughed. "This is good. I'll be able to use this for months."

Then she said, "I was just about to cook some breakfast. Would you like to come over and join me?"

CHAPTER THIRTY-FIVE

After breakfast with Polly, I went back to my motorhome, showered, shaved and got ready to start a new day.

I'd only been living in Serenity Cove for four days, and already had more excitement than I'd had in the previous two months.

On this day, I just wanted to relax. Spend a few hours catching up on some internet projects I'd been working on then maybe investigate some of the problems at Serenity Cove Anna had mentioned when she arranged my stay.

But first I needed to take a walk. Stretch my legs a bit.

If you check out the satellite view of Serenity Cove using Google Earth, you'll see it covers about four acres of land, laid out in a long rectangle. The shortest leg of the rectangle is on West Wentworth Street—where the main gate and office building are located.

From there, you take the paved driveway that makes a long loop through the park. As you drive the loop, you'll find all the RV sites are on the left, with the pool, tennis court, and pavilion on the right.

At the very back of the park, the road makes a slow 180 degree turn where it meets the waters of Lemon Bay. Here you'll find a narrow patch of grass between the road and the seawall that keeps the bay from spilling into Serenity Cove grounds.

Right off the seawall is an eight-foot-wide boat dock, used by residents to fish from and to occasionally dock boats. At low tide, the depth of the water in front of the dock is just over three feet—not deep enough for sail boats but enough for fishing and party boats.

While there aren't any RV sites on the waterfront, there are parking spots where residents and guests can park and have a picnic or load and unload their cars for fishing and boating.

From the waterfront, you head around the curve past another row of RV sites then end up back at the office and main gate.

I'd walked this loop several times with Polly and Oscar, but that morning I was walking it alone.

When I reached the dock on the waterfront, I stopped for a few minutes to take in the view. From my vantage point, I could look across the wide expanse of Lemon Bay to the white sand beaches of Manasota Key.

The scene of the swaying palms on the distant beach, with seagulls circling overhead and the occasional mullet breaking the water's surface, was the kind of view people up north came to Florida to see. Having it there at Serenity Cove made me realize how special the place really was.

Turning around and looking back toward the park, I could see that at one time Serenity Cove had been really nice. Wide RV sites shaded by mature palms. Pool, tennis court and picnic pavilion. Waterfront on Lemon Bay with easy boating access to the gulf.

The place had all the right ingredients to make it great.

But years of deferred maintenance had taken its toll. The pool was closed. The tennis court needed to be resurfaced. The office building needed painting and the dock needed new deck boards.

I was thinking about this when a voice behind me asked, "You going fishing?"

I turned to see Buck in his golf cart. In his right hand, he was holding a glass of what looked like iced tea.

"No, not fishing. Just checking out the dock. Thinking

about Serenity Cove."

Buck pointed back at the tennis courts. "This used to be a first class place. Had everything a person could want. But, lately, the owners have stopped doing maintenance. They've let things run down. It's like they don't care anymore."

I nodded in agreement then asked, "So tell me about last night. Did you have a good time?"

Buck tipped the front of his cowboy hat. "Sure did. Polly is a real peach. Fun to be around and smart too."

He was interrupted by the ringing of his phone. He looked at the caller ID and signaled he had to take the call.

Wanting to give him some privacy, I continued my walk around the park, making a mental list of the things that needed attending to.

CHAPTER THIRTY-SIX

Over the next four days, I spent most of my time either working on my computer or walking around the park taking notes. I didn't call Lucy, figuring she might need a few days without me around.

Most days I did see Polly walking Oscar, and on several occasions we walked loops around the park together. Our conversations were mainly about the weather or about Oscar and his desire to chase squirrels.

Polly did tell me that she was seeing Buck just about every day. Usually for breakfast or lunch, depending on what else they had on their individual calendars.

Buck's schedule was fairly simple, mostly revolving around his regular appointments with a chiropractor in Venice.

Polly's schedule was about the same, with most of her commitments related to the veterinary needs of Oscar or yoga classes on the beach with Lucy.

Each time yoga came up, Polly invited me to join her, but I always declined. It's not that I didn't like yoga or the beach or a crowd of women, it's just that I preferred to exercise alone. A solitary run was more my style.

At the end of that day's walk, Polly put a hand on my arm and said, "Walker, I mentioned my houseboat to Buck, and he wants to see the inside. I thought you might want to join us."

I nodded. "Polly, I would love to see the inside of your boat. But I don't want to be a burden on you and Buck. Are you sure you want me along?"

She smiled. "Well, actually, we can't go without you.

"See, to get out to the houseboat we have to use my dinghy. It's at Lucy's on a trailer. That's where you come in. We need someone to help us hook the trailer up to my minivan. Then, when we get to the boat ramp, we need help getting the dinghy in the water.

"Buck says he can do it, but I'm afraid he might hurt his back. If you came with us, you could do it. That'd keep me and Buck from getting hurt, and you'd get a chance to see the houseboat. It's still for sale, you know."

"Polly, I'd be happy to help. Just let me know when."

She smiled. "How about tomorrow afternoon? Around two? We can take my minivan, head over to Lucy's, hook up the boat trailer and then go to Chadwick Park."

I nodded again. "Sounds good to me. Just knock on my door whenever you're ready to go."

The next day the weather was perfect for going out on the water. One of those Florida spring days with bright blue skies, light puffy clouds, no humidity, and a slight breeze.

Just before two in the afternoon, Polly was at my door with Buck at her side. They were holding hands. "Walker, you ready to go out on the water?"

"Sure am. Let's go."

We loaded into Polly's minivan, Buck and Polly in the backseat with me driving. Before we left, I asked, "Oscar's not coming with us?"

Polly shook her head. "Not today. He's not good in the boat, so he's staying home."

I drove the two miles to Lucy's. As I pulled up into her driveway, Polly tapped me on the shoulder. "The boat's around back. Just drive across the grass. Lucy won't mind."

I drove across Lucy's lawn and around to the back of her house where the dinghy was stored. It was sitting on a single axle boat trailer, covered with a gray tarp.

Removing the tarp revealed an aluminum v-bottomed boat with a small outboard motor in the back. Inside the boat were three life jackets, a small first aid kit, and a metal case marked "Flares."

The boat had three metal bench seats—one back by the motor, one in the middle, and one near the bow. Even though the boat was small, it looked seaworthy.

Polly went to the back of the boat and checked the fuel level of the orange gas tank. "Tank shows almost full. That's good. Means we won't have to stop for gas. Before we get out on the water, let's see if we can get the motor started.

"Walker, come back here and help."

Polly pointed to the rubber fuel line. "Plug that into the motor. Then pump the primer bulb until it gets hard."

Polly watched as I followed her instructions.

"Good. Now, make sure the motor is in neutral, and pull out the choke. Then grab the starter rope and give it a good pull."

On the first pull, the motor coughed but didn't start.

"Don't worry, that's what it always does. Now, push the choke in halfway, and pull again."

This time, the motor started right up. It ran rough for about ten seconds until Polly pushed the choke all the way in. After that, the motor smoothed out into a steady idle.

After thirty seconds, Polly pressed the kill button, and the motor shuddered to a stop. "You got to love these old Mercury two strokes. They start every time and run forever."

She pointed to a paddle leaning against the back wall of Lucy's home. "Get that. Never know when we might need it."

With the paddle in the boat, Polly had me back the minivan up so we could hitch it to the trailer.

As I backed up, Buck stood near the trailer and guided me in.

"Slow. Slow. Straighten up. Good. Stop."

I put the van in park, killed the motor and headed back to hook up the trailer. Before I could get back there, Buck grabbed the tongue of the trailer and pulled it over to the van. He didn't have to move it far, but I could tell by the look on Polly's face she wasn't pleased.

She didn't want Buck hurting himself. That's why I was along, to do heavy lifting. But Buck had been quick and lifted the tongue of the trailer and dragged it over to the minivan before I could intervene.

When I caught up with him, he was lowering the tongue onto the ball of the trailer hitch. Once he had it set, he wiped his hands and smiled at me. "She didn't think I could do it. But I can."

He pointed to the chains hanging from the front of the trailer. "Since you're here, you can do the rest."

I knelt down and connected the safety chains and the light harness. When I got back up, Polly was standing behind me. I smiled and asked, "Anything else?"

She walked around the trailer, inspecting our work. "Everything looks good. Let's go."

The three of us got back in the minivan and headed to the boat ramp at Chadwick Park.

CHAPTER THIRTY-SEVEN

It took us less than ten minutes to reach the boat launch. The minivan had no problem pulling the trailer.

It took another fifteen minutes to get the boat launched. Polly supervised while I backed the trailer down the ramp, and then she showed Buck and me how to unstrap the boat from the trailer and get it in the water.

With the boat in the water, I used the bowline to guide it to the nearby dock so we could get in. Polly sat on the bench nearest the front of the boat, Buck took the middle, and I sat in the back and manned the motor.

With everybody in, I started the motor and backed away from the dock and headed out across the bay toward Polly's houseboat.

The little v-bottom boat quickly came up on plane, and we skimmed across the bay leaving only a small wake behind.

As we got closer to the houseboat, I throttled back and we glided toward its gleaming white hull.

Polly turned toward me and said, "Pull up close on the right side. But be careful. I don't want you bumping into my boat."

I nodded, showing I understood.

I brought us around to the right side of the *Escape Artist* and closed to within three feet of its hull. I then killed the motor. Our momentum kept us gliding forward toward the boat. When we got close enough, Buck reached out and used his hands to keep us from bumping into the houseboat's hull.

Polly pointed to the houseboat. "See that opening in the railing? I need you to move us down there. Don't start the motor, just grab the handrail and pull us down."

Pulling hand over hand, Buck and I moved the little boat toward the opening Polly had pointed out. When we reached it, she said, "That's far enough. Now hold the boat steady."

She stood and unlatched the section of the handrail that doubled as a gate, and pulled herself up on deck. Her momentum pushed our little boat away from the houseboat. We quickly floated out of Polly's reach.

"Oops," she said, "I should have tied us off before I got out. Throw me a line; I'll pull you back over."

Buck tossed her a line, and she was able to pull us back up close to the houseboat. She wrapped the line to a cleat on the houseboat's deck, to keep us from floating away.

She did the same with a line from the rear of the dingy. With both the front and the back of the dinghy secured, she stood and said, "You two wait here for a minute. I need to go get something."

She walked to the back of the houseboat and returned with two rubber boat bumpers. She snapped their lines onto deck cleats and then dropped them into the space between the two boats.

"Okay, guys. Come on aboard."

CHAPTER THIRTY-EIGHT

Buck went first, using the handrail on the houseboat to help make the step up from the dinghy. I followed.

Once aboard, we could see that just about every surface of the boat was freshly painted white. The contrasting blue curtains covering the many windows gave the boat a real nautical feel.

Polly unlocked the main cabin and invited us in. It was clean inside, but there was a slightly musty smell. Polly pointed to the windows. "Let's open some doors and windows so we can get some fresh air in here."

Buck opened the sliding door overlooking the front deck, while I opened the windows which wrapped around the main cabin.

While we were doing this, Polly went down a short set of stairs to an area below the main cabin. We could hear her opening and closing cabinet doors. A few moments later, she came back up and joined us.

"The main electrical panel is down there. You have to flip on the battery switch to have lights and power. When I leave the boat, I always turn it off, and when I come back, I turn it back on.

"To keep the batteries charged, I come out here and run the motors at least once a month."

She reached into her shirt pocket and retrieved a key ring that had three keys attached along with a bright yellow piece of rubber with the words "Boat US" printed in red.

"Walker, let me show you how to start the motor."

She stood behind the helm and inserted one of the keys into

167

the boat's ignition switch and turned it one click to the right.

"First, you start the fuel tank exhaust fan by flipping this toggle switch. That humming sound you hear means the fan is running.

"Next you start the fuel pump."

She flipped another toggle switch, this one labeled "Fuel pump," and we could hear a slight clicking sound from down below.

"Then you lower the motor into the water."

She pulled a large, white lever and we heard the deep humming sound of an electric motor followed by a splash.

"That splash means the motor is in the water. Now we'll see if it'll start."

She turned the ignition key to the far right, and we could hear the starter turning.

After five seconds, the motor hadn't fired up. Polly turned the key off, counted to ten, and then tried the starter again. This time the motor roared to life.

She smiled. "That's the way it's supposed to work. The first time primes it. The second time starts it.

"If you follow the steps just like I showed you, it'll start every time."

I nodded. "Seems pretty easy. Start the fan, run the fuel pump, lower the motor, and turn the key, twice."

She nodded. "That's right. Do it in that order, and you won't have a problem."

She then asked, "You guys ready for the tour?"

We both said, "Yes."

"Okay. I'll tell you what I know. This is a thirty-six-foot Sea Rover. It's a fiberglass tri-hull. They tell me that means low maintenance, more stability and a smoother ride.

"It's got a two-foot draft, which means we can go into pretty shallow water. That's good for around here because the water can be shallow up in the rivers and canals.

"Back when this boat was originally built, it had twin inboard motors, but the previous owner took them out and replaced them with a single outboard.

"He told me this made the boat lighter and easier to handle. It also opened more storage below. Supposedly the outboard is a better motor for the conditions here in Florida.

"I don't know if that's true or not, but that's what the guy said.

"Up here on the main deck, we have a small galley kitchen with fridge and microwave.

"Behind us is the head, with toilet and shower. Further back is the captain's quarters with a small bed and desk.

"Down below, there's a guest cabin with twin beds.

"Outside, we have a sun deck up front, a fishing deck out back, and a party deck up on top.

"Any questions?"

I raised my hand. "Why do you park it out here instead of the marina?"

Polly smiled. "Good question. I'd prefer to have it at the marina. It'd make it a lot easier to get to. But at the marina, they charge by the foot for dock space. For a boat this size, they charge four hundred fifty dollars a month.

"That's way more than I wanted to pay. So I anchor it out here in the mooring field where it doesn't cost me anything."

I nodded. "I guess that makes sense. But how safe is it to leave the boat out here?"

"Actually, it's pretty safe. Not many people bother to steal boats from the mooring field. Too much trouble to get to them, and there are almost always people around watching for that kind of thing.

"The big worry is tropical storms and hurricanes. If you see one of those coming, you do have to move the boat to safety.

"But so far, we've been pretty lucky in Englewood. Last big storm to hit this area was almost forty years ago."

Polly turned to Buck. "What do you think of her?"

He smiled. "From what I can see, this is a pretty sweet deal. A little getaway out here on the water. No one to bother you and all the comforts of home."

"Yeah," I said, "I agree with Buck. This is pretty nice. I'm impressed."

Then I asked, "Polly, would it be okay if I walked around, checked things out?"

"Sure, make yourself at home. Just don't use the toilet. I haven't turned on the pump and don't want to have to dump the holding tanks."

While Polly and Buck stayed on the upper deck, I explored. I started by going down the narrow set of stairs just behind the helm. This took me to the lower deck and the guest cabin.

It was surprisingly roomy, with twin beds, two closets, a night table and a lamp. Porthole windows on each side of the cabin provided light and cross ventilation as well as a water view.

To the rear of the guest cabin, right behind the night table, was a narrow door. Presumably this door led into the engine bays. I tried it, but it was locked.

Leaving the guest cabin, I headed back upstairs and checked out the captain's quarters—a small room overlooking the back of the boat. It had a single bed, a small desk and chair.

Windows on three sides provided ventilation as well as a good view outside the boat. With the door to the captain's quarters open, the captain would be just steps from the helm and have a clear view of the front and back of the boat.

Just outside the captain's cabin was a small bathroom, with toilet, shower and sink. Like all the other rooms in the boat, the bathroom had a window, but in this room it was placed high on the wall for privacy.

Going outside, I followed a narrow catwalk to the front deck

170

where Polly and Buck had pulled up two folding chairs and were talking.

Seeing me, Polly turned and asked, "So, did you see it all? Any questions?"

"I think I saw everything, and I'm really impressed. Much more room than I expected. My only question is about the air conditioner. I see you have one, but how do you power it?"

Polly pointed to the back of the boat. "There's a 4,500 watt gas generator in one of the engine bays. Whenever I need to run the A/C, I press a button on the helm, and the generator starts right up."

I nodded. "So how big is the boat's fuel tank? And how much fuel does she use when cruising?"

Polly smiled. "Those are the same questions I asked before I bought her. The previous owner told me it had a sixty gallon fuel tank. He said the boat uses about four gallons an hour while cruising.

"But I don't know if that's true or not. I've only taken it out once. Up to Sarasota Bay and back. Took about three hours and used an eighth of a tank."

I pointed over my shoulder. "Mind if I go back and check out the motor?"

"Check out whatever you like. Buck and I are going to sit up here and watch the dolphins."

I made my way to the back of the boat along the port side catwalk. About half way back, I heard Polly call my name. "Walker, you won't be able to get into the old engine bays. They're both locked. Keeps thieves from stealing the generator and batteries."

That made sense. Keep things locked, just in case uninvited guests make their way on board.

At the back of the boat, I stood on the fishing deck, right above the still running Honda four-stroke motor. It was surprisingly quiet, just burbling along at idle, spitting out a constant stream of water from above the prop.

Looking closer at the motor, I could see it was securely locked into a metal bracket that had been welded to the back of the boat.

This would tend to discourage would-be thieves, as would the large expanse of water they would need to travel across to get to the boat in the first place.

As I stood there, the motor suddenly stopped running. It had been running smoothly with no problems. Then it just stopped. Looking over my shoulder toward the front of the boat, I saw Polly standing at the helm. She had apparently switched off the motor.

Behind me, the motor lurched then slowly started tilting backwards, lifting up out of the water until the prop was a good eight inches above the surface.

Turning back toward Polly, I gave her a thumbs up, and she signaled me to join her. As I made my way to the helm, I could hear Buck closing the windows we had opened earlier.

When I reached Polly, she said, "It's about time to head back to shore. We don't want to be pulling the trailer back home after dark."

I frowned. "Seems like we just got here. We going back so soon?"

She smiled. "Walker, we've been out here almost two hours. It'll take us another hour to get back to shore and load up the trailer and get it back to Lucy's. By then it'll be close to dark."

I pulled out my phone to check the time. Polly was right. We'd been on the boat for two hours—a lot longer than I thought. Time had flown by.

I didn't want to leave. It was nice out on the water, and it wouldn't bother me a bit to stay longer. But I was Polly's guest. If she and Buck wanted to get back to Lucy's before dark, that's what we were going to do.

After Buck had closed all the windows and doors, Polly went

around and double-checked each of them.

She explained, "You have to check everything twice. Leaving a window just slightly cracked could cause a major problem. Rainstorms, birds, and uninvited guests will take advantage of any opening."

When she was certain that everything was secure, she locked the main cabin door and we headed back to the dinghy, which was still lashed to the side of the houseboat.

"Walker, you get in first. Get the motor started. Then Buck and I will get in."

I climbed down into the dinghy and, with one pull of the starter rope, got the motor up and running. Buck held Polly's hand as she stepped in, and he followed. Once we were all settled in, we untied the lines, pushed the dinghy away from the houseboat, and headed back.

A light chop had come up, and the ride back was a bit more bouncy as we crossed the open waters of the bay. But the light spray coming off the bow was invigorating, and we were all smiles as we headed in.

Upon reaching the boat ramp, Polly showed us how to get the dinghy back on the trailer. It took about ten minutes to get everything done to her satisfaction.

After checking everything twice, she said, "That's how we do that. Everything is secure, and everybody is back on dry land, safe and sound."

We got in the minivan and headed back to Lucy's to drop off the trailer. As before, I drove, with Buck and Polly side-by-side in the back seat.

They made a cute couple, and I was happy they had found each other. I heard Buck say, "Being on the water all day has got me in the mood for seafood. How about we all go to the Gulf View Grill tonight?"

Polly thought it was a good idea. "Sounds good to me. How about you, Walker?"

173

I shook my head. "I appreciate the invite, but I'm going to pass. I've got a few things I need to take care of tonight."

Truth was I really didn't have anything I needed to do that night. But I'd already spent most of the afternoon with Buck and Polly, and while I really enjoyed their company I didn't want to be a third wheel on their dinner date.

CHAPTER THIRTY-NINE

When we arrived at Lucy's, her 4Runner was parked in the driveway.

Polly smiled. "Looks like Lucy is home. Let me get out and talk to her while you two unload the boat. Think you can do it without me?"

"Yes," I said. "We can handle it. Go talk to Lucy."

After Polly got out, I pulled the minivan around to the back of the house and angled the trailer so that it was parked pretty much where it had been when we picked it up earlier that day.

After telling Polly we could handle unhooking the trailer, I wanted to be sure we actually could do it to her satisfaction.

Fortunately for us, unhooking the trailer was a lot easier than getting it in or out of the water. All we needed to do was lift the trailer off the hitch, roll it back to where it belonged, and crank down the trailer jack.

I took care of it while Buck watched. When I finished, he pointed to the tarp.

"It was covered this morning."

"Yes it was."

I grabbed one corner and Buck grabbed the other. Working together, we covered the boat using bungee cords to secure it to the trailer.

After we were done, we both looked around to make sure we hadn't forgotten anything.

Buck smiled. "Looks good to me."

I nodded. "I think Polly would approve."

When we drove back around to the front yard, Polly and Lucy were standing on the porch talking. As soon as they saw us drive up, Polly said something to Lucy that made her laugh. Then Lucy turned and waved at me. I waved back.

Polly tucked a loose strand of hair behind Lucy's ear and gave her a hug. Then she got back in the minivan with us. With everything taken care of at Lucy's, we headed back to Serenity Cove.

As we got close to Polly's trailer, she pointed and said, "Wonder what did that. It sure wasn't that way when we left."

There were two deep ruts where she normally parked her minivan. A trail of gravel led from the ruts to the road.

"Maybe a maintenance truck."

"No, I don't think so. I think someone's been inside my trailer."

"What makes you think that?"

"My inside curtains are closed. They were open when we left. Now they're closed."

Pulling to a stop just short of Polly's driveway, I asked, "Anyone else have a key to your trailer?"

"No. No one. Except for Lucy. And she didn't say anything about coming over here."

I nodded. "Okay, whoever it was, it looks like they're gone now. But just to be on the safe side, let me go in first."

Polly pointed to the car keys. "It's the silver one. Turn it to the right. And be careful."

Buck opened the door on his side of the minivan and started walking toward the Airstream. Looking back at us, he said, "Well, come on; let's see what we got here."

I caught up with Buck. He wanted to go in first, but I stopped him. I unlocked door and stepped in. Buck was right behind me, Polly a few steps back.

The place had been ransacked. All the cabinet doors stood

176

open, their contents dumped onto the floor. Photos had been removed from the walls. Tables and chairs upended, the couch cushions ripped open.

Everything from the kitchen cupboards and fridge had been opened and dumped out onto the floor.

The place was a real mess.

"Where's Oscar?" asked Polly.

"He should have met us at the door."

She called out his name. "Oscar. Oscar. Come on out. Come on out, Oscar."

There was no response. No Oscar.

"Maybe he's in the back."

Polly shook her head. "He usually comes when I call."

"Oscar. Mommie's home. Come on out."

No response. No Oscar.

Polly started to move around me, but I put my hand out to stop her. "Stay here. Let me go back and check. Make sure there's nobody back there."

I walked to the back of the Airstream, checking the closets and the bathroom to make sure no one was hiding. Much like the front, everything had been disturbed. Closets emptied, drawers dumped out.

It was obvious someone had been looking for something. But it looked like they were long gone.

And so was Oscar.

I went back to the front. "No one's back there, but it's a mess."

Polly pushed past me, her voice rising. "Oscar? Where are you?"

Buck stood beside me, shaking his head. "This is not right. Breaking in and making this kind of mess."

Looking around, I noticed a sheet of paper on the kitchen

counter with a small, black, domino-sized object on top of it.

On the paper was a handwritten message.

I called out to Polly, who had gone to the back of the trailer. "Polly, up here, I need to show you something."

She came up front, a hopeful look on her face.

"Did you find Oscar?"

"No. Something else. Check out the note."

I picked up the paper and handed it to her. She read it aloud.

```
"We got your dog.

We'll trade him for the package.

Wait for call.

No cops."
```

Polly's eyes welled up with tears. "They took Oscar."

I looked at her. "Polly, what's this about? Who are *they* and what's in the package?"

She walked away from the kitchen counter and started picking up some of the things that had been dumped on the living room floor.

I repeated my question. "Polly, what's this all about?"

She picked up the torn cushions and placed them on the couch. Then she sat down and patted the seat beside her.

Buck walked over and sat down. He took her hand and said, "It'll be alright. We'll get Oscar back."

Then he looked up at me.

I righted an overturned chair and pulled it up close to Polly. I leaned in toward her and asked, "Polly. Tell me. What's this about?"

She looked around and shook her head.

"It was two months ago. I was out on the houseboat. I'd

178

gone out there with Oscar and we'd spent the night. It was going to be a trial run to see how well we'd do on the boat.

"Things didn't go as planned. A storm came up, the waves got rough, and the boat rocked something fierce. I was afraid we'd get blown off our mooring.

"Oscar got seasick and he was throwing up all over the boat. He wanted to go home—but there was no way with the storm outside.

"It was a real mess. Neither one of us got any sleep.

"Sometime during the night we heard a loud boat anchor nearby. I figured they were just trying to get out of the storm.

"Then I heard another boat pull up beside the first one. They tied off to each other. We couldn't see much, but we heard voices and it sounded like they were moving things from one boat to the other.

"After about an hour, the smaller boat sped away, a few minutes later the big one left.

"The next morning, as we were getting ready to go back to shore, I noticed a package, about the size of an ice chest, floating in the water between the dinghy and the houseboat.

"It was wrapped in black plastic and had a number marked on the top.

"I fished it out of the water and figured it was drugs. Before I did anything, I used my phone to take a photo. I'm not sure why, but I wanted a photo of the package.

"Then, using a filet knife, I cut a slit in it. It was triple sealed in plastic. Hard to cut. But I was able to see what was inside. A brick of what I think was marijuana.

"I should have called the coast guard right away. Or the sheriff. But I didn't. Oscar was still feeling bad, and I just wanted to get off the boat and get back on dry land.

"So I decided to dump the package back in the water. Cut a few holes in the plastic and let it sink to the bottom.

"But before I sank it, I cut out a cigar box chunk of it—

about four inches all square. It was hard work—like sawing through wood.

"I put it in a plastic bread bag and stowed it with my gear. The rest I dumped overboard and watched as it sank to the bottom.

"I think that package is what this is all about. They want their drugs back."

Polly leaned forward and put her face in her hands. Sobbing, she said, "They've got Oscar."

Buck put his arm around her shoulder. "It'll be okay. We'll get Oscar back."

Looking at me, Buck asked, "How'd they know Polly was the one who found their drugs?"

I walked over to the kitchen counter and looked at the small object that had been sitting on top of the handwritten note.

"It's a GPS tracker. Smugglers sometimes use these to keep track of their shipments.

"This one must have been embedded in the piece that Polly kept."

Polly nodded. "I found that a week ago. I was worried that Walker was an undercover cop. I didn't want to have the drugs here in my trailer.

"I decided to break it up and toss it out with the trash. When I started pulling it apart, that thing fell out.

"I didn't know what it was, so I put it by the sink to look at later."

I nodded. "Must be activated by light. The sunshine coming in through the window turned it on, and they tracked it here.

"So what do we do now?" she asked.

CHAPTER FORTY

"They said they'd call. So my question is how do they know your phone number?"

Polly thought for a moment. "Oscar's collar. My phone number is on his collar."

"Okay. That's good. It might mean they don't know who you are. The GPS tracker led them to the trailer. But they don't know who lives here."

"What if they've been watching the trailer, waiting for me to leave? They'd know it was me living here."

I nodded. "That's possible. But I haven't seen anyone suspicious around here. Have you?"

She shook her head. "No one. Except Ponytail and Spider. Those two guys I told you about."

"When's the last time you saw them?"

"It's been at least three weeks. But maybe they watch at night, when we're asleep."

"Could be. But if the GPS tracker didn't activate until a few days ago, it might not be them. Could be someone else."

Polly and Buck nodded.

I took a deep breath. "No matter who it is, we've got a problem. They want their pot back, and we don't have it to give it to them.

"That means we've got to figure out a way to make them not want their missing pot and give us Oscar back."

Polly shook her head. "Walker, you and Buck don't have to get involved in this. It's my fault I'm in this mess and there's no reason to drag you two into it."

Buck stopped her. "That's not the way it works. You didn't do anything wrong. The guys who did this are at fault. And they're going to pay.

"Tell her, Walker."

"Buck's right. This is not your fault. You didn't do anything wrong. And we're going to take care of it."

Polly frowned. "But how? How are we going to take care of this? How are we going to get Oscar back?"

I looked at the mess in the trailer. "Polly, give me your phone."

"Why?"

"Because when they call, I'm going to answer. I'm going to tell them Oscar's my dog and I want him back.

"I don't figure them to be master criminals. My guess is all they want is the pot. They think you have it.

"That gives us some leverage. They'll keep Oscar safe until they get the pot. That gives us the upper hand—at least for a while."

Polly protested, "It should be me talking to them."

"No, it shouldn't. If a woman answers, they'll immediately think they have the upper hand. And they may not give us enough time to find Oscar.

"But if I take the call, they won't know who they're dealing with. They might be a bit more flexible. Maybe give us time to find Oscar on our own."

Buck spoke. "Polly, he's right. Let him take the call."

Shaking her head, Polly handed me her phone. "Don't make me regret this."

I wanted to tell her she wouldn't regret it. That we'd get this figured out. That Oscar would be safe and everything would be settled without any problems.

But I wasn't so sure. I didn't know who we were dealing

with or what they might do if things didn't go their way.

So I just said, "I'll do my best."

Part of doing my best meant working out a plan before the dognappers called. I figured it would be easier to do that next door without Buck and Polly around.

I told them, "I'm going over to my place. I need to check on a few things before they call. I'll come back as soon as I know something."

Outside, the sun had set and the evening had turned cool. A cold front had pushed across the state, bringing with it clear skies and a cool breeze from the north.

It was the kind of weather the snowbirds loved. Cool and no humidity.

I walked the short space separating Polly's Airstream and my motorhome, thinking about how I would handle the call.

Inside my home, things were just as I had left them. Unlike Polly's trailer, it hadn't been touched.

Bob came up front to meet me. He trotted over and rubbed his large body against my ankle.

"Yeah Bob, I missed you too. How's your food situation?"

Going back to the bathroom, I checked on his food and water. Everything was full. He'd be happy about that.

Back up front, I got out my laptop computer and set it on the kitchen table. I powered it up and brought up a Google Earth satellite view of Englewood. I wanted to have this in front of me during the call in case I needed help in seeing any location mentioned by the dognappers.

With the satellite view zoomed in on Serenity Cove and a bottle of water to clear my dry throat, I waited for the kidnappers' next move.

It wasn't a long wait.

Polly's phone chimed with an incoming call. No caller ID. I

answered on the third ring.

"Hello."

"We've got your dog."

"Yeah, I know. I want him back."

"Good. All we want is the package. We get that, you get the dog."

"Okay. How do you want to do it?"

"Where's the package?"

"It's not in my trailer."

"Yeah, we figured that. Where is it?"

"In a safe place."

"Good. Safe is good."

"What about Oscar?"

"Who's Oscar?"

"My dog. His name is Oscar. Where is he?"

"He's right here beside me."

"Has he been harmed?"

"No, he's in good shape."

"Good. Send a photo of him to my phone."

"You don't trust me?"

"I don't know you. You tore up my trailer pretty bad. There was no need for that. So send me a photo of Oscar or the deal is off."

"Okay, I'll send you a photo. But not until you send me a photo of the package."

"Hold on."

I scrolled through the images stored on Polly's phone and found the photo she had taken the day she found the pot. I forwarded it to the caller's phone.

"I just sent it to you. Now send me a photo of Oscar."

There was silence. Then the male voice on the other end said, "We'll call you back."

The call ended.

You'd think that now that I had the dognapper's phone number on my incoming call list, I could use it to track their location.

You can track a phone that way. But not nearly as easily as you see on TV. In reality, you either need to have real time access to phone company cell towers or be a federal spy agency that can hack into the phone company computers and pull the information they want.

But for civilians like me, who don't have this kind of access, tracking a phone's location isn't easy—unless the phone owner has installed a tracking app and provided you with the tracking password.

While it would have been nice for me to have some magic software on my computer where I could type in the dognapper's phone number and get his exact location, I didn't have that option.

But there are other ways to find the location of a cell phone without a warrant or specialized software. All you need is a recent photo from the phone.

If the phone's camera has geotagging enabled, the photo will have the exact GPS coordinates of where the phone was when the photo was taken.

That's why I demanded a photo of Oscar. I was hoping it would include GPS info embedded in it.

Five minutes after the call with the dognappers ended, Polly's phone beeped, telling me a text message had been received.

I clicked on the message, and it opened a photo of Oscar taken a few moments earlier. He appeared to be sleeping on a packing blanket in the back of what looked like a windowless panel van.

As I looked at the photo, the phone chimed with an incoming call.

I answered.

"You get it?" a rough voice asked.

"Yeah."

"So you ready to trade?"

"Yeah, when and where?"

"Nine tonight. At the hospital parking lot."

I paused. "Not tonight. Can't get the package until tomorrow morning."

"You can't get the package?"

"No, I can't. It's in a storage building. They locked the gates an hour ago. Won't open again until eight tomorrow morning."

A pause on the other end, then, "Don't be playing games with us. You either deliver tomorrow or you lose the dog. And no cops."

"I understand. But if something happens to Oscar, you'll have hell to pay."

Silence on the other end. Then, "Be ready in the morning. I'll call at eight thirty."

The caller disconnected.

CHAPTER FORTY-ONE

I'd gotten what I wanted—a photo of Oscar taken with the dognapper's phone.

After copying the photo to my laptop, I used Irfanview software to open it. Then I clicked on the "Image information" tab.

This opened a drop down window that showed when the photo was taken, it's resolution and file size. Just below that was a link labeled "EXIF Info."

Clicking that link produced the results I had hoped for—GPS coordinates showing where the photo had been taken. Just below the GPS coordinates, a button labeled "Show on Google maps."

I clicked the maps button, and my screen filled with a close-up map of Englewood, showing the exact location, with street address, where the photo was taken.

Definitely my lucky day. The phone used by the kidnappers had geo-tagging turned on.

I printed out the Google map, turned off the laptop, and headed next door.

I'd been gone for fifteen minutes, long enough for Buck and Polly to clean up the worst of the mess and to order a pizza. We hadn't eaten since leaving for her houseboat earlier in the day, and I was starving.

I grabbed a slice of pizza and handed the Google map printout to Polly.

"What's this?"

"That star on the map is where Oscar was about ten minutes

ago. I'm going to go see if he is still there."

Polly stood. "I'm going with you."

"No. You're not. And you're not staying here either. It's not safe. They might come back."

"So where do I go?"

Buck spoke. "She can stay with me. In my bus."

I shook my head. "No, that won't work. We need to get her away from Serenity Cove. In case they know who she is."

Using Polly's phone, I called Lucy.

She answered on the third ring. "Hey, Mom. What's up?"

"Lucy, it's me, Walker. Buck and I have to go take care of something and we don't want to leave your mom here alone. Would it be okay if she hangs out with you for a bit?"

"Sure, no problem. But why are you using her phone? Let me speak to her."

"She's busy right now. We'll be there in ten minutes."

I ended the call.

Hanging up on a woman is never a good idea. I'd probably lose a few points with Lucy for doing that. But maybe, when she heard the full story, she'd give me some slack.

Buck and I got in the Jeep and Polly followed us in her minivan. As we headed out, Buck said, "Stop at my place. I need to get something. It'll just take a minute."

Polly was behind me, she stopped when I pulled over in front of Buck's bus. We waited while he went in to do whatever he needed to do.

Three minutes later, he came back out. He had changed clothes. Instead of the white shirt and pants he had worn out on the boat, he was now wearing black pants, black T-shirt, a black sports jacket and was carrying a pair of black leather gloves.

"Wardrobe change?" I asked.

"Yeah. I figured, if we're going to be sneaking around

188

tonight, it might not be a good idea to be dressed all in white."

He was right.

Seven minutes later, we were sitting in Lucy's driveway. She was waiting for us on her porch and walked toward my side of the Jeep as Polly climbed out of her minivan.

"Walker, tell me what's going on."

Shaking my head, I said, "No time. Buck and I have got to go take care of something. Polly will fill you in on the details."

I put the Jeep in gear and headed down Old Englewood Road toward Dearborn Street.

"So," asked Buck, "what's the plan?"

I pointed to the map. "The house is on Pandora Street. It's a cul-de-sac with a turnaround at the end.

"I figure we'll turn off our lights and cruise slowly by. If it looks safe, we'll stop a few houses down, walk back and see what we can do."

Buck nodded. "Sounds good. But don't get us boxed in. Park so we can make a quick getaway if we have to."

We stayed on River Road until we reached Pine Street, where we turned right. Two miles down, we turned right again onto Pandora. I switched off the headlights and coasted to a stop.

Houses on Pandora were small. Stacked cinder blocks with asphalt roofs. Nothing fancy. Most had carports with room for only one car. Extra cars parked in the driveway or on the street.

The houses were close together, but only a few had lights on. Many looked vacant.

According to Google Earth, the house we were looking for was about halfway down the street on the left. I put the Jeep in gear, and with the headlights still off, we cruised down the street looking for house numbers.

"There it is. Sixteen Twenty-Two."

As we went by, we saw there were no cars in either the

carport or the driveway. No interior lights on. A 'for sale' sign in the yard suggested the home might be vacant.

The only sign of life were two old bicycles in the carport.

I looked at Buck. "What do you think?"

"Looks empty to me. No lights, no cars, and a 'for sale' sign out front. You sure this is the right address?"

"According to the GPS, it is."

Buck nodded. "When we get to the end of the street, turn around and come back. Drive past the house and park two doors down."

With our lights still off, I did as he suggested.

As we passed the house on our return, I cut the motor and coasted to the curb. We sat in silence taking in the sounds of the neighborhood. In the distance, we heard a solitary dog. One bark. Then nothing.

There were no streetlights on Pandora. The black Jeep was nearly invisible in the darkness of the night.

Not wanting to draw any attention, I moved the switch for the interior overhead light so it wouldn't come on when I opened my door.

After watching the house for five minutes, we hadn't seen anything that suggested anyone was inside. If there were people there, they were in the back rooms, not visible through the living room window.

I whispered, "I'm going to knock on the front door. See if anyone answers."

Buck reached inside his jacket and pulled out a large pistol.

"What's that?"

"357. Thought it might come in handy."

I shook my head. "No guns. We don't need that kind of trouble."

Buck laid the pistol in his lap. "We'll see."

Taking a deep breath, I slowly opened my door and quietly stepped out onto the street. I stood there for a moment, just waiting. For what I didn't know. But it felt good to wait.

I wasn't sure if there was anyone in the house or whether they would be armed or how they would react when I knocked on the door.

I wasn't in a big hurry to find out.

But it had to be done.

From the street, I walked to the yard of the neighboring home, which also appeared to be vacant. From there I headed up the driveway of the house where Oscar's photo had been taken.

From the driveway, I could see a blanket had been hung over the living room window, blocking the view into the home.

In some neighborhoods, a blanket over a living room window might draw attention. But not here. Not on Pandora Street. In this neighborhood, not all the residents would be spending money on curtains when a spare blanket or sheet over the window would do the job.

As I got closer to the front porch, I could see a flickering light behind the blanket. Candlelight. From inside the house.

If lights were on inside, even if it were only a candle, it meant someone was probably in the house. And possibly they had Oscar with them.

So I was going in.

I took a deep breath and moved up the driveway with intentions to knock on the front door. My path took me closer to the blanket covered window.

Just as I reached it, I saw shadows moving inside.

It was possible the occupants had seen me and were now moving in my direction. Not wanting to be exposed, I ducked down below the window. Almost immediately, the front door burst open and two men ran past me.

Neither seemed to have seen me and both were intent on

getting out of the house quickly. The first man jumped on one of the bicycles in the carport and pedaled away.

The second man hopped on the remaining bike but was stopped at the street when Buck stepped in front of him holding his pistol.

"What's your hurry?" he asked.

Seeing Buck with the gun, I stood, just in time to feel searing heat as the house exploded behind me.

CHAPTER FORTY-TWO

I was lying on the wet grass in front of the house, my face stinging from the blast. Behind me I could feel the warmth of a fire. My ears were ringing. Buck was kneeling over me, a stranger with a scraggly beard standing beside him.

I could see Buck's mouth moving but couldn't hear what he was saying. He was shouting. In my direction, up close, but all I could hear was a loud ringing in my ears.

Finally, I understood. He was saying, "Get up. Cops are on the way. We've got to go."

My head hurt, my eyes stung and my ears were ringing. I didn't want to go anywhere. Lying in the grass was fine with me.

Buck grabbed my right arm and pulled me to my feet. The stranger grabbed my left, and together they dragged me to the Jeep.

I was put in the back seat. The stranger got in on the passenger side, and Buck drove, lights out.

At some point, Buck took a left onto Pine Street and turned the Jeep's headlights back on; soon after, a sheriff's car with its siren blasting raced by.

Moments later, a fire truck and an ambulance followed. They were heading to the house we had just left.

Up front, I could tell that Buck and his passenger were having a heated conversation. I couldn't understand what they were saying but I could hear their voices. That was a good sign. It meant my hearing was coming back.

I leaned forward between the front seats and put my hand on Buck's shoulder to support myself. At my touch, he flinched.

"Damn, Walker. You scared me. Thought you were dead back there."

"Not dead yet, but I hurt."

I rubbed my face and my hand came away black with soot. "What happened back there?"

Buck pointed to the passenger. "Eddie here and his partner were cooking up meth. They got the mixture a little too hot. And it went boom."

Eddie grinned at me. "Same thing happened last time. Too much heat, and then 'boom'."

He used his hands to emphasize the "boom" part of his story.

When he smiled, Eddie's face looked familiar. I'd seen him before. But I couldn't remember where. My head hurt too much to even try.

Buck turned right on River Road, heading toward Dearborn Street. At the first stoplight, he turned into the Publix parking lot, drove around back and pulled in between two large produce trucks.

"Walker, do we need to take you to the hospital?"

I shook my head. "No, I'm okay. But what about Oscar? Was he in the house?"

Buck looked at Eddie. "Was there a dog in the house?"

Eddie shook his head. "No, but there was a wiener dog in the van with Darrell. When he came by to check on us, he showed us the dog and then left. Took the dog with him."

Buck cut his eyes toward me then back to Eddie. "Who's Darrell?"

"Don't know his last name. We just call him Darrell. He's the one that hired Peanut to cook the meth. Darrell gave us the key to the house, brought the ingredients by and told us when he wanted the crystal done."

"So Darrell has the dog?"

"Last time I saw him he did."

"Where's Darrell now?"

Eddie ran his right hand through his thinning, slicked back hair. "Darrell don't tell me none of his business. Even if he did, he'd be right pissed off if I turned around and told you."

Buck laughed. "Eddie, you and Peanut just blew up Darrell's house. He might already be right pissed off."

Eddie shook his head. "It weren't Darrell's house. It belongs to the bank. Darrell found out it was empty and figured nobody would care if we used it for a few days.

"Of course he might be upset we burned up all his meth fixins."

Buck nodded. "So, Eddie, here's the deal. That wiener dog belongs to a nice widow woman, and we want to get the dog back for her.

"Right now, you're the only person standing between us knowing and not knowing where that dog is.

"Since Walker almost got himself blown up because of you, maybe you could tell us where to find the dog."

Eddie looked at me, and recognition flickered in his eyes.

"I know you. You're the guy who saved my life! When I was riding my bike and that car hit me. It was you who stopped and took care of me."

I smiled as I realized where I'd seen Eddie before. On the ground, the day Lucy and I were taking the Jeep for a test drive.

I nodded. "You're right, Eddie, that was me. I saved your life. Now, do me a favor and tell me where we can find the wiener dog."

CHAPTER FORTY-THREE

"Walker, I owe you big time. I'd be dead if it wasn't for you stopping that day.

"So I'll help you find the little dog. But maybe we could stop over at the Shell station and get us some beer first. My throat's a little parched from cooking crystal. A cold beer would go down real good."

Buck looked at me. I sighed and then nodded. Might as well get some beer for our new partner in crime.

It took us four minutes to get to the Shell station. The parking lot was nearly empty so Buck pulled up near the front door. Removing the keys from the ignition, he turned to me and said, "You stay here with Eddie. I'll get the beer."

"Get Budweiser," Eddie said. "And some beef jerky sticks, the spicy ones. And a lotto ticket."

I just shook my head.

Buck went in and got a twelve pack of Budweiser and a handful of jerky sticks. He also picked up an eight pack of Zephyrhills water.

When he got back in the Jeep, he put the water in the backseat with me and gave the beer and jerky to Eddie.

Eddie started peeling the top off the twelve pack, but Buck stopped him. "Don't open it yet. Let's get someplace we won't be bothered."

"Go to Quirk," Eddie said. "Won't nobody bother us there."

"Quirk? What's that?"

"It's the public library on Dearborn. You know where that

is?"

"I know where the library is," Buck answered.

"Go there and park around back. Nice and private."

Eddie was right; the back parking lot behind the Elsie Quirk Library building was empty. The library was closed, and no one else was around.

As soon as we pulled in, Eddie grabbed a beer from the twelve pack, popped the top and took a long drink.

"Oh man, that hits the spot. You boys want one?"

I shook my head. "Not me. Think I'll just stick with water."

"Yeah," said Buck. "Water sounds good."

I pulled two bottles from the pack, handed one to Buck and kept one for myself.

The water was cold and felt good going down.

Buck took a long swallow then turned to Eddie.

"Now, Eddie, how about you tell us where the dog is? We need to get it back to its rightful owner."

Eddie took another long draw from his beer, finishing off the can. He reached for another, but Buck stopped him.

"Not yet. First tell us where the dog is."

Eddie looked longingly at the cold beers just out of his reach. "Palm Marina. That's where Darrell usually parks his van at night.

"If the dog's still in the van, that's where you'll find it."

"He works there? At the marina?" asked Buck.

"No, he keeps his boat there. He takes it out at night. Cruises around looking for things to steal.

"Ever since he heard about bales of pot floating in the bay, he's been going out there at night with a spotlight looking for them.

"Says he's got some kind of tracker device that tells him where the packages are."

Buck looked at me and nodded. We already knew why Darrell had visited Polly's trailer, the little, black tracking device we found on her kitchen counter.

Buck took his hand off the beer and smiled at Eddie. "Have another one. Just keep the can out of sight."

We pulled out of Quirk and headed toward Palm Marina. Like most places in Englewood, it was close. Not more than three miles away.

Eddie had finished his second beer by the time we pulled in the marina parking lot. Buck didn't stop him when he reached for his third. Eddie pulled the tab and began drinking it down fast.

Even though the marina facility was closed, the parking lot was a quarter full. Mostly pickup trucks belonging to fishermen who were still out on the water.

In the far corner of the lot sat a faded blue Chevy van.

Eddie pointed. "That's it. That's Darrell's van."

Buck coasted the Jeep over to the van and killed the motor.

"So you think Darrell is out on the water? He's not in the van?"

"Well, he does sleep in it sometimes. But usually not here."

Buck looked at me then opened his door and got out.

Being in the back seat of the two-door Jeep meant I couldn't easily follow unless either he or Eddie slid their seat forward.

Buck closed the door behind him and Eddie didn't make a move to get out. I reached into the front seat, grabbed what remained of the twelve pack of beer, and put it in the back seat beside me.

"Eddie, why don't we trade places? You get back here, and I'll get up there."

Eddie nodded. "Can do. But I gotta take a leak first."

He got out of the Jeep and walked over to the nearby chain link fence, unzipped his pants and let nature take its course.

With him out of the Jeep, I was able to tilt the front seat forward, giving me enough room to climb out. As soon as I was out, I walked over to the blue van and joined Buck.

"See anything inside?"

"No, there are curtains all the way around. Can't see inside."

I tried the back door. It was locked. Buck tried the two front doors. They were locked as well.

"Try this." I looked behind me and Eddie was standing there with a long screwdriver.

"This'll get you in. Just slip it between the two back doors and give it a twist."

Apparently Eddie had experience in these kinds of things.

CHAPTER FORTY-FOUR

I had just slipped the screwdriver between the back doors of the blue van when I heard a voice behind me say, "Better not do that."

I turned to see two men walking in my direction, one carrying a flashlight, and the other carrying what looked like a baseball bat.

Putting the screwdriver behind my back, I asked, "This your van?"

"Nope. Is it yours?"

Pointing back behind me, I said, "I think my dog's locked up inside. Trying to get him out."

The two men walked up closer and stopped about six feet in front of me. One had a ponytail, the other had spider web tattoos on both arms and around his neck.

I knew who they were. PT and Spider. The guys Polly had told me about. The ones who had been hanging out at Serenity Cove. The two guys I'd seen loading black suitcases into a boat when Lucy and I were having dinner at Zekes.

Ponytail waved his baseball bat in the general direction of Buck and Eddie. "Why don't you two move over a little closer to your friend here? That way we don't have to worry about you running off."

He turned to me and said, "You didn't answer the question. Is this your vehicle?"

I smiled, trying my best to win the two guys over. "No, it's not mine. I'm in the Jeep over there. But the guy who owns this van, his name is Darrell. I think my dog's inside. Just want to get him out."

Ponytail shook his head. "Your dog's not in the van. And you don't want to be breaking into it."

He pointed his baseball bat toward my Jeep. "It'd be best if all three of you got in your Jeep and got out of here before there's trouble."

Eddie started moving toward the Jeep, but Buck and I stood our ground.

I smiled at Ponytail. "We don't want any trouble. We just want to get our dog out of the van."

He shook his head. "Your dog is not in the van. It's time for you to go."

Buck looked at me and slowly moved his hand toward the inside of his jacket. I knew he was reaching for the gun that he wasn't supposed to be carrying.

I looked at him and shook my head.

He got the message, moved his hand away and pretended to be scratching an itch on his shoulder.

Looking up, I saw Ponytail shaking his head in disgust. He turned to Spider. "Call it in."

Spider pulled a phone from his back pocket, punched in a number and said, "We need a car."

I looked at Buck and he signaled with his thumb that it was time to head back to the Jeep.

I took a step toward the Jeep then quickly turned and slipped the screwdriver into the gap between the van's back doors. I twisted the screwdriver hard to the right.

That's all it took. One of the doors popped open. Not enough to see all the way in, but enough so I knew the door was now unlocked. If I grabbed the door handle, I could get it open.

A voice behind me, a lot closer than before, said, "Don't do it."

Ignoring the voice, I reached for the door, which, as it

turned out, was a major mistake.

With my back to Ponytail, I didn't see him swing the baseball bat that connected hard with my arm, knocking me away from the van.

As I fell to the ground, I saw Buck move toward me, and then saw Spider take him to the ground. I tried to stand, but Ponytail placed the blunt end of the bat on my chest, pinning me down.

"Look," he said, "we tried to warn you. Told you to leave. But no, you just had to look in the van.

"So I'm going to tell you again, the dog is not in the van. But now that you've jimmied the back door, you get to go for a ride and meet some of our friends."

Behind him, I saw a black, four-door sedan pull into the parking lot. Two middle-aged men got out and walked over to Spider, who was standing over Buck.

Spider did the talking. "These three. Take them and their Jeep."

The men said nothing, just nodded. Using plastic zip ties they handcuffed Buck, Eddie and me, and shoved us in the back seat of their car.

Eddie protested. "Listen here. I'm not with these guys. I was just walking along, minding my own business. I don't even know them."

Then he said, "That's my beer in the Jeep. Don't be drinking it."

The two men ignored him, locked us in the backseat, and went to talk with Ponytail.

After a brief discussion, one of the men checked the Jeep. The keys were still in the ignition. He climbed in the driver's seat, started it up and drove off. The other man came back to the car we were in, started the motor, and followed the man who was driving my Jeep.

Eight minutes later, we stopped at a deserted looking

warehouse on McCall Road, next door to Leonard's Roofing Supply. The driver of the Jeep got out, unlocked a padlock on a chain link fence, and rolled the gate open.

He got back into the Jeep and we followed until he reached a windowless cinder block building at the back of the gated yard.

Our driver walked to the lone metal door at the front of the building and pounded on it twice with his fist. A moment later, the door opened and a man stepped out. He looked at the car we were in and shook his head.

Then he signaled our driver to bring us in.

We were still handcuffed in the back seat. I was sitting closest to the door on the driver's side so they took me in first. They left Eddie and Buck in the car with a man watching over them.

I was led into the building through a small hallway and then into a large, well lit room. Several folding tables had been set up against the walls. Each table had a computer monitor and keyboard on it.

Men in various attire, ranging from Florida casual to business suits, monitored video feeds on the computer screens. Some wore audio headsets and were engaged in on-screen conversations.

"Where are we?" I asked.

The man guiding me said nothing. He pushed me past the computer stations and led me into a small, unoccupied room in the back. A metal table sat in the center of the room with a straight back chair on each side.

The man pointed at the chair on the far side of the table. "Sit. Don't go anywhere. Don't say anything."

He left, leaving me alone in the room. A moment later, another man stepped in. Medium height, receding hairline, bags under his eyes, a scowl on his face.

He looked at me, a faint smile replacing the scowl. "I'm agent Harris with Homeland Security. We've got a few questions for you."

"Homeland Security? Why is Homeland Security involved? We were just trying to get a dog back."

Harris shook his head. "You think this is about a dog? That's funny."

Then he pointed at the grass stains on my shirt and the soot on my face.

"Rough night?"

"Yeah, you could say that. Am I under arrest?"

"No. We don't arrest people. We might hold you for a while, but we don't do arrests."

Harris looked at me. "You going to be trouble?"

I shook my head. "No. I just want to get my dog back and go home."

"Good. That's what I want to hear."

From behind him, he produced a metal container about the size of a cigar box and slid it across the table to me. "Empty your pockets."

My hands were still bound behind my back. "Untie me."

Harris stood, pulled a small knife out of his pants pocket, and walked over behind me. "If you try anything, it won't end well."

I nodded.

With a flick of the blade, he cut the plastic zip tie from around my wrist. I slowly brought my hands around and shook them to get the blood circulating. I then placed them on the table in front of me.

Harris smiled. "You're doing good so far. Now stand up. Empty your pockets. Put the contents in the box, and sit back down."

I stood and did exactly what he said, emptying my pockets

into the box. My wallet from my left front pants pocket, Polly's cell phone from my right. I'd left my own cellphone back in the motorhome.

"What about your shirt pocket? Empty it."

Since moving to Florida, I'd adopted the local custom of wearing Columbia fishing shirts. The kind with two breast pockets held closed with hook and loop tabs. Rarely did I carry anything in those pockets. But that night was different.

Back at Polly's trailer, I'd picked up the GPS tracker she had found in the brick of pot. That tracker was now in my right shirt pocket.

Reaching in, I retrieved the tracker and placed it in the metal box.

"Is that everything?"

"Yep. That's it."

"Good."

Harris picked up the tracker. "Where'd you get this?"

"It's a long story."

"Good. I like long stories. So do my friends."

The door of the room opened and another man stepped in. He picked up the metal box and left the room with it.

Harris and I sat in silence for a moment. He was smiling, like he knew something I didn't.

Four minutes later, our silence was interrupted when the door opened and the man who had taken the metal box returned and placed my driver's license on the table in front of Harris.

Harris picked it up and looked at it carefully. Then he said, "Mr. Walker, want to tell me why you fire bombed the house on Pandora Street?"

CHAPTER FORTY FIVE

"Fire bombed a house? What are you talking about?"

Harris smiled. "We have witnesses. They saw you sneak around the house just before it exploded. So we know you were there. We just don't know why you blew it up."

I shook my head. "Yes, I was there. But I didn't have anything to do with the explosion. I was looking for my dog."

"Your dog? Why'd you think your dog was in the house?"

"It's a long story."

Harris smiled. "Like I said earlier, I like long stories. Tell me everything."

So I did.

I told him how Polly, Buck and I had gone out to her houseboat. And how, when we got back, we discovered someone had broken into her trailer and stolen her dog.

Harris interrupted me at that point. "Is the dog valuable?"

I shook my head. "Only to Polly. It's like her child."

Harris nodded. "What kind of dog is it?"

"A dachshund. His name is Oscar."

"So does this Polly person have a lot of money?"

"No, not that I know of."

"So if she doesn't have any money and the dog has no value, why'd they take it? What did they expect to gain?"

I took a deep breath. I needed to be careful with what I told him. I didn't want to get Polly in trouble.

"The dognapper thinks Polly has something that belongs to

him. And he wants it back."

"What would that something be?"

"A package she found floating in the Intracoastal."

Harris smiled. "Let me guess. Drugs."

I nodded. "Yes. Well, pot. She found it floating next to her houseboat. She didn't want to have anything to do with it, so she cut the package open and dumped most of it back in the water. But she saved a small piece as evidence.

"She took that piece back to her trailer and didn't know there was a GPS tracker embedded in it.

"Apparently, someone followed the signal to her trailer, searched for the pot, and when they didn't find it, they took the dog."

Harris interrupted me again. "She had illegal drugs in her trailer?"

"No, she'd already gotten rid of the pot. Dumped it. But still had the GPS tracker."

Harris smiled thinly. "So someone broke into her trailer and took her dog. Then what?"

"The dognapper called. He wanted to trade the dog for the pot. I agreed but said he needed to send me a photo showing the dog was still alive.

"He shot a photo with his phone and sent it to me. I used the GPS info embedded in the photo to track his location to the house on Pandora Street."

Harris rubbed his head. "So you went over there and blew up the house? Is that what happened?"

"No. I didn't blow up the house. I didn't have anything to do with it.

"When we got to the house, my plan was to go up and knock on the door to see if the dog was there.

"But just as I got to the door, the house exploded."

Harris held up his hand. "You say the kidnapper sent you a

photo of the dog?"

"Yes, it's on the cell phone."

Harris put his hand in the air and motioned with a finger. Apparently sending a signal to someone outside the room.

A moment later, an agent came in and handed Polly's cell phone to Harris.

"Show me the photo."

I took the phone and found the photo. "Here it is."

Harris took the phone back and looked at the photo I'd found. "Nice looking dog.

"So you somehow discovered the Pandora Street address from this photo?"

I nodded. "Yes. The dognapper's phone had geo-tagging enabled. That means GPS coordinates are embedded in the photo file."

Harris looked at me. "You some kind of computer expert?"

I shrugged. "I worked computer network security for ten years before I came to Florida. So, yes, I know a little about computers."

Harris started browsing the other photos on the phone. "What about this one? Is that the bale of pot the Polly woman found?"

I nodded. "Yes, that's the photo she took before she dumped it back in the water. We sent that photo to the kidnapper so he'd think we still had it."

Harris rubbed his eyes this time. "So, let me get this straight. Everything that happened tonight is about the dog. You just want him back. You're not involved in the meth lab on Pandora Street. And you really don't know anything about the owner of the blue van—except you think he has the dog."

I nodded. "That's right. It's all about the dog. Nothing else."

Harris heaved a sigh and said, "I'll be right back."

He left the room, leaving Polly's cell phone on the table.

CHAPTER FORTY-SIX

The phone was right there in front of me. No one had told me I couldn't use it. So I made a call.

Lucy answered on the third ring.

"Hello?"

"Lucy, this is Walker. Can't talk long. Oscar wasn't at the house on Pandora Street. We followed a lead to another location but it didn't pan out. We've got another lead to check out. I'll call you as soon as we learn more."

"Walker, don't hang up. Are you and Buck okay?"

"We're okay. Gotta go."

I ended the call before she could reply. That would be the second time I'd hung up on her that day. She'd be furious, but I couldn't tell her the whole story. Didn't have time and didn't want her to know we were being held by Homeland Security.

Moments after I put the phone back on the table, Harris re-entered the room.

He pointed over his shoulder. "Your friend out there is pretty famous. I've seen all his movies."

I nodded.

He continued. "I'm surprised he got mixed up in this. You'd think he'd know better. But the good news is his story matches yours.

I smiled. "So we can go?"

"No, not yet. You guys stumbled into one of our operations. We can't risk you going back out on the streets and messing this thing up.

"So, here's what we can do.

"We've had the man you know as Darrell under surveillance for two months. We know he took your dog, and we know where the dog is.

"It's safe. For now.

"But the thing is, we can't give you the dog back until we pick up Darrell and get him to tell us about some of his associates.

"We can't pick him up because we've lost track of him. We don't know where he is."

I interrupted. "Wait a minute. You just said you knew where the dog was. You said he was safe. But now you say you don't know where Darrell is?"

"That's right. We know the dog is with Darrell. We know he'll probably keep the dog safe until he gets the drugs from you. But at the moment, we don't know where Darrell is."

I shook my head. "You've got all that surveillance equipment out there, and you don't know where Darrell is?"

"That's right, we lost him. We followed his van to the marina and lost him when he took his boat out on the water. We were waiting for him to return to his van when you three stooges showed up.

"After you broke into it, we went ahead and searched it. It was empty. Like he wasn't planning on coming back.

"But now that we know you have something Darrell wants, there might be a way for you and me to work something out.

"According to Buck, Darrell expects to meet you in the morning to trade the drugs for the dog. That would be an ideal time for us to pick him up. Right after you give him the package he's expecting."

I shook my head. "Won't work. We don't have the drugs. Polly sunk the bale out in the bay."

Harris smiled. "That won't be a problem. We can create a package that looks exactly like the one in the photo. It'll be what he's expecting. You give him the package, and he gives you the dog.

"After the exchange, we'll pick him up, and you and Buck are free to go. But here's the thing. Since it could be dangerous, we can't force you to get involved.

"So it's up to you. Either you stay here until we find Darrell and hope your dog is safe or you take the call in the morning and go ahead with the exchange as planned. Your choice."

Harris sat back in his chair, awaiting my decision.

"What about Eddie? What happens to him?"

"Eddie? Which one is Eddie?"

"He's one of the guys from the Pandora house. He helped us after the explosion. Led us to Darrell's van."

"Oh. That Eddie. He's relatively harmless. Nothing's going to happen to him."

I was relieved. "That's good to know."

Harris was still waiting for my decision.

I wanted to get Oscar back and I definitely didn't want to hang around Homeland Security in what amounted to house arrest until they picked up Darrell.

So it was an easy decision.

"I'll do the exchange. But only if you promise we'll get the dog back unharmed. And if you keep Polly, Buck and Eddie out of this."

Harris smiled. "I was hoping you'd say that."

He stood, shook my hand and said, "Follow me."

CHAPTER FORTY-SEVEN

When we walked back into the main operations room, Buck was sitting on a couch surrounded by three agents who were listening to his stories.

When the agents saw Harris, they moved away from Buck and went back to their work stations. Buck saw me and nodded. "You hungry? We ordered pizza."

There were three slices of pizza in a box on the table in front of the couch, reminding me that it'd been a long time since I'd eaten.

So, yes, I was hungry. Enough so that I grabbed a slice of pizza and took a bite. It was cold and limp but still good. I finished the first slice and grabbed another.

While I was eating, Harris walked over to one of his men and spoke with him in a hushed voice. After their short conversation, both came over to me.

"Walker, don't take this the wrong way, but you look like a refugee from a bomb factory. You've got soot on your face, your clothes are singed, and you've got grass stains and mud on your back.

"If you show up looking like that tomorrow, Darrell will be suspicious.

"So Agent Jones here is going to escort you back to your place where you can shower and change clothes. Then he'll bring you back here and we'll wait for Darrell to call."

I smiled. "A shower sounds good. Let's go."

Buck stood to join us, but Harris stopped him. "Buck's staying here. He can call Polly and let her know everything is fine. But he stays here until after you meet with Darrell tomorrow."

I nodded at Buck. "You okay with that?"

"Yeah. These guys seem to be all right. I don't mind hanging around."

When we got outside, Agent Jones tossed me the keys to my Jeep. "You drive. Don't do anything stupid."

I slid into the driver's seat, got the Jeep started, and headed back to Serenity Cove. Jones was in the passenger seat, arms crossed, eyes on the road, not saying anything.

"So why is Homeland Security involved in this?" I asked.

He shook his head. "No idea. We just do what we're told. You should stop asking questions. The less you know about these things the better."

He was probably right. It wouldn't do me any good to know why Homeland Security was involved in this. The best I could hope for was to get Oscar back and forget all about Darrell, Agent Harris and Homeland Security.

When we arrived back at my motorhome, it was just as I had left it. The lights were out, no cars in the driveway, nothing strange had happened.

It was the same with Polly's trailer. No cars in her driveway and it didn't look like she'd had any visitors since we'd left.

When I went inside, Bob met me at the door. I bent over and gave him a pet, and he replied with a loud, "Meeeeoww."

I knew from the extra emphasis he placed on the "me" in "meeeoww" that he wasn't happy. Either his litter box was full or his food bowl was empty.

Either way, he wanted me to take immediate action. That's the way cats are. They are never in a hurry to do anything for you, but they expect you to be in a hurry for them.

Bob was still expressing his displeasure when Agent Jones followed me inside. This unexpected visitor startled him. He wasn't sure whether he should defend me or hide.

He made the easy choice. He ran and hid under the bed.

When I reached for the switch to turn on the overhead lights, Jones stopped me.

"No lights. Might make the neighbors suspicious."

He sat down in the chair Bob had just vacated. "Is this the only door? Any other way to get in or out?"

"No, this is it."

"Good, I'll sit here while you shower and change clothes. You've got ten minutes."

I went back to my bedroom and picked out a clean shirt and a pair of cargo shorts—my normal Florida attire. Then I went into the bathroom and took a quick shower and changed into the clean clothes.

My old clothes smelled like fire and weren't really worth saving. I wadded them up and dropped them in one of the plastic grocery bags I kept under the sink to use when cleaning Bob's litter box.

Before leaving the bathroom, I topped off Bob's food and poured him some fresh water. This would keep him happy for another ten to twelve hours.

Refreshed from the shower, I grabbed the bag of ruined clothing and walked back to the front of the motorhome where agent Jones was still sitting.

"What's in the bag?"

"My burned clothes. Can't leave them here, they'll stink up the place."

I picked up my car keys and said, "Ready to go."

Jones went out the door first. Stopping on the step, he scanned the area to make sure it was safe. Then he headed for the Jeep.

Behind him, I stepped out, locked the door, and looked up at the sky.

It was still dark, but in the distance I could see the faint glow of the coming dawn. Soon, if all went as planned, I'd be delivering a package and rescuing a wiener dog.

CHAPTER FORTY-EIGHT

Harris was waiting for us when we got back. "There's been a change of plans. We want one of our guys to do the exchange instead of you. It'll be safer that way."

I shook my head. "That won't work. Your guys look like cops. Even from a distance, your people look, walk, and talk like cops.

"Darrell will know and he'll bail. We won't get Oscar and you won't get Darrell.

"Let me do it as planned. He's heard my voice, he knows what to expect."

Harris studied me for a moment. "It could be dangerous. You sure you want to do this?"

"Yes, I'm sure."

"Okay then. Follow me."

He led me into the large room where his people were still monitoring video screens. Buck was sitting on a couch at the back of the room, donut in hand.

He smiled when he saw me. "Did they talk you out of it?"

"No, I'm doing this. I'm getting Oscar back."

He gave me a thumbs up, and I nodded.

Harris led me through a door to the right of the interrogation room I'd been in earlier. The room was filled with electronic gear, body armor, Kevlar helmets, and night vision glasses.

A metal table was positioned in the center of the room. Four chairs surrounded it.

Pointing at a chair, Harris said, "Sit."

He handed me Polly's cell phone. "We've paired this phone with one of ours, so we'll be able to listen in on any calls you get. We've also added a tracking app so we'll know where you are. Whatever you do, keep this phone with you.

"We're putting together a package that looks exactly like the one in the photo on Polly's phone. We wrapped it with the same kind of plastic and loaded it with high grade pot.

"We've put a GPS tracker in the package and we'll be following it until we get it back."

Harris sat in the chair across from me. "Look, we don't want you to get hurt. So don't do anything stupid. Just make the exchange and get out of there.

"If things go south, bail. Don't bother to look back. Just run."

I nodded. "I can run. But only after I get the dog back."

Harris sighed. "You and that damn dog."

He looked at his watch. "You've got two hours before the call. There's a cot over there. Get some rest."

I took his advice. After he left the room, I lay down on the cot and closed my eyes.

I must have slept because the next thing I knew Agent Jones was kicking one of the legs of the cot.

"Time to get up. Your guy should be calling soon. There's breakfast on the table."

Behind him, I could see a plate of donuts and a can of soda on the table. Not my usual morning meal, but on this day it looked pretty good.

I stood, stretched, walked to the table and grabbed a glazed donut and the soda. The donut was warm, the drink cold. A pretty good combination.

As I ate the donut, I started thinking about how just a few weeks ago my life had been simple. Living in my motorhome with Bob. No worries. No kidnappers, no exploding meth labs and no Homeland Security agents picking me up in the middle of the night.

Since moving into Serenity Cove, my life had gotten a lot more interesting. And a lot more dangerous.

The most dangerous part was coming up. In the next hour or so I would be handing off ten pounds of high grade pot to a drug dealer.

I decided a second donut was in order. This time I chose a chocolate-covered one. I washed it down with the rest of the soda.

Harris walked into the room. "Get a good nap?"

"Sure did. It's like the Hilton in here."

He smiled.

"So, you ready for the call?"

"Yes. Anything special you want me to say?"

"No, just get Darrell to set a time and place for the exchange and tell him you'll be there. Try to get a thirty minute lead time so we can get our guys in place."

"Will do."

In my previous conversation with Darrell, I'd told him I wouldn't be able to get the package until after eight in the morning because it was locked in a storage building. The truth was, when we'd spoken, I didn't have a package to give him. But now, thanks to Agent Harris and Homeland Security, I had the package he wanted.

Darrell said he'd call at eight thirty.

At eight fifteen, Harris and Jones sat with me at the table in the small room, waiting for Polly's phone to ring. Between the three of us, we'd finished off the plate of donuts.

Another agent had brought me a bottle of water to keep my throat from going dry. I was halfway through the bottle when the phone rang.

I answered on the third ring.

"Hello?"

"You got the package?"

"Yeah, I've got it. You keeping my dog happy?"

"Can't tell if he's happy. But he's right here beside me. Snoring."

"Snoring is good, means he's still alive. So when do you want to do this?"

"Nine o'clock. At the west end of Dearborn Street. Pull into the funeral home parking lot. Park near the water. Come alone. No cops. Keep your phone close."

Before I could reply, Darrell ended the call.

Harris and Jones had listened in on the conversation, and as soon as the call ended another agent came into the room with a laptop computer.

The screen on the computer displayed a Google Earth view of the funeral home parking lot at the end of Dearborn Street.

Harris pointed to the screen. "He picked an interesting location. There are at least three escape routes. He could go north on Harbor Street, south on Green Street or east on Dearborn. Each leads into a residential neighborhood.

"The funeral home parking lot backs up to Lemon Bay. There's a small boat dock there. Open water from there to the Intracoastal and the Gulf of Mexico."

Harris shook his head. "I don't like it. Too big an area for us to cover. We don't have enough people to do it right. No air support and it'll take us at least an hour to get a boat in position.

He looked at me. "I don't think you should be doing this. Too big a chance of something going wrong."

I shook my head. "I'm going. Whether you guys are ready or not, I'm going to be there."

Harris frowned. "I don't like it. But if you're good with it then it's a go."

He pointed at the Google Earth view of the parking lot. "Park here, near these trees. We'll get one of our guys back there. If things go south, head that way.

"When you park, back in. Make sure your Jeep is facing the road in case you need to leave in a hurry.

"Shouldn't be anyone else in the parking lot this time of day, but if there is, park as far away from them as you can."

He looked at his watch. "You've got twenty minutes to get there. If you need to use the facilities, now's the time."

After drinking the soda and a full bottle of water, a visit to the men's room was in order. When I came out, Harris and Jones were standing in front of one of the video monitors.

Pointing to the screen, Harris said, "We're moving our guys into position but haven't been able to set up a video feed yet. May not be able to get it done. Not enough time."

He picked up a green duffel bag, opened it, and showed me what was inside.

"This is what we made up for you. It looks and weighs the same as the package Polly found.

"You'll want to be careful with this. Street value is around forty thousand dollars. If you're caught with it by the local police, you can expect to spend some time in jail."

Before handing me the duffel, Harris put the package inside and dropped it into a large Walmart shopping bag. "Keep it in this. Draws less attention."

I picked up the bag. It had some weight to it. "What's to keep me from selling this and skipping town?"

Harris didn't smile. He said, "Twenty years in prison."

I'd tried to make a joke, but no one was laughing.

He looked at his watch. "Time for you to go. Don't forget we're tracking both you and the package."

I nodded and headed for the door.

CHAPTER FORTY-NINE

Out in the Jeep, the first thing I did was put the Walmart shopping bag behind the passenger seat. It had ten pounds of pot in it and I felt better having it out of sight.

The drive to the funeral home lot took me down Dearborn Street. Familiar territory. Palm trees overhead, small shops on the left and right, a local barber offering nine-dollar haircuts.

Small town America. The kind of place you'd feel safe leaving your car unlocked. But not me. Not today. Not with forty thousand dollars of contraband behind the seat.

At the end of Dearborn Street, I pulled into the parking lot behind the funeral home. It was empty. No other cars. No people.

The far side of the lot backed up to the waters of Lemon Bay and the Intracoastal Waterway that runs through it. A calming view for those visiting the funeral home.

Darrell had told me to park close to the water. That would be easy. Every parking spot in this lot was close to the water. The very closest were those on the back row. That's where I parked, backing in so the front of the Jeep faced the street.

This would give me a view of other cars entering the lot and allow me a quick getaway if it became necessary.

After parking, I rolled down my window and waited for Darrell to show up. It was a nice day to be sitting outside. Deep blue skies, no humidity, and just a slight breeze over the water. Perfect Florida springtime weather.

The waves of Lemon Bay rolled in against the rock seawall behind me. The rhythmic sound helped calm my nerves.

Truth was, I wasn't as nervous as I probably should have been. I was still thinking of Darrell as a small time hustler trying to make a buck. Probably not dangerous.

Harris said at least one of his agents would be hidden behind the bushes on the north side of the parking lot. Looking in that direction, I saw a tall stand of thick bamboo screening the parking lot from the nearby residential neighborhood.

I looked but didn't see anyone back there. Probably a good thing. If I could see an agent hiding back there, Darrell might see him as well and call off the exchange.

After ten minutes of waiting and no sign of Darrell, I started to wonder if he'd show up. Maybe he'd been tipped off to the presence of federal agents.

Or maybe he had called with a change of plans and I missed the call. I checked Polly's phone. No missed calls, full battery charge, signal strength at five bars.

Darrell was now twelve minutes late. No sign of him anywhere. Had we somehow gotten our signals crossed? Maybe I was supposed to meet him somewhere else.

I decided to get out of the Jeep, walk around the parking lot, see if I'd missed anything. Stepping out, I immediately heard a phone ringing. Not Polly's. The ringing came from another phone, somewhere nearby.

Turning, I tried to zero in on the ringing. It didn't come from the street or the bushes on my left. Nor from inside the funeral home.

When I turned toward the water, I realized the sound was coming from the small boat dock that stretched out over Lemon Bay. I walked toward it and noticed a small hand-painted sign reading, "Serenity Pier."

The phone continued to ring. Since no one else was around, I figured the call might be for me.

Walking out onto the dock, I saw a white plastic bag tied to the leg of a bench. The ringing sound came from inside the bag.

By the time I got the phone out of the bag, the ringing had stopped. I'd missed the call.

Looking back at the Jeep, there was still no sign of Darrell. No one else in the parking lot.

The phone rang again and this time I answered.

"Hello?"

"Took you long enough to answer."

It was Darrell.

"Here's the deal. I'm watching you right now. I can see everything you do.

"I want you to reach into your front pants pocket and pull out the cell phone you had earlier. Not the one you found in the bag, but the other one."

Following Darrell's instruction, I pulled out Polly's cell phone.

"Now drop the phone over the rail and into the bay."

I hesitated. It was Polly's phone and she'd be pretty upset to lose it and everything on it, including her photos.

"Can't do that. Too nice a phone. Paid too much for it. If you want, I can put it back in the Jeep."

"No. If you want your dog back, drop the phone in the water."

I wanted the dog back. The phone I could replace but not the dog; I dropped the phone over the rail into the salty water below.

"Good. Now, reach into your other pockets and empty them onto the bench in front of you."

I did as instructed. The only thing I was carrying was my car keys and wallet.

"Are you sure that's all you have?"

"Yes, that's it. Just my keys and wallet."

"Put them back in your pocket."

Again, I did as instructed.

"Where's the package you were supposed to bring?"

I pointed over my shoulder. "In the Jeep."

"Good. Go back and get it. Bring it out on the dock. Leave your keys and wallet in the Jeep."

As I walked back to the Jeep, I scanned the area trying to locate Darrell. If he could see me, he had to be nearby. But looking around, I couldn't see him anywhere. Maybe he was on top of one of the nearby buildings.

Wherever he was, I hoped Homeland Security agents were watching him.

When I got to the Jeep, I took four twenty dollar bills out of my wallet and stuffed them in my pocket. Then I put my wallet in the glove box and locked it. I put the car keys under the driver's seat.

I grabbed the plastic Walmart bag and headed back out onto the dock, raising the bag up over my head.

Darrell was still on the phone. "Is the package in that bag?"

"Yes. But you're not getting it until I'm sure Oscar is safe."

Darrell didn't answer. He ended the call.

CHAPTER FIFTY

A moment later, the phone buzzed signaling an incoming text message. I clicked on the message and saw a photo of Oscar lying on a white, sandy beach, a rope attached to his collar, tied to a palm tree.

The phone rang.

"You see the picture?"

"Yes. Where is he?"

"Right here with me. Just follow my instructions and you'll have him back in a few minutes."

"Okay, what do I need to do?"

"Jump into the water."

"What?"

"Put the phone down. Jump into the water. Go completely under. Then climb back up on the dock and pick up the phone."

"I'm not getting in the water. It's cold."

"Either get in the water or the dog dies."

Darrell had the upper hand. I put the phone down and stepped off the dock into the chilly saltwater.

I stood for a moment then quickly ducked down until I was totally submerged. I silently counted to ten.

I understood why Darrell had asked me to do this. Any electronic device I might be carrying would be ruined by the salt water. If I had a GPS tracker on me, it wouldn't work when I got out.

The fact that Darrell knew this meant he was a little smarter than I had originally thought.

After twenty seconds I came back to the surface, waded over to the ladder and climbed back up on the dock. I was dripping wet, the cool breeze quickly chilled me to the bone.

I picked up the phone.

Darrell was still there. "Was the water cold?"

"Come over here, I'll show you."

"No need. We'll be seeing each other soon enough.

"Take the package and walk to the end of the dock. There's a small flat bottom boat. Get in it."

I'd noticed the boat earlier. I figured it belonged to the funeral home. Maybe they used it to spread ashes of loved ones over Lemon Bay.

Following Darrell's instructions, I climbed over the dock rail and stepped down into the boat. The boat shifted under my weight. With one hand holding ten pounds of pot and the other the cell phone, I struggled to stay upright.

The wobbling of the small boat almost sent me overboard. I dropped the bag with the pot onto the floor of the boat and used my free hand to grab the dock.

From the phone, I heard a chuckle.

Then, "Behind the back seat there's a foil lined freezer bag. Put the pot in that bag and hold it up so I can see it."

I carefully stepped to the back of the boat and found a large bag, the kind sold in grocery stores to keep frozen food cold. Opening the bag, I placed the brick of pot inside then held it up in the air to show I'd completed the task.

From the phone I heard Darrell's voice. "Good. Now untie the boat, start the motor, and head south, hugging Manasota Key until you get to Stump Pass State Park.

"Shouldn't take you more than ten minutes.

"When you get to Stump Pass, keep your eyes peeled for a

man wearing an orange vest standing on a sandbar to your left. He'll be alone.

"Pull your boat up on that beach. That's where you'll find your dog.

"Any questions?"

I shook my head. "No. No questions. Ten minutes, I'll be there."

I set the choke on the motor and pulled the starter rope. The engine sputtered to life. I reset the choke, untied the lines and slowly motored out into the bay.

Glancing behind me, I hoped Agent Harris and his men were watching.

They wouldn't be able to track me using the GPS app they'd installed on Polly's phone. The phone was sitting at the bottom of Lemon Bay. And it was possible that the foil lining of the freezer bag would block the signals from the tracker in the brick of pot.

I didn't have time to worry about any of this. I had ten minutes to get to Stump Pass State Park. As I reached the channel, I brought the boat up on plane and headed south.

Four minutes later, I passed under the Manasota Key drawbridge where the wide waters of Lemon Bay began to narrow toward Stump Pass, a natural cut into the Gulf of Mexico.

Much like a funnel, the waters from the gulf roar through the pass at low and high tides, creating strong and sometimes dangerous currents. Those currents weren't a problem for large boats, but the little flat bottom I was in would have a tough time if the tides caught it.

If Darrell's directions were accurate, I didn't have to worry about the pass. I would reach the sand bar long before the pass. But there were other things to be wary of in these waters.

The channel leading to Stump Pass is dotted with the broken stumps of trees sheared off during tropical storms. At low tide,

231

most of these stumps are visible and easy to avoid. But at high tide, many are hidden and pose a significant danger.

Hitting one of these in any size boat would be bad. But in my little boat, with its thin metal hull, hitting a stump would spell disaster.

As soon as I saw the first stump, I throttled back and steered toward the center of the channel. This gave me more water depth below the boat and less chance of hitting a stump.

Being in the center of the channel had its own risks. It put me in the path of northbound boats. The small ones I wasn't worried about. I could get out of their way.

The larger ones could be a problem, creating fast moving wakes that could easily swamp the little flat bottom boat I was in. Fortunately, there didn't seem to be much boat traffic that morning and I didn't have far to travel.

As I neared the park, I cut my speed and started scanning the sandbars on my left for a man in an orange vest.

The sandbars were created when the Corps of Engineers dug the Intracoastal Waterway back in the nineteen fifties. They dredged the sand to create a deep, navigable channel and dumped the excess on the sides, creating small spoil islands.

Over the years, the spoils had become overgrown with tropical plants and home to flocks of native birds.

I studied each of the islands, looking for a flash of orange. Against the white sandy beaches, it shouldn't be hard to spot.

After passing six islands, I started to worry. I hadn't seen a single person. The further south I went, the more I felt the current picking up strength, pulling me toward Stump Pass and the Gulf of Mexico.

If I didn't spot Darrell soon, I'd have to make a decision. Either turn around and head back or get closer to the pass and risk getting caught by the currents and swept through the pass.

After passing yet another empty island, I decided I had missed him. I started to swing the boat around when the phone buzzed, startling me.

I answered with a question. "Where are you?"

"Just ahead on your left. I can see you from here."

Looking ahead, I saw a man wearing an orange vest step out from the thick undergrowth. Behind him, just at the tree line, a dog on a leash. Oscar.

I steered my boat in his direction and watched as he took off the vest and stuffed it into a green pack.

He was wearing a white fishing shirt, khaki wading pants and a fishing hat with a neck flap. His face was completely hidden behind a white sun mask.

If he were to walk into a bank dressed like that, he'd be arrested on the spot. But out here on the water, he fit right in. Just another fisherman dressed to cut his exposure to the sun.

As I got closer, he pointed to the sand in front of him. He wanted me to beach the boat at that spot.

I steered to where he pointed and gave the motor enough power to push the flat bottom up onto the sand. With the boat beached, I killed the motor, stood and started to step off into the water.

The man, who I assumed was Darrell, shook his head. "Hold it right there. Both hands in the air."

He had a small silver revolver, pointed straight at me.

With my hands in the air, I said, "I'm unarmed."

The man waggled his gun in my direction. "Let's check for sure. Turn around. Slowly."

Balancing myself in the boat, I did a slow three sixty turn.

"See, no gun. I'm not armed."

Still pointing the gun at me, he said, "Toss me the package."

I lobbed him the foil bag. Catching it in his free hand, he said, "Stay in the boat while I test this. If it's good, you can have the dog and be on your way."

He backed up a ways and squatted to begin the process. It seemed to take forever. He had to keep one eye on me and the gun within reach while he cut through the wrapping around the package and pulled out a small sample.

After placing the sample in a test tube, he added several drops of liquid from a small plastic bottle. Then he shook the test tube vigorously.

"Now we wait. See what color it turns."

As we waited for the results, a large trawler made its way up the Intracoastal. Three teenaged girls in bikinis on the top deck waved at us, and I waved back.

Darrell looked at me. "They with you?"

"No. But when cute girls wave at me, I always wave back."

I pointed at the test tube. "So what's it show?"

The contents had turned a deep purple.

"You're in luck. It tested good. Get out of the boat and go get your dog."

He didn't have to tell me twice. I hopped into the shallow water and headed toward Oscar. Even before I reached him, he was wagging his wiener dog tail hard enough to shake his entire body.

"Oscar, you okay?"

In response to my question, he dropped to the sand and rolled onto his back so I could rub his belly. It needed doing so I obliged him.

Behind me, I failed to notice that Darrell had put his gear in the boat and pushed it off the beach.

When I heard the motor start, I turned just in time to see him wave as he powered away toward the Gulf of Mexico, leaving Oscar and me stranded on the sand.

I had rescued Oscar. But who was going to rescue me?

CHAPTER FIFTY-ONE

"How about it Oscar? Think we can swim across?"

He didn't answer. He didn't have to.

The outgoing tidal currents along with the cool water temperature would make swimming across the channel a risky move—especially since neither of us had a life jacket.

Even if I could make it across, I was pretty sure Oscar and his stubby little legs didn't stand a chance. There was no way I was going to leave him behind.

The way I figured it, there was no reason to risk either of our lives trying to swim to safety. Sooner or later, Agent Harris or some of his men would show up. He had assured me they would come to my rescue should I need their help.

I needed their help now, so I was pretty sure they were on their way. So I did the smart thing. I found a nice, shady spot under a palm tree, and Oscar and I stretched out on the sand to await their arrival.

I'm not sure how long I slept. It could have been a few minutes or a few hours. But judging by the shadows cast by the palms trees, I was pretty sure it was past noon. That meant we'd been stranded on the sandbar for more than three hours, and neither Harris nor his men had swooped in to rescue us.

So maybe they weren't coming. Or maybe they didn't know where we were. Either way, I was tired of waiting.

I'd already decided not to risk swimming across the channel. I could probably make it but Oscar couldn't, and I wasn't going to leave him behind.

Our other option was to try to wave down a north bound

boat and hitch a ride. The only problem with this plan was there hadn't been much boat traffic that day. Of course, I'd slept through most of the morning, so I really didn't know how many boats had passed.

But it really didn't matter how many boats had already gone by. What mattered was how many boats would pass by in the next hour or so. And how many of those boats would have a shallow enough draft to reach us there on the sandbar.

I explained our situation to Oscar and he didn't seem too concerned. He stood, shook the sand off his shiny, brown coat and slowly trotted toward the water. When he reached the edge, he plopped down in the wet sand. He had found himself a cool spot and he was happy.

I stayed in the shade of the palm tree where I could watch for north bound boats. Sooner or later the right one would come by, and we'd find someone who would either take us across to Stump Pass State Park or drop us somewhere further north where we could find a phone and call for help.

During the next hour or so, we saw two large trawlers and three sailboats—all headed south, the wrong direction for us.

There'd also been three teens on jet skis heading north, but they'd been traveling so fast they were gone before I could get their attention.

We'd seen three other boats that would have worked—all were charter fishing captains coming back off the gulf with clients. I waved to get their attention and they waved back. But none of them had stopped.

Oscar didn't seem to be bothered by any of this. He slept, licked his parts, and slept some more.

I, on the other hand, was anxious to get back to the mainland and to my normal day-to-day life. One that didn't involve drug dealers and Homeland Security agents.

Settling back on the sand, I sighed. And maybe dozed off again.

I drifted awake to the faint strains of Jimmy Buffet singing "Cheeseburger in Paradise". I wasn't sure whether I was hearing the song in my head because I was hungry or if it was actually coming from the water.

When the song got louder, I realized it was coming from a boat. Hopefully one that might stop and pick us up.

I walked down to the beach and stood beside Oscar. Looking south, I saw something heading our way. As it got closer, I could see that it was a boat, unlike any I had seen before.

Someone had added a tiki hut with a palm frond roof to a party barge. Under the shade of the tiki hut, a shirtless man with shoulder length hair stood at the helm. Behind him, three women in bikinis held water pistols.

This was the kind of rescue I was hoping for.

As the boat got closer, I started waving my arms to get the attention of captain and crew. Oscar decided to help by singing along with Jimmy Buffet. I'm not sure which was more effective, but it worked.

One of the women saw us and squirted the man at the helm with her water pistol. When he turned to squirt her back, she pointed at us.

Seeing us on the beach, he immediately reduced speed, turned down Jimmy Buffet, and picked up a microphone. "Ahoy, there. You need help?"

"Yes! We're stranded."

He turned and consulted briefly with the three women, then turned back to me. "Stay put. We'll come to you."

The man steered the boat toward shore and brought the tips of the pontoons up onto the sandy beach. With beer in hand, he walked to the front deck and opened the gate.

"I'm Captain Jim. The girls and I are heading up to Chadwick Park. You're welcome to ride along with us."

I smiled with relief. "Chadwick Park would be perfect."

After lifting Oscar up onto the boat, I climbed onto the

front deck and started to take my shoes off. I didn't want to track sand into their boat.

Captain Jim shook his head. "Don't worry about that. Sand is part of life out here. We're used to it."

I nodded. "I really appreciate you stopping for us."

Captain Jim smiled. "No problem. But how'd you come to be stranded?"

There was no way I could tell him about the drug deal, so I thought fast. "Oscar and I got out to explore the island, and while we were gone, someone took our boat.

"We've been out here most of the morning, hoping to hitch a ride."

Captain Jim shook his head. "That just ain't right. What kind of person steals your boat and leaves you stranded?"

I didn't answer.

"So if you've been out here all morning, you must be pretty thirsty. We've got water and beer. Your choice."

I smiled. "Water sounds good. And maybe a bowl so I can pour some for the dog."

One of the women produced a plastic jug of water and a small bowl. Handing both to me, she said, "If you're not in a hurry, you could spend the day with us. We're celebrating."

A celebration sounded good. But not that day. "Sure wish I could join you, but I've got to get the dog back home. He's had a rough day."

She somehow managed to smile and pout at the same time. How do women do that? "Well, if you change your mind, let me know."

Behind us, Captain Jim revved the engine, signaling we were about to start moving. He backed away from the beach, and then steered the boat north, toward Chadwick Park and home.

CHAPTER FIFTY-TWO

The small motor on the party barge didn't move the boat very fast, but according to Captain Jim, they really weren't in any hurry to go anywhere. They were coming up from Port Charlotte and were just out to enjoy the ride and have a little party.

It took us about twenty minutes to get to the Chadwick Park boat launch and another five minutes to securely tie off the boat.

After we'd reached shore, I needed to call someone to come get me. But my cell phone was back in the Jeep. And Polly's phone was at the bottom of Lemon Bay.

I turned to Captain Jim. "I hate to ask this, but do you have a cell phone I could borrow?"

He shook his head. "No I don't. One of our rules is no cell phones when we're out on the boat. They're too distracting. So we travel naked—no phones."

He pointed to a convenience store across from the public beach parking lot. "I'm going over there to get some beer. If you want, the girls can watch your dog while you go over there with me. I'm pretty sure they've got a phone."

I nodded. "That sounds good."

I reassured Oscar I was coming back and asked the girls to make sure he stayed on the boat while I was gone. I wasn't too worried about him jumping ship. His little legs weren't long enough for him to get off the boat and up onto the dock.

As Captain Jim and I were walking toward the convenience store, he asked, "You jump off a drug boat?"

"What? No! Why do you ask that?"

"Because when we came through Stump Pass there were Coast Guard and DEA boats stopping and checking everyone.

"I figured something was up. They were looking for somebody and when I saw you stranded on the sandbar, I thought maybe you were involved."

I shook my head. "They weren't looking for me."

Captain Jim smiled. "If you say so."

When we reached the convenience store, I wasn't surprised to see that there was no pay phone. Most of them disappeared years ago.

Inside, I asked the clerk if I could borrow his cell phone. He shook his head. "Nope. Nobody uses my phone but me."

He pointed to a display on the counter. "Forty dollars will buy you a phone with sixty minutes talk time."

I'd left my wallet in the Jeep. But I had four twenty dollar bills in my pocket. A little wet from wading in the water, but otherwise still intact.

I put three twenties on the counter. "I'll take one."

The clerk smiled. "What color?"

"I don't care."

He reached for the pink one.

"Not pink. Give me black."

The clerk grinned, took my money, and rang up the sale. He handed me my change and I stepped aside as Captain Jim put a twelve pack of beer on the counter.

I pulled out a twenty. "I've got this."

Jim smiled. "Well, all right then."

We headed back to the boat where the girls were waiting. As soon as they saw us, they started waving. We waved back and made our way onto the boat.

Captain Jim asked, "You sure you don't want to come with

us?"

I shook my head. "I wish I could. But I need to get Oscar back home."

He nodded. "I understand."

He pulled out his wallet and handed me a business card.

Captain Jim Morgan

Attorney at Law

Port Charlotte, Florida

The card had his phone number, email address and office location.

"If you ever need legal help, call me. The girls and I can take care of just about anything."

I thanked him, picked up Oscar and stepped off the boat. Captain Jim and the girls waved as they pulled away from the dock. Jimmy Buffet was singing, "It's Five O'clock Somewhere".

The phone I'd purchased showed the local time as three pm. Six hours since I'd made contact with Darrell in the funeral home parking lot.

I hadn't heard from Agent Harris or any of the Homeland Security agents who were supposed to be tracking me during the package exchange. That bothered me. But it wasn't something I could do anything about.

I needed to call someone to come get me and Oscar. My first inclination was to call Buck. But I didn't have his unlisted number with me. It was on my phone, which was back in the Jeep.

I could call Polly. She'd be thrilled to learn that Oscar was safe. But she didn't have her cell phone. I'd dropped it into Lemon Bay that morning.

Next on my list was Lucy, Polly's daughter. This time of day she'd probably be hard at work, selling trucks.

I punched in her number and made the call. She answered

on the third ring.

"Hello?"

"Lucy, it's me, Walker."

"Walker, where have you been? We've been worried sick. Have you got Oscar?"

"Yes, I've got him. We're here at Chadwick Park and we need a ride."

"I can be there in fifteen minutes. Don't go anywhere."

She hung up.

Two minutes later, she called back. "Is it okay if I call Mom and let her know you and Oscar are safe?"

"Yes, call her. Let her know Oscar's fine. A little hungry, but otherwise in good shape."

"Good, she'll be so happy. And Walker, what about you? You okay?"

"Yep. Just come get me and I'll tell you the whole story."

Fifteen minutes later, Lucy's white 4Runner pulled into the Chadwick Park parking lot. Oscar and I were sitting in the shade of the pavilion. When Lucy saw us she flashed her headlights and headed over.

As soon as she stepped out of her car, she ran over and gave me a big hug. She released me and stood back with tears in her eyes. "We were so worried. Buck said the feds lost track of you. They weren't even sure if you were alive or not."

She hugged me again. This time longer than before. I hugged her back. It felt good.

When she finally released me, she took a step back and looked down at Oscar.

"Oscar, your mom is going to be so happy to see you. Would you like a treat?"

His little tail went into overdrive. He knew what the word "treat" meant. And, yes, he wanted one.

Reaching into her pocket, Lucy pulled out a dog biscuit and flipped it to Oscar, who caught it in his mouth.

"I always keep treats on hand for Oscar."

I nodded. "What about me? What'd you bring me?"

She smiled. "I'm here. What else do you need?"

"A burger and fries would be nice."

After loading Oscar into Lucy's 4Runner, we agreed our first priority was to get him back to Polly.

According to Lucy, Polly hadn't slept since we'd called her the previous evening, and as the hours passed without hearing from me, she'd grown more and more worried.

Seeing Oscar healthy and alive would be a huge weight off her shoulders. Seeing me wouldn't hurt either.

Lucy was driving; I was in the passenger seat. Oscar was in the back.

"I wasn't joking about the burger and fries. I'm starving."

"Really? You want me to stop?"

"Yes, I don't care where as long as they have food."

There aren't many fast food places in Englewood, but there is a Burger King. It was right on our way. Lucy pulled into the drive through lane.

She ordered a Whopper and a Coke for me and a Whopper Junior for Oscar. After paying at the pickup window and getting our food order, Lucy pulled into a parking space.

She handed me the Whopper and gave the meat patty from the Whopper Junior to Oscar.

He gobbled it down then looked at me, hoping I was going to share my Whopper with him. That wasn't going to happen. I ate it slowly and enjoyed every bite.

Lucy waited patiently while we ate and then pulled out of the parking lot to head home. Turning to me, she said, "Don't tell Mom I gave Oscar a burger."

I nodded.

Two minutes later, we pulled into Lucy's driveway; Polly was outside waiting for us. I could tell she had been crying, but upon seeing us her face broke out into a smile.

Without waiting for us to get out, she rushed up and opened the 4Runner's back door where she found Oscar happy to see her.

While she was busy with Oscar, I got out and went over to talk with Buck, who had come out of the house.

He met me with a handshake. "Glad you made it back alive. You had us worried."

"I was worried too. Where were Harris's agents? They were supposed to back me up."

Buck pointed to the back yard. "Let's go around there and talk."

I followed him around the house and we stood beside the small boat we had taken out just one day earlier. It felt like weeks had passed.

Buck started telling me the story.

"After you left for the funeral home, Harris got a call from Washington. He was ordered to drop everything and to assist the Coast Guard. Apparently something big had come up.

"Harris pushed back. Said he had an active mission with a civilian in the field. Said he couldn't leave you out there without backup.

"The people in Washington didn't care. They ordered him to back off. Said it was an all-hands-on-deck situation with the Coast Guard.

"Harris had to follow orders. So everyone in the office loaded up into cars and took off. No one was left to track you.

"I had to call Polly to get a ride home. We haven't heard from Harris or his agents since."

I was stunned. They had abandoned me in the middle of a

mission. They'd left me on my own after assuring me they had my back.

When I was in the military we were always taught, "No man left behind." Surely Homeland Security had the same rules.

"So let me get this straight. They left me out in the field with ten pounds of pot, no backup, no protection, and no rescue?"

Buck nodded. "Yes. That's exactly what they did."

CHAPTER FIFTY-THREE

Buck and I went back to the front of the house where Lucy and Polly had Oscar up on the porch, taking turns rubbing his belly.

Seeing us coming, Polly came over to me. "You're my hero. You saved Oscar. I can't thank you enough."

She hugged me then returned to the porch to be with her beloved dog.

Lucy looked at me and shook her head. "You going to tell us what happened? Why you were gone so long?"

"Sure, but there's not much to tell."

Lucy smiled. "Always the modest hero. Come inside. I want every detail."

We went inside and I told them the whole story. Starting with me driving to the funeral home parking lot and ending with me being rescued by a Parrot Head legal team blasting Jimmy Buffet.

When I was done, Polly spoke first.

"My phone is at the bottom of Lemon Bay? It's gone forever?"

I nodded. "Yes, it's gone. But it was either your phone or Oscar, and I figured you could always get another phone."

Polly patted Oscar. "You're right. I can get another phone. You did the right thing."

She stood and yawned. "I didn't get any sleep last night. It's time for Oscar and me to go home."

She turned to Buck. "You riding with me?"

"Yes, as long as it's okay with Walker."

I nodded. "Fine with me. But I need a ride to my Jeep. It's still in the funeral home parking lot."

Lucy reached over and touched my shoulder. "I'll take you. I'm going that way."

We all loaded up into our various vehicles and headed out.

On the ride over to the Jeep, Lucy kept glancing over at me but not saying anything.

Finally, I asked, "Okay, what's up? Why are you looking at me like that?"

"Just trying to figure you out. You show up pretty much out of nowhere. No job, no visible means of support, and living in a RV.

"Then you start rescuing homeless people and saving damsels in distress. You fix my mother up with a movie star. And then you volunteer to chase down a drug dealer for the sake of a dog.

"So I'm just wondering. Is this what life with Walker is usually like?"

I shook my head. "Lucy, for the most part my life is pretty boring. But since moving to Serenity Cove, things keep happening. Hopefully, it'll stop soon.

"Right now, all I want to do is to go home, feed Bob and go to sleep. No rescues, no damsels in distress, and no finding lost dogs."

Lucy smiled. "Good. Go home and sleep. No heroics for a few days. Can you do that?"

"I'll try."

When we reached the funeral home parking lot, my Jeep was still where I'd left it. No one had touched it.

Lucy pulled up beside it, and as I reached for the door to get out, she stopped me.

"Walker, you were amazing today."

Then she leaned in and kissed me on the cheek.

248

"Now go home. Take a shower. Get some rest."

Smiling, I got out and walked over to the Jeep. I suddenly felt very happy, not tired at all.

Instead of driving off, Lucy waited until she saw me start the Jeep. She wanted to make sure I wasn't stranded twice in one day.

As soon as she heard the Jeep start, she waved and drove off.

While the Jeep warmed up, I opened the glove box and pulled out my cell phone. Five messages. One from Lucy, one from Agent Harris and three from Anna.

I'd listen to them later. At that moment I just wanted to pick up some food for dinner and get back to Serenity Cove.

CHAPTER FIFTY-FOUR

All was quiet when I got back to the motorhome. Bob met me at the door, purring for a change instead of demanding immediate food service.

I rubbed the top of his head with my thumb then headed to the back bedroom, Bob right on my heels. Apparently he wasn't going to let me out of his sight.

I topped off his food and water bowls on the way. He would need more attention later, but not right away.

My plan was to take a hot shower and rinse off the sand, salt and wet dog smell I'd picked up during the day's adventure.

After the shower, I changed into clean clothes and plopped down on the living room couch. Bob settled in beside me. I checked the messages on my phone, starting with the one from Lucy.

"Walker, where are you? We're worried. Give me a call as soon as you can."

She had called while I was stranded on the island.

I'd talked to her since, so no need to call her back. I deleted the message.

The next message was from Agent Harris at 12:28pm.

"Walker, we were reassigned at the last minute. Call me as soon as you can. It's not over."

No apology for leaving me stranded without a backup. No explanation. Just telling me it wasn't over.

I pressed the call button. After three rings, a voice answered.

"Harris."

"What do you mean it's not over?"

"Walker, good to hear from you. We were starting to get worried."

"You left me out there without backup."

"I know and we didn't want to. But something came up. An all-hands-on-deck kind of thing."

"So that's the way you operate? You stick someone in the field then abandon them?"

"No, that's not the way we operate. I didn't want to leave you without backup. But it wasn't something I had control over. It sounds like you made it back just fine.

"So, how did the exchange go? Did you get the dog?"

"Yeah, I got the dog. And I spent five hours stranded on a sandbar down by Stump Pass."

"What about the drugs? You still have them?"

"No, of course not. I exchanged them for the dog, just like we planned."

"So you don't have the drugs in your possession?"

"No, I do not."

"Well, that's not good. We signed them out to you. We either need to get them back from you or find the guy you delivered them to."

I couldn't believe what Harris was saying. Somehow I was responsible for getting the drugs back? That was definitely not part of the deal. I was to do the exchange, get the dog back, and then I'd be out of it.

"You've got to be kidding me. You planned this whole thing. I did my part. It was your guys who bailed. As far as I'm concerned, my part's over."

Silence on the other end of the line. Then, "Walker, let's get together tomorrow and talk this through. I'll call you then. In the meantime, don't leave town."

He ended the call.

I couldn't believe it. Homeland Security came up with the plan, they supplied the drugs, they told me what to do, and then they took off at the last minute and left me on my own.

And now I was somehow responsible for getting either the drugs or the guy holding the drugs back to them?

That was crazy.

Looking for something to take my mind off the mess, I turned on the TV and tuned to the local news. The screen showed an aerial view of a Coast Guard cutter approaching a large yacht. A scrolling message across the bottom of the screen read, "Coast Guard stops vessel carrying missile."

Turning up the volume, I listened as a local reporter told how authorities had received a tip a vessel in the gulf was transporting a shipment of shoulder mounted surface-to-air missiles.

The Coast Guard, in conjunction with officials from Homeland Security, had searched for the vessel and eventually located it seven miles offshore.

When they approached it, shots were exchanged, and one crewman on a Coast Guard boat was injured. The suspect vessel was eventually disabled and boarded by Coast Guard and Homeland Security agents.

Upon boarding the vessel, several crates of weapons were found. No other details were available, but the reporter assured viewers they were on top of the story.

Apparently, this was the reason Harris and his agents had been ordered to drop everything and assist the Coast Guard. Finding missiles was more important than helping me rescue a dog. I didn't like it, but I understood.

The next story on the news concerned the building of a new baseball stadium in Tampa. I wasn't interested so I turned the volume down.

Almost immediately, my phone chimed with an incoming call. The caller ID showed it was from Anna. I answered.

"Anna, what's going on?"

"Walker, I was about to ask you the same thing. I've been trying to reach you for two days, and you haven't called me back."

"Sorry about that. I've been away from my phone and just got back today."

"You been on a trip?"

"Kind of. Been on a boat, no phone."

"Sounds like fun. But we've got a problem."

CHAPTER FIFTY-FIVE

"What kind of problem?"

"The owner of Serenity Cove called me this morning. She said the park manager didn't deposit this month's rental checks in the bank. He didn't pay the park's electric bill either.

"When the owner called the manager's office to talk to him about it, no one answered. She said she called ten times and still no answer.

"She called me to have you check it out. I couldn't reach you. She's in a panic, wondering what's going on down here.

"Since you're living in Serenity Cove and supposed to be keeping an eye on things, tell me what's going on."

Anna was upset. She had told the owner I would watch over things. I'd be their 'undercover' guy at the park.

And I'd missed something important.

"Anna, I haven't seen the manager in a few days. I don't know if he's sick or if he's taken off with the money. How much are we talking about?"

"A lot. About eighteen thousand dollars. It should have been deposited five days ago. But it wasn't.

"There's another problem. Serenity Cove's bank account looks like it's been cleaned out. There was ten thousand dollars in it. Now it's gone."

"Here's the worst part. Without the monthly rent deposit, the owner is going to have a hard time paying this month's mortgage payment and utility bills.

"She said she might be able to hold off on the loan payment

for another thirty days, but if the electric bill isn't paid, they'll turn it off.

"That means no electricity for anyone staying in the park."

I could understand why the owner was in a panic. No money, bills due, and soon no electricity in the park.

"Anna, how long before they shut off the electricity?"

"Thirty days at most. Last month's bill wasn't paid either."

"So how much is the bill?"

"About six thousand. And another thousand for the water bill.

"The owner doesn't want to deal with these kinds of problems. If the rent money isn't found, she'll be in trouble. Her personal home was used as collateral for the loan.

"That's why she's in a panic. She said she may have to sell the place to land developers to cover the loan. If she does, they'll close the park, kick everybody out and put up condos."

I'd only been living in Serenity Cove for three weeks, but I'd come to enjoy the lifestyle it offered and the people I'd met there. I'd have hated to see it sold to developers and replaced with high rise condos.

"Anna, see if you can stall the owner for a few days. I'll look for the manager and the missing money."

"Walker, do that. If you find out anything, call me immediately."

We ended the call.

I'd planned on an afternoon of rest after what had been a long day following a sleepless night. But it was not to be.

After learning about the missing rent money, I decided to check the manager's office. Maybe he was sick or something and wasn't able to answer the phone or go to the bank.

I decided to find out.

It took me less than two minutes to walk from my motorhome to the Serenity Cove office. When I got there, the front door was locked, no lights were on.

Walking around the building, I checked all the windows. They were locked and shades had been pulled preventing anyone from seeing inside.

At the back of the building, a six-foot wooden fence surrounded a small courtyard which led to the back door of the manager's apartment. The gate on the fence wasn't locked, so I pushed it open and went in.

Inside the courtyard, I found two broken lawn chairs and an empty trash bin. Nothing else. The metal door leading into the apartment was locked as was the small window beside it.

So far, I'd seen no sign of life. No indication that anyone was in the office or the apartment. I needed to make sure, so I knocked loudly on the apartment door.

There was no response. I knocked again, this time even louder.

After thirty seconds, no response.

Either no one was inside or they were unable to answer the door. I knocked one more time, just to be sure.

Again, there was no answer.

I pulled out my phone and called Anna. She answered on the second ring.

"Anna, I'm at the manager's apartment. No one seems to be here. All the doors and windows are locked.

"Think I should try to go in?"

"Walker, do you have a key?"

"No. I was thinking about maybe taking the door off the hinges."

"And you're asking my permission?"

"Yes."

"I'll call you right back."

Anna hung up.

While waiting for her call, I went back to my motorhome and grabbed a hammer and the battery powered drill I kept in one of the outside compartments.

With these in hand, I headed back to the manager's apartment and waited for Anna to call.

I didn't have to wait long.

"Walker, I spoke to the owner. She says do what you need to do to get inside. She said if you find the manager, don't hurt him and don't get the police involved."

"Got it. I'll call you back and let you know what I find."

Using the drill, I removed the screws from the door hinges and lifted the door out of the frame. Then I stepped inside and announced myself. "Anyone home?"

No response.

Finding a light switch on the inside wall, I flipped it on.

I was in the kitchen. Nothing askew. No dead bodies. Just a kitchen. Small kitchen table. Stove, microwave, an old fridge.

Exactly what you would expect to see in a small apartment.

Venturing further in, I headed toward a short hallway that I suspected would lead to a bathroom and a bedroom.

Again, I announced myself. "Hello, anyone here?"

No answer.

Flipping on the light in the hallway, I saw that it indeed led to a small bedroom. Inside, an unmade bed, an empty closet, and a dresser with empty drawers.

No sign that anyone was still living there.

Checking the bathroom, I found the same thing. Nothing. No personal items on the counter or in the medicine cabinet over the sink.

Back in the kitchen, I pushed open the door that led into the business office of Serenity Cove.

The office was undisturbed. Pretty much the way it had

looked when I had checked in earlier that month. Nothing seemed to be missing. Nothing unusual.

Except there was no manager.

And no sign that anyone had been there in the last week or so.

I checked the manager's desk looking for any clues as to when he might have left or where he had gone.

In the desk drawers, I found the things you would expect. Notepads, pens and pencils, rental forms, and handouts for new guests.

But nothing of a personal nature from the manager.

It was like he had never existed. There was no sign of his presence anywhere.

On the corner of the manager's desk, a red, blinking light on an ancient answering machine got my attention. Looking closer, I could see the number "Twenty-three" below the red light. Twenty-three new messages.

Most likely these were calls from park residents, potential guests, and the park owner. Someone would need to listen to them and make sure the manager hadn't left a message.

But not me, at least not then.

I walked through the office area, seeking any clues as to the manager's reason for not being there. Nothing stood out. No signs of a struggle, no blood, not so much as a file cabinet or chair out of place.

I continued my search for ten minutes. The only unusual thing I found was a set of keys on the manager's desk. They were marked "Serenity Cove."

I picked them up and put them in my pocket.

Satisfied I hadn't missed anything obvious, I turned off the office lights and headed back into the manager's apartment where I did another search, looking for anything that might help me find the manager or the missing money.

But the place was clean. No personal items of any kind. No food in the fridge. No dirty dishes in the sink.

I'd been inside the building for twenty minutes and hadn't found anything.

I called Anna.

"Did you find him?"

"No. There wasn't anyone inside. No sign that the manager is living here. It looks like he's moved out."

"That's not good."

"I was thinking the same thing.

"I tried to find the company checkbook, but it looks like it's gone too. You'll probably want to have the owner close the account in the morning. Report the checks as being stolen."

Anna sighed. "No telling how many checks he's written.

"When I call the owner and tell her about this, she's not going to be happy. She's probably going to want to sell the place."

I nodded. "I don't blame her. Losing that much money has to hurt."

Anna took a deep breath. "You know, Serenity Cove could be a good investment for you. Fix it up a little, and you could get a pretty good return."

She caught me by surprise. I'd been looking for a place to buy but hadn't considered a commercial property like Serenity Cove.

Still, it might be worth investigating.

"Anna, I might be interested. But the price is probably more than I can afford. This place has got to be worth a lot of money."

"Walker, if the power gets turned off, the residents will have to move out, the rental income stops, and the place will lose half its value.

"The owner doesn't want that to happen, so she's thinking of setting a low price to get a quick sale. She knows she can't afford to draw this out.

"The price might be within your reach."

"Maybe. Find out what she wants for it then let me know."

"Will do."

We ended the call.

When I'd first met Anna over on the Treasure Coast, and we had found our gold coins, we daydreamed about what we would do with the money we'd make from selling the treasure.

Anna said she was going to move to Englewood and sell real estate. I had joked that I might buy an RV park.

Anna's dream had already come true. She was selling real estate. It looked like mine might come true as well. I might end up owning Serenity Cove.

Or not.

CHAPTER FIFTY-SIX

I went to bed early, trying to catch up on sorely missed sleep. Bob didn't disturb me during the night, so my sleep was good. Just not enough of it.

My phone chimed me awake with an incoming call. The caller ID showed "Unknown," so I didn't bother to answer. The way I figured it, if the call was important, it would be from someone I knew.

A few minutes later, the phone chimed again. Same caller ID, "Unknown." I let it ring until it went to voice mail. If they wanted to hide their identity, they could leave a message.

And they did.

It was Agent Harris. His message was short and to the point. "Call me."

I didn't want to return his call, but how long can you ignore Homeland Security? They'd already proven they could pluck me off the street in the middle of the night. No telling what they'd do if I didn't return their call.

I pressed redial and Harris answered on the first ring.

"Walker. Nice of you to call me back."

"Yeah, right. You called to apologize for leaving me in the field without backup?"

"Walker, we didn't have a choice. Missiles always trump drug cases."

"So why call me if you're not apologizing?"

"There are some loose ends we need to deal with."

"Loose ends?"

"Yes, loose ends. Things we need to take care of. In person.

"So I was thinking it would be good if we could get together at ten this morning at Lemon Bay Park. Think you can meet me there?"

"Sure, I can make it. But why aren't we meeting in your office?"

"Too much going on there with this missile thing. Things you don't need to see. The park is a better place. Be there at ten."

He ended the call.

Almost as soon as the call ended, my phone chimed with another incoming call. The caller ID showed it was from Anna.

"Morning, Anna."

"Walker, I just got off the phone with Serenity Cove's owner. She's pretty upset about the manager disappearing. She's worried there's no one there to keep the office open. No one to collect rents and check in new guests.

"She wants me to find someone to take over until a replacement can be found. Is there any chance you want to play office manager for a few days?"

"Anna, I can't do it. I've got something else I have to deal with. But I do know someone who might be able to handle the job. She lives here in the park and she owes me a favor."

"Really? You've only been there a few weeks and you've already got women in the park who owe you favors?"

"Anna, you know how it is. These things happen."

"Yeah, right. So is this woman trustworthy?"

"You've met her. My next door neighbor. The one who took care of you the morning after I brought you home from Rusty's Raft."

"Polly? That's her name, right?"

"Yeah, Polly. If you want, I can ask if she wants to play park manager for a few days."

"Walker, Polly might be perfect for the job. Let me know what she says."

"Will do. But what if she asks how much it pays?"

Anna laughed. "The park's bank accounts are empty so there won't be any pay. But how about free rent for the next month?"

"Sounds good. I'll talk to her."

We ended the call.

The two calls had pretty much set my schedule for the first half of the day. I'd meet with Agent Harris at ten, and, before that meeting, I'd try to talk to Polly about being the temporary park manager.

She usually walked Oscar around eight thirty each morning, and I figured that would be a good time to talk to her about the job.

It was already five after eight, so I needed to get going. I got up, took a quick shower, pulled on some clean clothes, and headed for the kitchen.

For breakfast, I poured myself a bowl of cereal and covered it with white grape juice—my usual fare. I stood and ate by the window, keeping an eye on Polly's Airstream.

Right at eight thirty, she and Oscar came out.

I put down my bowl and went outside to greet them. Polly grinned when she saw me.

"Walker, how are you this fine morning?"

"Good. How about you?"

"Wonderful. Now that Oscar is back, life is great.

"You going to walk with us this morning?"

"Sure, if you don't mind."

With Oscar leading, Polly and I headed out for our morning walk around the park. As usual, we walked in the center of the road, while Oscar zoomed from one side to the other, sniffing the grass for messages left by other dogs.

Occasionally he'd stop and mark a spot, letting other dogs know he'd been there. Polly carried a small plastic bag, ready to retrieve any larger clues Oscar left.

As we walked past Buck's bus, I asked Polly about him. "How's Buck doing?"

She smiled. "He's doing well. In fact, he says our little adventure has inspired him to write a movie script. Involving dognappers and drug dealers.

"Says he wants to tag along with you next time you go out so he can beef up the plot."

"Funny you should mention that. Something has come up, and I need to ask you a favor."

"Walker, any favor you need, you've got it."

"Good. But feel free to say, 'No.'

"Here's the deal. The manager of Serenity Cove is gone. He left without giving notice and there's no one to run the office. So they're looking for a temporary office manager.

"I thought maybe you might be interested in the job. It won't involve much work. Just answering the phone, checking the mail, and keeping everyone here in Serenity Cove happy.

"You can keep Oscar with you in the office, and you can come and go as you like.

"So what do you think?"

Polly shook her head. "I never trusted that manager. I always thought he was up to no good. Are you sure he's gone?"

"Pretty sure. They need a replacement starting right now. If you're interested, the job is yours. You'll be the Queen of Serenity Cove."

She laughed. "Queen of Serenity Cove. I like the sound of that."

"So you think you might be interested?"

"I'm not sure. Let me think about it."

We were about halfway through our walk and the park office

building was just ahead. I reached into my pocket and pulled out the keys I'd found the night before.

"You want to go in, see what it's like?"

She shook her head. "I already know what the office looks like. I've been in there many times. What I really want to know is, are you're absolutely sure the old manager won't be coming back."

"He's not coming back. I can guarantee that."

"Well, if you're sure, we can go in, take a look around."

I unlocked the door and we went in. Me first with Polly following and Oscar in tow.

The office looked the same as it had the night before. No sign anyone other than me had been there recently.

She flipped on the overhead lights and looked around.

"So if I agree to be the manager, what am I supposed to do?"

"The normal stuff. Answer phone calls, reply to emails. Check in guests.

"You'd also be in charge of everything that went on here in the park. So if a guest had a problem or needed something, they'd come to you."

She nodded. "I'd be in charge of everything?"

"Yes, for the most part, you'd be in charge. But there is something you need to know, and you can't tell anyone about this.

"The manager took off with this month's rents. About twenty thousand dollars. He didn't pay the park's utility bills. Electric or water. So you might get some calls about that.

"If those calls do come in, just tell them the owner is making arrangements to pay the bills. Don't tell anyone the manager ran off with the money."

She frowned. "The manager took off with all the rent money? Does that mean there's no record of who paid and who didn't?"

267

"That's a good question. One the new manager will have to find the answer to."

Polly pointed at the office computer. "Whenever I paid my rent, he'd entered it into the computer. So maybe it's all there. If it is, it shouldn't be too hard to straighten things out."

I nodded. "So what do you think? You interested in being the new manager?"

She smiled. "I wouldn't mind being Queen of Serenity Cove. But only if you're sure the old manager is not coming back."

"Polly, he's not coming back. But just to be on the safe side, as the new manager you can have someone come in and change the locks today.

"If you want, I can get business cards printed up showing you as the manager. So what do you think?"

She bent over and gave Oscar a pat on the head then stood back up to face me. She had a smile on her face.

"I'll do it."

I handed her the office keys. "You are now officially the new Serenity Cove park manager. Any questions?"

"Yes, what's the job pay?"

"Polly, as Queen of Serenity Cove, you'll get free rent, and if I can arrange it, a starting salary of two thousand dollars a month."

She smiled. "Free rent is good. And the salary isn't too bad.

"Just one more question. Can Oscar and I go back to our trailer? I didn't know I'd be starting a new job today and would like to get changed into something nicer."

I laughed. "Polly, as Queen of Serenity Cove, you can do anything you like. You're in charge."

She smiled again. "In charge. I do like the sound of that."

CHAPTER FIFTY-SEVEN

When I got back to my motorhome, I called Anna.

"Anna, good news. Polly agreed to take over as temporary park manager. She's going to start today and will be working to get everything caught up."

"Walker, the owner will be happy to hear that. But what about the missing money? I spoke to the owner last night and she said if the money doesn't show up soon, she'll have to sell. She's still thinking the quickest way is to sell to a developer."

"Anna, you already told me that. Has she given you a price yet?"

"No, not yet. As soon as she does, I'll let you know."

We ended the call.

I was supposed to meet Agent Harris at ten, which gave me just under an hour to get things ready. He hadn't said to come alone, and I figured having a witness might be a good idea, so I decided to pay Buck a visit.

Polly had told me Buck enjoyed our little Homeland Security adventure and wanted to tag along next time I went out. So maybe he'd want to go with me to meet with Harris. Buck could be my wing man—a witness should something unexpected happen.

I walked down to his bus and pressed the doorbell. Instead of the normal "Ding dong," the doorbell played the first few bars of the theme song from Buck's long ago TV show. Funny how, after all these years, I still recognized the tune.

A moment later, Buck met me at the door wearing a silk western shirt, jeans, cowboy boots, and a smile on his face.

"Walker, good to see you. What have you got going on today?"

"I'm meeting with Agent Harris in about an hour. Thought you might like to come along. Not sure what the meeting's about, but it could be interesting."

Buck smiled. "That sounds like fun. Let me grab my things and we can head out."

"Buck, no gun. Leave it here."

Buck shook his head. "Couldn't take my gun if I wanted to. Homeland Security took it from me the other night, and they still have it. Maybe Harris can get it back for me."

I nodded. "Yeah, maybe."

While Buck got ready for our meeting with Harris, I walked back to my motorhome, got the Jeep and took it up to Buck's place.

He was waiting when I pulled into his driveway. He got in the Jeep and said, "Walker, hanging around with you is like being a character in one of my movies. You just never know what's going to happen next. I like it."

We arrived at Lemon Bay Park about ten minutes early. There were no other cars in the parking lot, and unless he was hiding, Agent Harris hadn't shown up yet.

I got out of the Jeep and walked over to the park bulletin board to check out the park map. It showed several walking trails, a kayak launch, and something called "Alligator Pond".

I turned to Buck. "They've got an alligator pond. You want to go over there and take a look?"

He shook his head. "No. I've seen plenty of gators. You go ahead, I'll wait here."

He stayed in the Jeep while I walked to Alligator Pond. The trail wound through a tropical forest bounded by tall ferns and shaded by oaks and large palms. Thirty feet in and it felt like civilization was a thousand miles away.

After a hundred yards, the trail rose slightly to a narrow,

wooden bridge overlooking a pea-green water feature. A small placard on the bridge railing said, "Alligator Pond."

Visitors were warned not to feed the alligators or to swim in the water. You'd think a warning sign near an attraction called "Alligator Pond" would be unnecessary. But having seen my share of tourists doing stupid things, the sign was definitely needed.

In the six months I'd lived in Florida, I'd seen several alligators, mostly around creek banks and in slow moving rivers. I was always amazed these prehistoric creatures lived close to so many humans and yet there were so few alligator attacks each year.

I was thinking about this when I heard a horn back in the parking lot. Buck letting me know Agent Harris had arrived. Not wanting to keep them waiting, I turned and walked back the way I had come.

When I reached the parking lot, I saw that a black, four-door Suburban with heavily tinted windows had pulled up beside my Jeep. Agent Harris had gotten out and was standing near the passenger side of the Jeep, talking with Buck. They were both smiling and acting like old friends swapping war stories.

I walked up to Harris. "I see you made it."

He smiled. "Yeah, just got here. See any gators in the pond?"

I shook my head. "No. But I don't doubt there's at least one in there."

Harris nodded. "There is. I've seen it."

He pointed toward his Suburban. "Let's me and you have a talk."

"Sure, but let's talk out here."

Harris frowned. "I'd rather talk to you privately. Inside the car."

I shook my head. "No, I'd like Buck to hear whatever you have to say. Just in case there is a misunderstanding later on."

Harris looked around. There were no other cars in the lot. No reason not to talk out there.

"Here is fine."

He looked up at the blue sky then back at me.

"Walker, here's the thing. We lost you and the drugs. The GPS tracker in the package doesn't seem to be working.

"Since we have to account for the drugs, we need to find them or the person who has them.

"Since you were the last person who had the drugs, we start our search with you.

I nodded. "That makes sense."

"So, Walker, the question is, do you still have the drugs?"

I shook my head. "Of course not. I did the exchange as planned. You know that."

"No I don't know that at all. In fact, all we really know is we gave you the drugs and you were supposed to do the exchange in the funeral home parking lot. But it didn't go that way, did it?"

I shook my head. "No, it didn't go that way. If your guys had been there as planned, they would know that Darrell called and had me meet him on an island near Stump Pass.

"That's where the exchange took place."

Harris nodded. "But where's the proof? How do we prove the deal went down the way you say it did?"

I was starting to get angry but didn't want to show it. I took a breath then said, "Look, if your guys were in place, like you promised, they would have seen everything. They would know the exchange took place on the island."

Harris smiled. "Okay, so let's say I believe you. What did the guy look like? The one you gave the drugs to?"

I shook my head. "I don't know. He was wearing a mask."

"A mask? What kind of mask?"

"A full face fishing mask. The kind that fishing guides wear to protect them from the sun.

"The mask covered his face, dark sunglasses hid his eyes. A long sleeve shirt covered his arms. Other than him being about two inches shorter than me, there's not much else I can tell you."

Harris frowned. "So let me get this straight. You exchanged ten pounds of pot, worth about forty grand, with some guy wearing a mask?"

When he put it like that, it did sound kind of fishy. But it was the truth. I didn't hesitate to tell him so.

"Harris, I delivered the drugs to Darrell. I got the dog back. Your guys screwed up, not me."

Harris crossed his arms and stared at me. He pressed his lips together and slowly shook his head.

A minute passed then he said, "Tell me everything. Start with when you got to the funeral home parking lot."

I told him the whole story, leaving out no detail. From the time I reached the funeral home parking lot until I was rescued at Chadwick Park.

When I finished, he said, "I've got a couple of questions.

"First, what did you do with the phone you found on the dock? The one that Darrell used to give you instructions?"

"I left it in the boat. Darrell has the boat now and the phone."

"Okay, after you gave him the drugs, you say he headed south toward Stump Pass?"

I nodded. "That's right, he went south."

Harris shook his head. "See, there's a problem with that. The Coast Guard was set up at the mouth of Stump Pass and checked every boat that came through.

"Your guy never made it to the checkpoint."

I thought about it for a moment. "Well, maybe he turned

around, went behind the island and headed back north. That'd make more sense than him taking the small boat through the pass."

Harris nodded. "Yeah, he could have done that. But the Coast Guard had another checkpoint at the Manasota Key Bridge. If he had gone north, they would have stopped him there.

"So no matter which way he went, he should have run into a Coast Guard checkpoint. But there's no record of someone in a small boat being stopped that morning.

"That creates a problem for you. We can't verify you gave the drugs to anyone. For all we know, you kept the drugs for yourself."

I shook my head, the anger threatening to boil over. "I can't believe this. You set this whole thing up. It's your fault your guys weren't there to see it happen. And now you blame me?

"I didn't keep the drugs. I followed the plan and traded them for the dog. Then I sat out there on that sandbar for hours waiting for your guys to rescue me, and they never showed up.

"And there *are* witnesses to the exchange. At least one trawler went by while I was on the beach with Darrell. Three girls on top waved, and I waved back.

"If the Coast Guard stopped all the boats, they'll have a record of the trawler. Contact the boat's owner. Ask him what he saw."

Harris smiled. "Walker, I believe you. But the problem is we don't have the guy or the drugs. Somebody has to take the fall for the missing product."

Buck had stayed quiet until he heard this, but at this point he'd had enough. "Walker isn't going to take the fall. He didn't take the drugs. He got the dog back. He's got witnesses that saw the deal go down.

"If you try to pin this on him, I'll go to the media. I'll tell them everything. How you put this plan in motion and then pulled your agents and left Walker hanging out there without backup.

"With me involved, this'll be a national story. All the networks will want a piece of it. It'll be a media feeding frenzy. 'Feds abandon civic-minded volunteer to fend off drug cartel on his own.' How does that sound?"

Harris studied Buck for a moment.

"There's no need to get the press involved. Maybe there's another way we can resolve this.

"All you need to do is find Eddie."

CHAPTER FIFTY-EIGHT

"Eddie? Why do I need to find Eddie?"

Harris smiled. "Because Eddie is your connection to Darrell. If you can find Eddie, maybe he can lead you to Darrell."

I shook my head. "So why aren't your guys out looking for Eddie? He's your confidential informant. Don't you know where he is?"

"Walker, believe me, if we weren't involved in this missile thing, we'd be out looking for him. But we're kind of short-handed right now.

"But you and Buck should have no problem finding him. You were with him the night the house on Pandora blew up. And before then you were there when he crashed his bike into the car on River Road.

"So I figure you and Eddie must be good buddies."

I laughed. "You've gotta be kidding. I've only seen Eddie twice in my life. That was two times too many. I have no idea where he lives or hangs out."

Harris shook his head. "That's too bad. Because if you could find Eddie, and Eddie could find Darrell, we could go pick him up.

"And you, Mr. Walker, would be off the hook. This thing would be over."

I shook my head. "I cannot believe how messed up this is. You want *me* to do *your* work for you? To go track down Eddie and then Darrell?"

Harris didn't answer. He just smiled.

Buck tapped me on the arm then whispered, "This is good. I can use it in my movie script. Let's do it."

I turned to Harris. "Okay, so let's say we're able to find Eddie and he tells us where Darrell is. Then what?"

Harris reached into his pocket and pulled out a phone. "Use this to call me. There's only one number programmed into it. Mine. Don't call anyone else, just me. Don't try to apprehend Darrell on your own. Just locate him and call me."

I took the phone and shoved it into my pants pocket. "Got it. Locate Darrell. Call you and we're out of it, right?"

Harris nodded. "Yes, if you can find Darrell, we'll pick him up and you'll be in the clear."

He then looked at his watch. "Well guys, it's always good to see you. But I've got somewhere I need to be right now. Walker, don't leave town until this is resolved."

He tossed us a salute, walked to his Suburban and drove off.

Buck looked at me and smiled. "That went well."

I frowned. "What are you talking about? He blames me for losing the pot. I can't leave town. He wants me to do his job and find the drug dealer."

Still smiling, Buck said, "It could've been a lot worse. He could have put you in cuffs and hauled you off to wherever Homeland Security keeps people these days.

"As it is, you're still free. And I got my gun back."

"You got your gun back? When did that happen?"

"When you were over at the gator pond. Harris drove up and I asked about my gun.

"He had it with him. Gave it back to me. No bullets though."

"So you got your gun back, and I got screwed. Doesn't seem quite fair."

"Walker, look at it this way. Homeland Security is asking for your help. All you have to do is find Eddie and ask him where

Darrell is.

"That shouldn't be too difficult. You've got me to help. Plus we've got insurance."

"Insurance? What kind of insurance?"

Buck reached into his shirt pocket and pulled out his phone. He pressed "Play" on the audio recorder app.

The phone began playing back my conversation with Harris, starting with, "See any gators?"

"You recorded it?"

"Yep, got everything. This will be our insurance. We can give this to the media if Harris doesn't honor the deal."

Suddenly relieved, I shook my head and laughed. "I like it. We've got insurance. Now all we have to do is find Eddie. Any suggestions for how we should start?"

Buck smiled. "I was in a movie once where we had to track some people down. We started by having lunch. It worked out fine.

"So I suggest we start by calling Polly. Ask her if we can bring her lunch. She's probably getting hungry about now; what with all the work you've got her doing in the Serenity Cove office."

Buck was right. It was nearly lunchtime, and it would be a good idea to offer to take some food to Polly.

"You want me to call her?"

Buck smiled. "Let me call."

He punched her number into his phone and walked away a few steps so I couldn't hear the conversation. Probably sweet nothings I didn't want to hear anyway.

When the call ended, Buck walked back over. "She said bring her a turkey sandwich and a Coke, please.

"She said she's found something on the computer you'd be interested in. She didn't say what but said you'd definitely want to see it."

Maybe Polly had located the missing money. I sure hoped so.

Buck and I got into the Jeep and headed to the local deli to pick up lunch. From there we headed back to Serenity Cove, by way of Dearborn Street. As we passed the library, I remembered what Eddie had told us about the place.

He said the back parking lot was a good spot to hang out after dark. Nobody hassled him there, and if he passed out, he'd get a good night's sleep without being disturbed.

Maybe we'd find Eddie there later on that night.

When we pulled into Serenity Cove, we could see the lights in the manager's office were on and the "Open" sign had been placed on the front door once again.

Inside, Polly was sitting at the desk, entering something into the computer. She looked up at us and smiled.

I wasn't sure whether she was happy to see us or happy to see the food we had brought with us. Either way, it was good to see her smile.

Buck walked over and kissed her on the top of the head. "We brought you lunch."

He started to spread the sandwiches out on her desk, but she stopped him. "Oh, no you don't. I've just finished cleaning this up and you're not going to mess it up with food."

She pointed to the open door behind her. "We're going into the apartment to eat like civilized people at the kitchen table."

She led the way and we followed.

When I walked in, I noticed the change. The night before, the room had been dark and uninviting. But with Polly as manager, it was totally different. The shades had been opened and sunlight streamed in. The windows had been raised and a fresh breeze had replaced the stale air.

The counter tops, sink, and kitchen table gleamed. The floor looked like it had been swept.

"So," asked Polly, "what do you think?"

I smiled. "I can't believe it. In just a few hours, you've totally transformed this place. It actually looks livable. You didn't have to do all this."

She smiled. "I know. But once I got started, it was hard to stop. And being the Queen of Serenity Cove, I wanted things to be nice around here. There was no one else to do it, so I did it myself.

"And you know what? I liked it. In fact, I was even thinking I might apply for the permanent position. Queen of Serenity Cove."

I smiled. "Be careful of what you wish for; because if you apply, you just might get the job."

She started unwrapping her sandwich then stopped. "Wait until I show you what I found. You're going to be amazed."

Intrigued, I asked, "What? Tell me."

She shook her head. "Not now. I want to eat first. Then I'll show you."

We took our time eating our sandwiches. It was good to sit around a kitchen table with people I liked.

After we finished and cleaned up our napkins and wrappers —at Polly's insistence—we went back into the front office.

Polly sat down at the manager's desk and pointed to the computer screen. "While working this morning, I found a spreadsheet that showed monthly income and expenses for Serenity Cove.

"Among other things, it breaks out monthly rental income for each site in the park. Right away, I noticed it showed ten sites as being vacant and not producing any income.

"But if you walk through the park, you'll see that none of those sites are actually vacant. In fact, we don't have any vacancies.

"I called one of the people on the list and they assured me that they had been paying rent. They even offered to show me their canceled checks.

"Each of those spots rents for $500 a month, which means the manager was under reporting monthly income by at least $5,000.

"I checked the previous four months, and it was the same. And it doesn't stop there. If you look at expenses, you'll see there's a $500 entry each month for pool services.

"I know for a fact no one has serviced the pool for months. I called the pool company and they said the service was canceled more than a year ago. That means the manager was showing expenses and cutting checks for work that wasn't being done."

Polly swiveled her chair to face us. "The way I figure it, he was scamming the owner out of well over five thousand a month. And he was being paid a salary to do it."

Buck was impressed. "You figured out all this since this morning? Maybe I ought to get you to go over my books."

She beamed with pride.

I smiled. "Polly, you are amazing. But don't tell anyone about this. And keep digging. If you find anything else, let me know."

She smiled. "That's not all I found. Check this out."

She swiveled her chair back around so she was facing the computer screen. "I checked the browser history to see what the manager had been looking at on the web, and I found this."

She clicked a link and the screen showed a sales page from Amazon for a full face sun protection mask. The kind Darrell had been wearing on the beach.

I was stunned. "You've got to be kidding me. The manager was looking at fishing masks on Amazon? Can you tell if he bought one?"

She clicked a few keys, and the page reloaded displaying a message that read, "Instant Order Update. You purchased this item on. . ."

The date shown was ten days ago. The item had been shipped directly to the Serenity Cove office.

CHAPTER FIFTY-NINE

"So, the embezzling manager of Serenity Cove ordered a face mask just like the one Oscar's dognapper was wearing? Are you sure?"

Polly pointed at the computer screen. "That's what it shows on Amazon. He ordered the mask ten days ago using this computer. He had it shipped here and it arrived three days later."

I leaned in and saw that the mask looked exactly like the one worn by the man I'd met on the beach.

"That's pretty interesting."

Polly looked up from the screen. "I thought so. It means that S.O.B. manager is probably the one who broke into my trailer and took Oscar."

I shook my head. "Polly, we don't know that for sure. Just because he ordered a fishing mask doesn't mean he's the guy. But it is pretty strange that he ordered the exact mask the guy was wearing.

"It's also strange that he disappeared about the same time Oscar was taken."

She shook her head. "I never trusted that man. I knew he was up to no good, but I never imagined he would pull something like this."

Buck put his hand on her shoulder. "Polly, we don't know for sure he's the guy. But Walker and I are going to find out. We'll be out looking for him tonight."

"What do you mean you'll be out looking for him tonight?"

Buck looked at me then back at Polly, "We're on a secret

mission for Homeland Security. They picked us out special for this.

"They want us to find this Darrell guy. Maybe he and the former manager of Serenity Cove know each other—or are the same person. Either way, we're going to be looking for him starting tonight."

Polly looked up at me. "You agreed to this?"

I nodded. "We weren't really given a choice. They said it was my fault they lost track of Darrell, and it was up to me to find him."

She stared at me for a moment then asked, "How can I help?"

Before I could answer, my phone rang. It was Anna.

I excused myself and stepped outside.

"Anna, what's up?"

"I just spoke to the owner of Serenity Cove. She's in a panic and wants to sell right away. She's afraid she's in too deep.

"She was depending on this month's rent to catch up on the payments, but now that the money is gone, she doesn't see any other option but to sell."

"Anna, what's the number? How much will it take to buy the place?"

"Walker, she said it's worth at least one point three million. But she thinks at that price, it'll take maybe a year or more to sell. And she can't wait that long.

"She told me if she could get six hundred fifty thousand for it, she'd sell it today. But she can't wait long. She needs the money now.

Anna paused then said, "Walker, would you be interested in buying at that price?"

"Maybe. Does the six fifty include your commission?"

"No. With commission, it'll come out to six hundred eighty-two thousand. When you add closing costs, figure seven hundred thousand dollars all in. That's less than you'd pay for a nice waterfront home. If I were you, I'd jump on it."

It was a good price. I had a little more than that in the bank, which meant I could buy Serenity Cove and pay cash. But doing so would deplete most of my funds. I wouldn't have much left.

"Walker, you still there?"

"Yes. Just thinking this through. Can I call you back in an hour?"

"An hour? Yes, I can hold her off for an hour. But not much longer. Call me back no later than two."

We ended the call and I walked back into the office.

Polly looked up. "Important call?"

"Kind of. I'll tell you about it later. But right now, I need to ask you another favor.

"I need you to look at the Serenity Cove books and tell me if this place can be profitable. I also need to know if there are any outstanding debts or upcoming major expenses that have to be covered.

"And I need to know all this within an hour."

Polly looked at me. "An hour? You need to know all this in one hour?"

"Yes, sooner if possible. It's important."

Polly sat down at the computer. "I'll try. But you two need to get out of here. Let me get to work."

Buck and I took the hint and stepped outside. After we were back in the Jeep, Buck turned to me. "What's up? Why do you need the numbers?"

"I'm trying to save Serenity Cove."

Buck frowned. "Why would Serenity Cove need saving?"

"Because the owner is in trouble and needs money fast. She's thinking about selling to developers who'll shut the place down and build condos.

"So, I'm trying to save it."

Buck looked at me. "How do you plan to do that?"

"I'm thinking about buying it."

"Buying it? That's going to take a lot of money. You got that kind of juice?"

"Maybe. But first I need to know if this place can be profitable. That's why I asked Polly to run the numbers."

"Well, if you need an investment partner, I might be interested. I've got a little money put away and would be willing to help to keep Serenity Cove alive."

"Good to know. But right now, I think I've got it covered."

Buck nodded. "So, when are we going to start looking for Eddie?"

"How about we start right now? I've got a newspaper clipping at my place that might help us find him."

The local newspaper had run an article about my "heroic" rescue of Eddie after he was hit by a car. Lucy had clipped the article and given it to me the day after it had run.

If I remembered correctly, the article had Eddie's full name in it. That could be helpful in finding his home address or maybe locating a relative who knew where he was staying.

Back at my place, I pulled into the driveway and turned to Buck. "I'll be right back. Gotta get something from inside."

I expected Bob to meet me at the door, but he was a no show. Most likely he was in the back, sleeping. Just to be sure, I checked. As expected, he was asleep on the bed. Curled up with his little feet tucked up under his chin.

Not wanting to disturb him, I went back up front and tried to remember where I'd put the article Lucy had given me. She had presented it to me in a small picture frame, but I didn't think she really expected me to hang it on the wall—and I hadn't.

I'd stuffed it in one of the drawers or one of the overhead

cabinets that lined the walls of the motorhome. I couldn't remember which one.

I started by looking in the most likely places. The junk drawer in the kitchen. The catch-all cabinet above the couch, the magazine rack near the reading chair.

It was in the magazine rack. A quick glance showed the article did indeed include Eddie's last name.

Booth. Eddie Booth.

Back out in the Jeep, I showed the article to Buck.

"You had it framed?"

"No, Lucy had it framed. A memento of our first night out together."

Buck took it from me. "So why is the article important?"

I pointed to the text below the photo.

"Eddie Booth. That's the guy we're looking for."

Buck frowned. "So we know his full name. But there's no address. That doesn't help much."

"Sure it does. It means we can go online, do some searches, see if we can find a phone number or a home address. Who knows, he might even have a Facebook page."

Buck shook his head. "You're kidding, right? You don't really think Eddie, a guy who lives on the street, has a Facebook page?"

I smiled. "Stranger things have happened. And it won't take long for us to find out."

I got out of the Jeep and headed for the motorhome. Buck hesitated then followed.

Inside, I fired up my computer and invited Buck to sit on the couch while I searched the internet for Eddie Booth.

"Make yourself at home. You need a drink or anything?"

Buck said no. "Too early for a drink, but if you have bottled water, that'd be good."

"It's in the fridge. Help yourself."

Behind me, I heard Buck get up and go to the fridge where he found the water. Then, instead of going back to the couch, he asked, "You got a bathroom in here?"

"Yes, it's in the back."

While Buck headed for the bathroom, I did a Google search for "Eddie Booth Englewood Florida."

Turns out, Eddie did *not* have a Facebook page. Nor did he show up as having a listed phone number.

But a quick search of Sarasota county records showed that an Edward Booth of Englewood had been arrested for public intoxication. The arrest report showed his address as "Unknown."

A second arrest report showed he had been picked up for loitering. And again, the home address was listed as "Unknown."

Neither of these would help our cause.

But a third arrest record for Edward Booth proved useful. The charge was "unlawful entry", and was filed by a woman claiming to be Eddie Booth's girlfriend.

The responding officer reported that Mr. Booth arrived at his girlfriend's home in an intoxicated state and she refused him entry. He then went to the back of the home, entered a screen porch, and passed out on a mattress on the floor.

After the responding officer questioned the complainant and determined there had been no violence, he wrote a ticket for unlawful entry, and left Mr. Booth to sleep it off.

The police record was dated just three months earlier and the street address for the girlfriend was listed.

"Hey Buck, I found something."

No response. He hadn't returned from the bathroom. He'd been in there at least ten minutes.

I sent the police report to my printer and got up to go check on Buck.

From the kitchen, I could see the bathroom door was open. Buck wasn't in there.

Going to the bedroom, I found Buck lying on my bed. His eyes were closed. Bob rested on his chest, purring.

My first thought was that Buck had a heart attack. But as I stood there looking at him, he opened his eyes and looked up at me with a sheepish grin.

"Your cat likes me."

I nodded. "It looks like he does. You okay?"

"Doing just fine. Wanted to rest a bit, and this cat decided to join me. I'm ready to go whenever you are."

"Don't get up yet. I've still got a few things I need to do on the computer."

I went back up front and picked up the printout of the police report with Eddie's girlfriend's address. I entered the address into Google and printed out a street map.

Almost an hour had passed since we'd left Polly in the office, and I wondered if she'd been able to run the numbers on the potential profitability of Serenity Cove.

As I was reaching for my phone to call her, it chimed an incoming call. From Polly.

"I was just about to call you. What have you found?"

"Good news, I think. I ran the numbers for the past three years, backing out the false expenses and adding back in the missing rents, and it painted a pretty good picture.

"It shows the average income after expenses should be around eleven thousand a month. It'll be a little lower in the summer and a little higher during snowbird season.

"The annual income before taxes would be about one hundred thirty thousand dollars a year."

I let this sink in. Serenity Cove could be a very profitable business. At a hundred thousand a year profit, it could repay my investment in less than eight years.

"Polly, that's pretty impressive. Serenity Cove should be a profitable business."

"It would be, as long as you don't have a manager stealing you blind."

"So, Polly, what kind of unexpected expenses could the park owner face?"

"I figured you might ask that. The three biggies are utilities, property taxes and liability insurance.

"Since the park is primarily a vacant lot with forty-eight parking slabs and just one small building, property taxes aren't bad.

"Insurance is a different story. It's been going up every year. Having a pool, water frontage and paying guests means higher rates. It works out to about fifteen hundred a month.

"The biggest bill is park utilities. Over the course of a year, they average about six thousand a month. Lower during the winter and spring, and higher in the summer.

"Still, with forty-eight sites paying an average of five hundred a month, the income more than covers the expenses and leaves a pretty good profit."

"Polly, that's definitely good news. Just one more question. If I bought Serenity Cove, would you consider being the full-time park manager?"

CHAPTER SIXTY

"Walker, you're really thinking about buying Serenity Cove?"

"I am. That's why I asked you to pull together the numbers."

She frowned. "I didn't know Serenity Cove was for sale."

"It wasn't. But the owner isn't too happy with the manager running off with the rents. She says she doesn't want to deal with it anymore and was talking about selling the place to developers.

"I don't want to see that happen, so I'm thinking about buying it myself just to keep it out of their hands.

"So, Polly, if I buy Serenity Cove, would you consider being the full-time manager?"

She didn't hesitate. "Yes, in a heartbeat. I'd love to do it.

"And Walker, if you need some help buying the place, let me know. I've got some money saved up and Serenity Cove sounds like a pretty good investment."

"Polly, it does sound like a good investment. With you as the manager, it'll be even better. I'll let you know how it works out."

We ended the call.

Buck was standing behind me holding Mango Bob. "Who was that?"

"Polly. I asked her if she would consider being the manager of Serenity Cove if I bought it."

"What'd she say?"

"She said yes. Even said she'd like to help me buy the place."

Buck smiled. "She's a smart woman. Investing in Serenity

Cove might be a good move."

I nodded. "I notice you're holding my cat."

"I am. He wanted me to pick him up, carry him around. So I did. He's been purring ever since."

I shook my head. "Bob usually doesn't let anyone pick him up. Including me. He's pretty particular that way."

Buck smiled. "Well, he seems to like it now. So that's his name? Bob?"

"Yes. Mango Bob."

Bob heard me say his name and decided he had been held long enough. He pushed on Buck's chest with his front paws, and Buck put him down on the floor.

We watched as Bob trotted back to the bedroom. After he disappeared, I turned to Buck.

"While you were back there charming my cat, I found something that might help us find Eddie. He's got a girlfriend here in Englewood, and I found her address."

I showed him the printout of the police report.

Buck pulled a pair of reading glasses from his pocket and looked at the report.

My phone chimed with another incoming call. This time from Anna.

"Anna, I was just getting ready to call you."

"Good because I have the listing for Serenity Cove in my hands, and am about to enter it into the MLS."

"Don't do that. I'll buy the place. Write up the offer and I'll be over in a few minutes to sign it."

"Walker, are you sure about this? She's listed it at six hundred eighty thousand. She's looking for a cash deal. No time to wait for a buyer to arrange financing."

"Anna, I'm sure. Write it up as an all cash offer. Conditioned on no liens, no liabilities, clean title and survey."

"Walker, you're sure? All cash?"

"Yes, all cash. I can write you a check for the full amount."

"Walker, you're full of surprises. Unemployed, living in a motorhome, and able to pay cash for a waterfront resort."

"Anna, it'll take most of what I have, but I think it'll be worth it."

"Walker, Serenity Cove is going to be a good investment, you'll see. I'll write the offer and have it ready by the time you get here. Let's get it signed and in her hands before she changes her mind."

We ended the call.

Buck was still standing behind me with the police report in his hands. "So you're buying Serenity Cove?"

"It looks that way."

"You need any help? Because I've got money to invest."

"Thanks for the offer, but I think I can do it on my own. I'll let you know if that changes."

He nodded. "What about us finding Eddie? Has that changed?"

"No. We're still going to do that. We just need to stop by Anna's office so I can sign the offer. Then we'll go look for Eddie."

Buck smiled. "Good. Can we take Mango Bob with us?"

"No. Bob stays here."

Buck and I headed over to Anna's office which was four miles and one stoplight from Serenity Cove.

As promised, she had the offer ready when we arrived.

"Here it is. Full price, all cash."

I scanned the offer and saw she had added the contingencies I'd requested. She'd also added, "Expires in twenty-four hours."

"Nice touch on the expiration. It'll encourage the seller to

293

accept and we can get the deal done quickly."

I signed the offer and handed it back to Anna.

She smiled. "I'll call and let her know. Hopefully we can get her to accept it before the day is over."

"Good. Call me as soon as you hear back."

She pointed to my Jeep in the parking lot. "Who's your friend out there? He looks familiar but I can't place him."

"That's Buck. I'll introduce you later. But right now we're in kind of a hurry."

She gave me a hug. "If this deal goes through, you'll have to help me celebrate another big commission check."

I smiled. "Plan on it."

Back out in the Jeep, Buck was looking at a street map of Englewood.

"Where'd you get that?"

"They had a rack of them outside the real estate office. I figured it might be helpful to have a map of the whole town."

I nodded. "You find the street that Eddie's girlfriend lives on?"

"Yep. It's off East Dearborn, three streets up from Publix. You drive; I'll show you where to turn."

We headed out. No real plan. Just flying by the seat of our pants.

It took seven minutes to reach the stoplight at Dearborn. It was red when we got there.

"Turn left here then get in the left lane."

When the light turned green, I let ongoing traffic clear, and then turned left and stayed in the left lane.

Buck pointed ahead. "Look for Lee Circle. It'll be on the left."

He was right. Lee Circle. On the left.

"Look for 121. That's her address."

Lee circle was a cul-de-sac. A fancy name for a dead end street that ended with a turning circle.

The houses on the street were modest, one-story, block construction. Most showed pride of ownership. Yards were well kept, lawns were mowed, no junker cars parked in the street.

The house numbers started at 60 and went up. We were looking for 121. Buck called off the house numbers as we cruised slowly down the street.

"70. 75. 80. 85. 90. 100. 115. 120. 125."

I stopped. "Where's 121? Did we miss it?"

Buck looked over his shoulder. "Back up. It's gotta be between 120 and 125."

Putting the Jeep in reverse, I backed up until we reached the driveway that had 120 painted on the mailbox. An older man stood in the yard with a water hose in his hand. He looked up and waved.

I turned to Buck. "I'm getting out. See if the neighbor knows where 121 is."

I walked over to the man in the yard and greeted him with a smile. "I think we may be lost. We're looking for 121 Lee Circle."

The man laughed. "You must be looking for Eddie or Edith. They always give their address as 121. But there's no 121."

I nodded. "So that's why we couldn't find it."

He looked at me and then at the Jeep. "You the law? Eddie in trouble again?"

"No, I'm not the law. As far as I know, Eddie's not in trouble. We're just trying to find him."

"Friends of Eddie, huh? You don't look like the kind of people Eddie generally hangs out with."

I took that as a compliment.

I smiled. "Eddie's not in trouble. We just need to talk with him for a minute."

The man looked at my Jeep. "That your Jeep?"

"Yes sir, it is."

"Had it long?"

"About a month."

"You the one who rescued Eddie when he was hit on his bicycle?"

"How'd you know about that?"

"It was in the paper. Eddie showed us the picture. Had your Jeep in the photo."

I nodded. "Yes sir, that was me."

"Well, I guess it won't hurt to tell you where Eddie and Edith live."

He pointed toward an overgrown vacant lot at the end of the street. "They live down there. Park on the street and follow the path back to the house.

"Used to be a driveway, but neither of them have a car, so they let it get overgrown. Edith says she likes it that way."

I thanked him and went back to the Jeep.

Buck looked at me. "You find out where they live?"

"Yep, down there behind that vacant lot."

"We going to drive in or walk?"

"Walk. Edith doesn't like cars back there."

"Who's Edith?"

"You're about to find out."

CHAPTER SIXTY-ONE

We parked the Jeep on the street and headed down the overgrown path. What had once been a well landscaped lot with carefully placed palms, palmettos, and citrus trees had through neglect become a tropical jungle.

According to the neighbor, this was the way Edith and Eddie liked it. It gave them privacy and made their home invisible from the street.

I wondered about dogs. People who like their privacy often have dogs. Big ones. I hadn't asked the neighbor whether Edith and Eddie had dogs or not.

I should have.

Forty feet in, the path curved to the left and led us to a clearing. In the center stood a small cottage, white with lime-green shutters, metal roof and a small screened-in front porch.

It wasn't what I expected. The house was well maintained, the porch spotless. No appliances in the yard, no abandoned cars, no junk lying around.

We stopped and took it all in.

Buck spoke first. "Not what I expected."

"Yeah, a pleasant surprise."

"You think this is the right place?"

"According to the neighbor, this is where Eddie lives. With Edith."

"Think they're home?"

"One way to find out."

As we got closer to the house, the crunch of our footsteps on the white shell path alerted a dog to our presence.

Fortunately, the dog was small and inside the screened-in porch. It could see us, and it could bark, but it didn't look like it was going to cause any trouble as long as we stayed outside.

The dog continued to bark as we got closer to the house, and a heavy-set woman, maybe in her fifties, wearing cut off sweat pants and a white T-shirt, came out into the porch.

She pointed at the dog. "Hush up, baby."

The dog immediately stopped barking and moved to the woman's side.

She pushed the screen door open and the small dog rushed us, wagging its tail as it ran. It went straight to Buck and sat down in front of him, apparently waiting to be petted.

"You boys looking for Eddie?"

"Yes ma'am. We are."

"You the law?"

"No ma'am. We're not."

The woman opened the screen door and stepped out cigarette in hand.

"What do you want with Eddie?"

Buck, who had been leaning over petting the dog, stood up and walked past me.

"Ma'am, My name is Buck Waverly. I'm in town scouting movie locations, and Eddie was helping us."

The woman smiled. "I know who you are. I've seen all your movies. Especially the ones with that girl actor. What's her name again?

"Eddie told me he met up with a movie star the other night, but I didn't believe him. Eddie's always coming up with wild stories."

She took a drag on her cigarette. "So, you're the movie star?"

"Yes ma'am, I am. And we need Eddie's help. Plus we may

have a part for him in our movie."

"Really! Eddie in a movie. Wouldn't that be something?"

"Yes ma'am, it would be. Anyway, we need to talk to Eddie about it today. Can you tell us where we can find him?"

The woman took a final drag of her cigarette, and dropped the butt in a coffee can beside the door.

"So this movie? How much does Eddie get paid for doing it? And don't call me ma'am. My name is Edith."

Buck smiled. "Well, Edith, if we can find Eddie and if we can get him in the movie, he'll get paid three hundred dollars a day. We might need him for three or four days."

Edith paused as she calculated how much money we were talking about. Then she asked, "What about me? Any parts in that movie for me?"

"Maybe. But only if we can find Eddie."

She smiled. "What part would I play in the movie?"

Buck looked over at me then back at Edith. "Eddie's girlfriend. You could be his girlfriend in the movie."

Edith smiled. "How much would that pay?"

Buck explained the movie was still in pre-production, and if he couldn't find Eddie that day, there wouldn't be parts for either one of them.

Edith frowned then said, "Well, if you're looking for Eddie, you probably won't find him until after dark.

"During the day, I don't know where he goes. He says he has a job washing trucks at the roofing company, but I don't believe him.

"He also says he has a job cleaning the bait tanks at the convenience store on Dearborn. That might be why he sometimes comes home smelling like fish.

"All I know for sure is by dark he's usually made enough money to buy a twelve pack of beer, and he'll hang out behind the library and drink with his friends until it's all gone. Then he'll come staggering home to me. Usually just before sunup."

Buck nodded. "Edith, does Eddie have a phone?"

"Yeah, he's got one. It's inside on the kitchen counter. He never takes it with him. Never checks his messages. I doubt he's turned it on in the past month.

"If you want to find him, come back here around eight tomorrow morning and you'll likely see him sleeping on the back porch. Or look around Dearborn Street after dark tonight."

Buck pulled a business card from his pocket and wrote a number on the back. He handed it to Edith. "If you see him, have him call this number."

As Buck turned to go, Edith reached out and grabbed his arm. "Wait. You can't leave yet. I need to get a picture!"

She pulled a cell phone from inside her bra and pointed it at Buck.

"Go over there and pick up my little Taco. I want to get a picture of you petting him."

Buck smiled and walked over to the dog. As soon as Buck got close, the dog lay down, rolled over onto its back and put his feet in the air.

"Ain't that just the sweetest thing!" Edith hollered. "Rub his belly!"

Buck rubbed the dog's belly, and Edith took a photo.

Edith beamed. "That came out real nice. Wait till Eddie sees it."

We thanked Edith for her help and walked back to the Jeep. After we were buckled in, I asked, "You gave her your phone number?"

Buck laughed and shook his head. "No. I gave her yours. She'll probably be calling you about a part in a movie."

We'd spent thirty minutes at Edith's and learned we'd probably have the best chance of finding Eddie after dark.

Since we had two hours of daylight left, we decided to go back to Serenity Cove and check on Polly.

When we arrived at the office, she was inside and in a good mood. "You just missed the locksmith. He changed all the door locks and checked the windows. Found two broken locks in the back, which he fixed. The bill is on my desk. He said we could mail in the payment."

She dangled a set of keys. "He gave me two sets of keys for the new locks. You want me to keep one?"

I nodded. "You're the office manager. You'll need office keys."

My phone chimed. Anna.

I stepped outside to take the call.

"Walker, just talked to the seller. She's signed the offer. But with one condition. You can't call the police on the former manager. She doesn't want anything on record about what he did."

I shrugged. "Fine with me. I wasn't planning to call the police anyway. It's her money that was taken, not mine. It'd be up to her to press charges, not me. Not sure why she'd even bring that up."

"I agree; it's strange she made me include it in the offer. But she was adamant. No police."

"Anything else?"

"Yes. She's already contacted her bank and told them about the sale. They're going to work to push it through quickly.

"We might be able to close within ten days—as long as you can come up with a certified check for the full amount."

"I can do that. Just let me know a day ahead so I can get to the bank."

"Will do."

We ended the call.

When I stepped back inside the office, Buck was sitting on

Polly's desk, his back to me, whispering to her. When Polly saw me, she asked, "Good news?"

I nodded. "Yes. It looks like I'm going to be the new owner of Serenity Cove. Probably close the deal within two weeks."

She smiled. "That's great! Does that mean I'll still be the park manager or will you be taking over?"

I shook my head. "I'm not the manager type. You've got the job for as long as you want it."

CHAPTER SIXTY-TWO

Buck told Polly about our day. How we'd met Edith and where we'd have the best chance of finding Eddie after dark.

"So," asked Polly, "you're going to go out and look for Eddie tonight?"

"Yes," I answered. "That's what I'm going to do."

Buck stood. "And I'm going with him."

I shook my head. "Buck, you've had a long day. Why don't you stay home with Polly tonight? I can hunt for Eddie by myself."

Buck seemed hurt by my suggestion. "Walker, I may be a few years older than you, but that doesn't mean I can't keep up. Don't ever think otherwise. You're not leaving me behind. I'm going with you tonight to find Eddie."

I nodded. "Okay, if you're sure. I'll pick you up around eight thirty."

Polly stood and jangled the office keys. "Guys, it's after five. Time to close up and go home."

After Polly locked the doors, we got in my Jeep and headed into the park. Buck was in the front seat, so I dropped him at his place first.

After he got out, he walked around to my window and said, "Don't forget. I'm going with you tonight."

I nodded. "I won't forget. I'll pick you up at eight thirty."

Buck gave me a thumbs up, turned and headed for the door of his bus.

Once he was inside, I drove Polly back to her trailer. Before she got out she turned to me. "Walker, I'm trusting you to make sure nothing bad happens to Buck. He's in this because of me and I don't want to see him get hurt."

I smiled. "Polly, I don't want to see Buck get hurt either. We'll take it easy, and if things go south, we'll come home."

She pointed her finger at me. "I'm counting on you. Don't let him get hurt."

Bob was waiting for me at the door. He nudged my ankle with his head and then ran to the back bedroom. Expecting me to follow.

I would, but I wanted to check something else first. Ever since Polly's trailer had been trashed, I felt like mine was going to be next. So far, I'd been wrong.

Still I had a feeling I needed to check just to be sure. I flipped on the lights and saw all was well. Nothing had been disturbed. Everything was in its place, just as I had left it.

Bob was still in the back, waiting for me to join him. Not wanting to disappoint him, I went back to see what he had to show me.

As soon as I walked into the bathroom, I knew what it was. I'd neglected his litter box for three days, which was two days too many. It was full, and Bob didn't like a full box.

When he isn't happy, he'll let you know about it. If you didn't fix the problem, he wouldn't let you sleep. And if you neglected his litter box too many days in a row, he'd leave you a little present—somewhere you wouldn't miss it. Like in a shoe.

He'd only done this once before, and I learned real quick. When Bob says his litter box needs to be cleaned, it's time to clean it.

Using the plastic scoop I kept near the box, I cleaned out the lumps, raked the sand, and poured in new litter.

Bob would be happy.

After I washed my hands, I microwaved a frozen dinner and ate while checking my email. I didn't find anything important, just the daily load of spam—which I deleted.

After turning off the computer, I cleared away my dinner and stretched out on the couch.

Three hours later, I woke to someone knocking on my door. "Walker, you in there?"

It was Buck. "Yeah, I'm here. Give me a minute."

I stood, shook off the sleep, and opened the door. Buck was standing there in a black shirt, black pants, and a black ball cap.

"You were supposed to pick me up at eight thirty. Almost an hour ago. You been sleeping?"

"Yeah, I must have dozed off."

"Well, it's dark outside. Time to go round up Eddie."

I nodded. "Let me grab my shoes."

Buck laughed. "You were worried about me keeping up with you? Looks like you're the one who needed to stay home tonight."

He was right. I'd had a busy few days and it would have been nice to stay in that night. But that wasn't going to happen. We needed to find Eddie.

I grabbed a bottle of water, keys, wallet and phone, and followed Buck out the door. I took special care to lock the motorhome behind me. Didn't want to make it too easy for anyone to break in.

Inside the Jeep, Buck asked, "So, what's the plan? We heading to the library first?"

"Yeah, that's what Edith said. Look there first."

It took us just six minutes to get from Serenity Cove to the Elsie Quirk Library. Three streets, no stoplights, and almost no traffic.

The library, a large, one-story, buff brick building, was surrounded on four sides by a paved, well-marked parking lot. A wide sidewalk wrapped around the entire building, making it easy for patrons to reach the front door, regardless of where they parked.

Floor to ceiling windows on the front and back of the building provided natural light as well as an open and airy feel for those inside. A row of six foot tall, well-manicured wax myrtles between the sidewalk and building shielded the inside from the hot Florida sun.

This time of night, the library was closed. There were no patrons inside and no cars in the parking lot.

We cruised around the building. No sign of Eddie.

Buck spoke first. "Doesn't look like he's here."

I nodded. "Let's get out. Check behind the bushes."

I pulled up on the north side of the building and parked next to a large air conditioning unit. We got out and decided it would be safer if we stuck together.

We didn't expect problems, but there was no need to take chances.

Checking the back of the building, we found a six-foot-tall wood fence around the library's dumpster. I checked behind it but no Eddie.

We continued our walk around the building, and didn't find any signs that anyone had been hiding out or drinking. No beer cans, no bottles, no trash.

Back around front, we checked the space between the row of wax myrtles and the big, plate glass windows.

Buck saw it first. "There's a bike."

I nodded. "Could be Eddie's."

We slipped into the space behind the wax myrtles. Four steps in, we heard a voice. Someone singing softly.

It was Eddie.

Not wanting to scare him, I cleared my throat, making a sound just loud enough that he would know we were there.

Hearing me, he grabbed the twelve pack of beer in front of him and started to jump up. Apparently, he didn't expect strangers and was prepared to run if anyone approached.

"Eddie, it's us," I whispered.

He turned toward my voice, a puzzled look on his face. Then he smiled. "What y'all doing over here?"

"We're looking for you."

"Well, you found me. Come on in, have a seat."

We squeezed between the wax myrtles and joined Eddie. Buck leaned against the building, while I squatted down across from Eddie.

"Am I in trouble?" he asked.

I shook my head. "No, you're not in trouble. I just need to ask you about Darrell."

Eddie took a sip from the beer he was holding. "Darrell. I figured you might have a few questions about him. You get the dog back?"

"Yep, we got him back. But I still need to find Darrell."

Eddie shook his head. "I don't think Darrell wants to be found."

"What makes you think that?"

"That's what he told me. Said too many people were looking for him. Said he's leaving town in the morning."

"You've talked to him?"

"Yep, talked to him this afternoon. Over at the convenience store. I was cleaning the bait tanks like I always do, and Darrell showed up.

"Said he was buying supplies for his trip north."

"Did he tell you where he was staying?"

"He didn't have to tell me. I know where he's staying."

"Where? Where's he staying?"

"He's in the *Toot Toot*."

Up until this point, Buck had stayed out of the conversation.

Keeping quiet, letting Eddie talk. But no longer. Upon hearing Eddie's answer to my question, Buck burst out laughing.

"The *Toot Toot*? What the hell is the *Toot Toot*?"

Eddie laughed along with Buck. Then, after catching his breath, he said, "It's from the Popeye song."

Then he started singing.

> "I'm Popeye the Sailor Man,
> I'm Popeye the Sailor Man.
> I'm strong to the finish
> 'Cause I eats my spinach.
> I'm Popeye the Sailor Man.
>
> Toot Toot."

By the time he finished singing the song, all three of us were laughing so hard we were almost crying.

I regained my composure first. "Okay, I get it, but what does that have to do with where Darrell is?"

Eddie smiled. "It's the name of his boat. The *Toot Toot*.

"It looks like a little tug boat. The kind Popeye had. So they named it *Toot Toot*. The name's painted right on the back of it."

Each time Eddie said *Toot Toot*, Buck snorted with laughter. In fact, we all laughed. It was funny.

"So Eddie, where do we find the *Toot Toot*?

Eddie pointed. "It's out on the water over past the bridge. With all them other boats."

"You mean the mooring field?"

Eddie shook his head. "I don't know what they call it. It's where you can park your boat for free. That's where Darrell keeps the *Toot Toot*."

"Is he out there tonight?"

"Don't know for sure. He usually sleeps out there. I reckon he'll be there tonight."

"Anybody with him?"

"I don't know. He don't tell me everything.

"All I know is he's got to get out of town. Supposedly he stole some money from his work and is scared the cops are looking for him."

I looked up at Buck; we were both thinking the same thing.

"He took money from work? Where'd he work?"

Eddie smiled. "You don't know? He works at the trailer park. Told me he was the manager there."

CHAPTER SIXTY-THREE

Eddie had told us what we needed to know. Darrell was hiding out on the *Toot Toot*, and planning on leaving in the morning.

I still had a few questions.

"Eddie, how did Darrell come to own the *Toot Toot*?"

Eddie took a swallow of his beer and answered. "When his dad died, his mom got the trailer park and Darrell got the boat."

I shook my head in disbelief. "So you're telling me Darrell's mom owns the trailer park where he was manager? And he stole money from her?"

"Yep, that's what he did. Stole money from his own momma. He hadn't ought to do that. I told him so. You don't steal from family.

"He said he felt real bad about it. Said he was taking the boat up to see her. Give her some of the money back. At least what's left of it."

This explained a lot. Darrell's mom owned the trailer park—Serenity Cove. Even though Darrell stole money from her, she didn't want him arrested.

"Eddie, you've been a big help. Anything you need?"

He smiled. "Not really. I got enough money to keep me happy, but not so much that I'd get myself in trouble."

"Well, if you need anything, give me a call."

I pulled a slip of paper out of my pocket and wrote a number on it and handed it to him.

Buck and I left Eddie where we found him, in his little nest behind the bushes. He kept it clean and didn't seem to be bothering anyone. It wasn't up to us to do anything about it.

Back out in the Jeep, Buck asked me, "You gave Eddie your phone number?"

I shook my head. "Nope, I gave him yours."

Buck laughed then pulled out his phone.

"Who you calling?"

"Polly. I figure we need a way to get out to the *Toot Toot*."

He made the call.

"Polly, this is Buck.

"Yeah, we're doing fine. Just need to ask a favor.

"Can we borrow your boat?

"You sure it's no problem?

"Okay, tell her we'll be over there in five minutes."

He ended the call.

"She said we could use the dinghy. Said to ask Lucy for the key to the houseboat while we're at it. Just in case."

When we arrived at Lucy's, she was waiting on the front porch.

"What have you guys gotten into now? You're taking the boat out at night?"

Buck said, "Yeah, we're taking the boat. We're going to see the *Toot Toot*."

Lucy rolled her eyes. "Whatever. Mom said to give you the keys. Said to tell you to please be safe.

"She also said to remind you there are no lights on the dinghy, so use a flashlight. And wear life jackets."

Lucy was shaking her head when we drove off with the boat trailer behind the Jeep. She didn't approve of us being out on Lemon Bay in a small boat without lights after dark.

I didn't blame her. It really wasn't a smart thing to be doing.

The Chadwick Park boat launch was the quickest access to the mooring field, so that was where we headed.

As we crossed the Manasota Key Bridge, we slowed to see if we could spot the *Toot Toot* in the mooring field, but it was too dark and too far to read the names on any of the boats anchored out there.

When we reached the park, I backed the Jeep down the boat ramp and between the two of us we were able to get the dinghy off the trailer and in the water.

I parked and locked the Jeep then met Buck back at the boat. He'd already put on one of the life jackets and handed me the other.

"Put it on."

There was no argument from me. We were going out on the water after dark in a small boat without lights. Wearing a life jacket seemed like a pretty good idea.

Our plan was to go straight across the bay to the mooring field and tie off on Polly's houseboat. From there, we hoped to be able to pick out the *Toot Toot* from the other boats anchored nearby.

The ride across the bay in the dark was an adventure. From my seat in the back, I couldn't see more than about fifteen feet in front of us, and even then all I could see was darkness.

Buck sat up front and held the flashlight. I relied on his hand signals for my navigation.

After seven minutes, he frantically motioned me to slow down, and I cut the power. Our little boat quickly came off plane and we coasted as I awaited Buck's next signal.

He pointed left, and I turned the boat in that direction. Then he moved his hand across his neck, and I killed the motor. He gave me a thumbs up and pointed the flashlight ahead.

We had reached the *Escape Artist*. Polly's houseboat.

We tied off as we had two days before and climbed aboard. Buck used the key Lucy had given him to unlock the main cabin door. He went in first, and I followed.

With all the curtains drawn, it was pitch black inside. Buck still had the flashlight and used it to point to the helm.

"Walker, you remember how to power up the boat batteries?"

"You think we'll need them?" I asked.

"Depends on how long we're going to be out here. I'd rather have the batteries powered up and not need them than need them and not have them."

Buck was right. It was probably a good idea to have power in the boat. Using Buck's flashlight, I went below and found the closet where the battery switch was and turned it to the "On" position.

I called to Buck. "Try the lights."

He flipped on a cabin light. "That's it. Come on back up."

Back in the main cabin, Buck pointed toward the curtains. "Let's keep the lights off and the curtains closed. Don't want to draw any attention."

I agreed.

We turned off the interior light and crept out onto the deck. It was a cloudless and moonless night. Very dark, except for the stars and the occasional flashing lights of jets thirty thousand feet above.

It took a few minutes for my eyes to adjust to the darkness.

Buck whispered, "Look over there. Lights."

Turning to where he was pointing, I could see one of the boats in the mooring field had its interior lights on. The window shades on the boat weren't drawn and we could see inside.

From where we were standing, we could make out a man working inside the boat. But we couldn't see clearly enough to know whether it was Darrell or not.

Buck whispered, "You think Polly has binoculars?"

I nodded. "Probably, I'll go look."

I went back into the cabin and rummaged around until I found a pair of Minolta Marine binoculars on a shelf under the helm. Taking them outside, I handed them to Buck.

"Take a look," I whispered.

He adjusted the binoculars, focusing on the man inside the boat.

"Yep, that's him. The manager of Serenity Cove."

"Okay," I said, "we've found him. Now what?"

Buck pointed to the cabin door indicating he wanted to go back inside. We turned on a low power lamp and sat down at the map table.

I spoke first. "Agent Harris said to call him when we found Darrell. That's what I'm going to do."

Buck nodded.

I pulled out the phone Harris had given me and made the call.

After ten rings, Harris answered.

"You find him?"

"Yes."

"Where?"

"He's on the *Toot Toot*."

"Say again."

"He's on the *Toot Toot*."

"Walker, are you on drugs? What the hell are you talking about?"

"It's a boat. The *Toot Toot* is a boat. Right now it's in the mooring field across from Chadwick Park. Darrell's on it. He's leaving tomorrow morning. You need to come get him now."

There was a pause on the other end of the phone. Then Harris said, "Walker, I'm glad you found Darrell. But it'll take me a few hours to arrange a boat and get my guys out there.

"Stay with him. Don't try to apprehend him. Just follow

315

him if he leaves."

He ended the call.

I looked at Buck and shook my head. "Looks like we're spending the night out here."

CHAPTER SIXTY-FOUR

"You want me to go back to shore? Get some food, maybe something to drink?"

We were sitting in the main cabin of Polly's houseboat, the *Escape Artist*. I had just told Buck what Harris had said to me. We were to stay and keep an eye on the *Toot Toot* until Harris was able to get his crew together and take over.

According to Eddie, Darrell planned to take his boat north in the morning. If he left before Harris showed up, it would be up to us to follow him.

We hadn't planned on being out all night and hadn't brought any food with us; I'd asked Buck if he wanted me to go back to shore and get some.

"No. It's too late to go back into town. Won't be anything open this late anyway. It's not like we're going to starve if we don't eat until morning."

He was right. We weren't going to starve.

He pointed to his phone. "I'm going to call Polly and let her know what's going on. She'll be worried otherwise."

"Good idea."

He made the call and filled her in on our situation. When the call ended, he smiled.

"She said there's food in the pantry. Still there from when she planned her trip. Canned beans, jerky, salami, crackers, some bottled water. Maybe other stuff too."

We checked the pantry and found the jerky and bottled water. Neither one of us was hungry enough to eat the salami, but bottled water sounded good.

With refreshments in hand, we each grabbed a folding chair and headed out on the back deck so we could keep an eye on the *Toot Toot*. For the next two hours we sat, watched the stars overhead and listened to the waves gently lapping against the hulls of nearby boats and made sure the *Toot Toot* didn't leave.

Right around midnight, the *Toot Toot* went dark. Apparently it was bedtime for Darrell.

After a few minutes, Buck whispered, "Let's go inside." He went in, and I followed.

We sat at the map table and I spoke first. "No need for both of us to stay up all night. You want to do the first watch or want me to?"

Buck yawned. "You do the first one. Wake me in three hours."

I nodded.

Buck headed off toward the guest cabin while I remained at the map table and thought about what I needed to do.

Knowing it was going to be a long night, I put my phone in vibrate mode and set two alarms. One in three hours, and a second one for twenty minutes before sunrise.

The alarms would be my insurance. If I fell asleep while on watch, the first alarm would wake me. If Buck dozed off during his watch, the second alarm would alert me before dawn.

I figured there was no way Darrell would sail off in the *Toot Toot* before daybreak. With a moonless sky and no lights on the Intracoastal, it would be foolhardy to take off in a big boat in the dark.

Still, there was no shortage of fools in this world, so it was possible Darrell would leave before daybreak. I grabbed the seat cushions from the map table and went outside on deck. I arranged the cushions so I had something soft to stretch out on, and lay down.

Out there it was so quiet that if Darrell started the motors on the *Toot Toot*, I would definitely hear them. Even if I were asleep.

Three hours later, my phone vibrated me awake. I had dozed off during my watch. I didn't know whether I'd been asleep for a few minutes or for the full three hours.

Either way, there was no harm. The *Toot Toot* was still anchored where it had been earlier. It hadn't moved.

The skies were still dark. No moon but lots of stars. The slight breeze kept the mosquitoes and no-see-ums away and added a slight chill to the early morning air.

I saw no reason to wake Buck. I had slept through my watch and felt refreshed enough to stand watch for the next three hours. With my phone set to chime twenty minutes before sunrise, it provided backup should I fall asleep again.

Three hours later, my phone chimed me awake. Again, I had slept through my watch. Looking over, I could see the *Toot Toot* was still anchored. But the cabin lights were on and there was movement on deck. As I watched, I heard the motors on the *Toot Toot* rumble to life.

Darrell was preparing to leave. We needed to be ready to follow him.

I went inside and found Buck sleeping in the guest cabin. I shook his bunk. "Buck, time to get up. Darrell is getting ready to leave."

When I was sure Buck was awake, I headed back to the main cabin and called Agent Harris.

After twelve rings, he answered.

"What?"

"Darrell is leaving. Your guys need to get here now."

"Not gonna happen. We have other priorities today."

"What do you mean 'other priorities'? You told me to find Darrell and I've found him. Now you say you have 'other priorities'?"

"That's right, Walker, we have other priorities today. That's all I can tell you. It's going to be up to you to handle this. Either follow Darrell until we can get some of our guys involved or get the drugs back from him yourself. Your choice."

He hung up.

Buck came into the cabin. "Walker, the *Toot Toot* is leaving."

Raising the window shade, I could see he was right. The *Toot Toot* was pulling away. Heading north on the Intracoastal.

It signaled its departure by sounding its horn.

Toot toot.

Just like the name of the boat.

Buck pointed at the helm of the *Escape Artist*. "You remember how to start this thing?"

I nodded. "Yeah, I think so."

Polly had shown me the steps three days earlier and I was pretty sure I remembered them.

Buck pointed at the helm. "You get the boat started and I'll get everything else ready."

Looking at the console in front of me, I followed the steps as I remembered them. I lowered the motor into the water. Turned the blowers on. Turned the fuel pump on. Set the choke. Then turned the starter key.

The motor came to life. Running rough at first, until I remembered to adjust the choke. Then it settled down into a smooth purr.

Buck gave me a thumbs up. While I'd been working with the motor, he had raised the blinds on all the windows and opened the curtains on the big sliding doors overlooking the front of the boat.

"Walker, what do you want me to do next?"

"Tie the dinghy to the mooring ball, we'll leave it here. Then unhook us and I'll get the anchor up."

Buck went to the dinghy, pulled it around to the front of the boat and latched its line to the mooring ball. Then he

320

unsnapped our line, releasing the *Escape Artist* from the ball.

While he was doing this, I found the switch on the helm labeled "Anchor." When I pressed the switch, I heard the hum of an electric motor as the anchor chain was hoisted from the bottom.

The depth of the water in the mooring field was just shy of twelve feet. It took less than a minute to raise and lock the anchor.

With the *Escape Artist* no longer tethered to the mooring ball and with the anchor up, the boat started to float free. The current of the Intracoastal began pushing us toward the nearby mangroves.

Buck came back into the cabin. "Walker, he's getting away."

I put the gear selector in forward, pushed the throttle up and steered toward the main channel. The *Escape Artist* responded. Moving slowly but not turning. I gave it a bit more power. The boat finally started to turn in the right direction.

Buck pointed at a blank display screen built into the console. "Turn that on."

I pressed the power button on the display, and after a few seconds, the screen lit up with a full color map.

"That's your GPS. The green line shows the center of the Intracoastal. Try to stay on that line. The large numbers below the map show the water depth. Make sure it stays above three feet."

I nodded.

The steering on the houseboat wasn't very responsive. When I turned the wheel it would take a few seconds for the boat to respond. This meant I needed to plan ahead to change direction.

Following the GPS track would help me stay on course, but I still needed to keep alert for obstacles, floating debris and other boats.

Fortunately, there wasn't much boat traffic that early in the morning. The sun had just come up, and the only boats we'd seen so far were small fishing boats.

The *Toot Toot* had an eight-minute head start on us, and we'd already lost sight of it.

I was shaking my head when Buck said, "We'll catch him. That tug boat of his can't go very fast and there's nowhere for him to turn off in this part of the channel."

Nodding, I pushed the throttle up another two notches and felt the *Escape Artist* slowly pick up speed.

Polly had told us the *Escape Artist* could run at nine or ten knots. Maybe even faster. Its shallow draft and light weight gave it speed that other houseboats didn't have.

Buck was standing beside me. "Just follow the line on the GPS screen. We'll catch him."

The question was, when we caught him, what then?

CHAPTER SIXTY-FIVE

For the most part, the Intracoastal Waterway from Englewood to Venice is a long, narrow canal. There are no exits to the gulf and no shortcuts.

Only after you pass the three Venice drawbridges and reach the jetty at Nokomis can you leave the Intracoastal and move out into the open waters of the Gulf of Mexico.

Unless you're an experienced sailor with the right boat and know the weather conditions, going out into the gulf—especially with a one-person crew in a tug boat—is not a good idea.

We figured Darrell probably knew this and would stay in the Intracoastal as long as he could.

It was unlikely he knew we were following him, so chances were good he was moving at a slow and safe pace and would be doing so most of the morning.

That was our big advantage.

We were behind him and knew where he was headed. Because we were behind him, we could increase our speed until he came into sight.

Twenty minutes after leaving our anchorage in the mooring field, we finally saw the *Toot Toot* in the distance. We had already passed under the north Manasota Key drawbridge, and, according to the nautical maps, we were entering the narrow section of the Intracoastal that split Venice mainland from Venice Island.

If we could catch up with the *Toot Toot* in this narrow section, we might have a chance of boarding him. Or at least getting him to stop.

Buck pointed ahead at the *Toot Toot*. "Walker, will this thing go any faster?"

To answer his question, I pushed the throttle all the way forward. The boat didn't immediately react but the speed display on the GPS showed we had reached ten knots.

For most boats at full power, ten knots is pretty slow. But we weren't in most boats. We were in a houseboat. For us, ten knots was good.

Fortunately, the *Toot Toot* was moving even slower than we were. We were starting to catch up with Darrell. If he were to look behind him, he'd see us about a hundred yards back.

I pulled the throttle back two notches, slowing the boat.

Buck looked at me. "You're slowing down?"

"Yeah, I've got an idea.

"Let's see if we can hail him on the radio. Let him think there's a Coast Guard inspection boat ahead.

"Tell him they have drug sniffing dogs and are looking for a boat carrying contraband. Maybe it'll scare him and he'll dump the drugs overboard."

Buck smiled. "You think it'll work?"

"Maybe. He probably has his marine radio on since he needs it to contact the drawbridge operators.

"You can hail his boat by name, ask him to go to a different channel, and then tell him the Coast Guard is dead ahead."

Buck smiled. "I like it. We'll trick him into dumping the drug package, and he'll never know it's us."

I nodded. "All you have to do is convince him the feds are up ahead and they're going to inspect his boat."

Buck smiled. "Hey, I'm an actor. I can make him believe anything."

Our marine radio was already on and set to channel nine, the channel used by boaters and bridge operators. This would be the channel Darrell was monitoring,

I handed the microphone to Buck.

In a voice straight out of a *Smokey and the Bandit* movie, Buck spoke into the radio. "Breaker channel nine, this is Top Hat. Hailing the *Toot Toot*."

No response.

"Breaker channel nine. This is Top Hat. Hailing the *Toot Toot*."

No response.

"*Toot Toot*, come in."

This time we got a response.

"This is the *Toot Toot*."

"*Toot Toot*. I have a private message for you. Go to channel thirty."

"Yeah. Changing to channel thirty."

Buck changed the radio channel to thirty.

"*Toot Toot*, you there?"

"Yeah, this is *Toot Toot*. Go ahead."

"*Toot Toot*, just a friendly warning. The Coast Guard is set up three miles ahead of you doing boat inspections. They have drug dogs."

No response.

"*Toot Toot*, do you copy?"

No response.

Buck looked at me with a "What now?" expression.

I pointed ahead. "He's slowing down. He's thinking about what to do next."

We slowed down as well. Didn't want to get too close or pass him.

"Buck, go back to channel nine. Use another voice; say something about the Coast Guard stopping boats. Get people talking about it."

Buck flipped to channel nine. With a distinct southern accent, he said, "If any of y'all boaters are carrying wacky tobacky today, better get shed of it. The coasties are stopping all boats and boarding."

Then, in a Brooklyn accent, he replied, "Yo, I just got stopped. They got them dogs. Nobody's getting by them today. If you got anything, dump it before you get to da jetty."

Then, in yet another voice, he said, "They just set up another checkpoint at the north Manasota Bridge. Won't be able to get by them today."

Up ahead, we could see the *Toot Toot* coast to a stop. I put our boat in neutral and just watched.

Buck brought out the binoculars he'd used the night before.

"Darrell's just come onto the back deck."

"He's holding a package."

"He's looking around."

"He just went back into his cabin. Still has the package."

We waited.

A voice on the radio asked, "The coasties working both ends of the Intracoastal? They still there?"

It was Darrell's voice.

Buck put down the binoculars and picked up the microphone.

"They're still there. Seem to be looking for someone in particular."

Buck put the microphone down and picked up the binoculars.

"He's back out on deck. Carrying the package."

"He's moving to the right side of the boat, close to the sea wall."

"He just dumped it! He tossed it up on the rocks. Now he's back in the cabin."

"The *Toot Toot* is moving. He's heading out!"

I smiled. Our plan had worked.

"Buck, think you can handle this boat? Think you can get me close to where he threw the package?"

"I'll give it a try."

Buck took over the controls and brought our speed up to just above idle. I used the binoculars to guide him in.

"A little to your right. We're getting close."

"Okay. See if you can hold it here. I'm going in after it."

Grabbing the mooring line from the front of the *Escape Artist*, I slipped over the side into the chilly water. I could see the package up on the rocks, no more than ten feet in front of me.

Holding the mooring line, I swam toward shore. As soon as I could touch bottom, I stood and walked to the rock seawall and grabbed the package Darrell had discarded.

Pulling the package behind me, I swam back to the *Escape Artist* and tossed it up on deck.

Buck had dropped a ladder over the side and I used it to climb back aboard.

I was wet and chilled, but it didn't matter. I had recovered the package and could deliver it to agent Harris.

An hour later, Buck and I were tying the *Escape Artist* up back in the mooring field in Englewood.

"Well," said Buck, "we made it."

"Yeah, that was quite an adventure. You going to call Polly, tell her we're safe?"

He nodded and pulled out his phone.

While he was calling Polly, I called Agent Harris.

He answered on the third ring.

"What?"

"When can I drop off the package?"

"What package?"

"The ten-pound package."

"You got it back?"

"Yeah, I got it back."

"What about Darrell? You get him too?"

"Nope. Not my job."

"You know where he is?"

"Last time I saw, he was heading north on the Intracoastal in the *Toot Toot*."

"Good, I'll let our friends know. Let them deal with him. You really got the package back?"

"Yes, I've got it right here."

"Good. Bring it by my office. You've got thirty minutes."

He ended the call.

I turned to Buck. "What did Polly say?"

"She said she was glad we made it back safely. Said it was time to come home to Serenity Cove."

I nodded. "Harris said we had thirty minutes to get the package to his office."

Buck smiled. "Well, we better be on our way then."

After Buck and I secured the *Escape Artist*, we took the dinghy back to Chadwick Park and loaded it onto the trailer behind the Jeep.

Our next stop was Lucy's, where we dropped the trailer off. She wasn't home so it didn't take us long to get the job done.

From there we headed to Agent Harris's office. Buck went in with me and acted as my official witness as I handed the package over.

He made Harris produce and sign a document stating I had

returned the package as requested and that everything we had done had been at the request of Homeland Security.

The document might not have been official, but if anything ever came up about me transporting pot for the federal government, it would be my 'get out of jail free' card.

CHAPTER SIXTY-SIX

Three weeks later, we gathered in the office of Serenity Cove to celebrate the sale of the park.

Surprisingly, I wasn't the new owner.

Before the deal closed, Buck and Polly had come to me and presented a convincing argument of why they should buy the place instead of me.

Not only did they have enough money, they had lived in Serenity Cove a lot longer than I had, and felt they would be better stewards of the property than me.

They were probably right about that. Chances were good they'd live in Serenity Cove for the rest of their lives, while I would eventually chase an adventure that took me somewhere else.

For that reason alone, it made more sense for them to buy Serenity Cove instead of me.

That night we were celebrating their purchase. The office was filled with friends. Anna was there and so was Lucy and of course Buck and Polly, along with Oscar the wiener dog.

During the celebration, Polly announced that, based on advice from their attorney, they would be changing the name of Serenity Cove to something else.

Polly said she wanted to name the place Oscarville in honor of Oscar the wiener dog.

Buck had said no. "Nobody wants to come to Florida and live in a place called Oscarville. And they don't want to live in Wiener Town either."

"How about Mango Bay? In honor of Walker and Mango

Bob?"

Polly thought that was a great idea. She said, "I never liked calling the place Serenity Cove. Sounded like a cemetery. Or a place where old people go to die.

"But Mango Bay—now there's a name that suggests excitement and some major adventures ahead."

And she was right.

We never learned what happened to Darrell. According to Agent Harris, his people dealt with him and we were off the hook. That was good enough for us.

Eddie called to ask about his part in the movie Buck had told Edith about. He was disappointed to learn there were no movie roles for him or Edith.

Polly did offer Eddie a job doing maintenance and clean-up work around the park. He took the job but soon decided he liked cleaning the bait tanks at the convenience store better than working at Mango Bay, so he quit, to the great disappointment of Edith.

Buck finished the movie script he was working on and started shopping it around to different Hollywood studios. There'd been some interest in it but no buyers.

Buck wasn't worried. "It's got a wiener dog, a boat name *Toot Toot*, a cat named Mango Bob. It takes place in a trailer park in Florida. The perfect combination for a hit movie."

Maybe he was right.

Lucy and I still saw each other occasionally, but it didn't look like it was going to get serious any time soon.

Anna was still selling real estate, and her sale of Serenity Cove had pushed her into contention for the top agent in Englewood for that year.

My life in Serenity Cove, now known as Mango Bay, settled down a bit. No more visits from Homeland Security and no damsels in distress.

I did buy the *Escape Artist* from Polly and started making

plans for a trip in it to the Keys.

All in all, life was good. Nice and peaceful.

But as I was about to find out, it never stays that way for long.

The adventure continues . . .

Follow the adventures of Walker and Mango Bob in the Mango Bob series of books found at Amazon. Find photos, maps, and more from the Mango Bob adventures at http://www.mangobob.com

Facebook: https://www.facebook.com/MangoBob-197177127009774/

If you liked Mango Bay, please post a review at Amazon, and let your friends know about the Mango Bob series.

Other books in the Mango Bob series include:

Mango Bob

Mango Lucky

Mango Bay

Mango Glades

Mango Key

Mango Blues

Mango Digger

Mango Crush

Mango Motel

Mango Star

Mango Road

Made in the USA
Las Vegas, NV
15 November 2021